The Problems

with

Prophecies!

D. Alan Petersen

Linellen Press
265 Boomerang Road
Oldbury, Western Australia
helen.iles.linpress@gmail.com

Contents

The Problems with Prophecies!

The interminable swaying and jostling ended. Inside the monstrous All-Terrain Vehicle, its passengers celebrated by stirring its air with a collective exhalation of relief.

For six months, the various away teams, under the guidance of Mission Control in the expedition's orbiting spaceship, had been scouring every speck of land, from continents to the smallest, remotest island, for signs of survivors.

The team Ditar commanded had been allocated South America, and had checked every city, village, settlement, mine site, bunker and cave, all without finding any signs of intelligent life. This stop would be their last chance of doing so.

Alone in the last row of the blessedly stationary ATV, Ion delayed disembarking, stymied by a reluctance to face the probable demise of their last hopes. As the team's psychologist and historian, he still struggled to understand the causes, historic and social, for the calamity that had desecrated and depopulated Mother Earth.

Perhaps today they'd find survivors, hopefully one who was lucid enough to provide an explanation for what had happened. If not survivors, then at least some illuminating documentation. On both counts, he wasn't optimistic.

Jojo, at the wheel, interrupted Ion's gloomy speculations.

'This is it, folks, our last job is down that gravel path. And the sooner we get there, the sooner …' Jojo's booming joviality faltered in the arid silence emanating from those behind him. Glancing in the rear mirror, he encountered three pairs of tired, disenchanted eyes. In more sober tones, he continued, '… the sooner we can relax and enjoy a convivial meal, and an early night.'

Ditar, in the co-driver's seat, after stretching his shoulders and back, added his wisdom, 'Jojo's right. But let's not get ahead of ourselves. We don't know what's awaiting us. It could be another Rio de Janeiro.' He paused, letting the gravity of his remark sink in, then added, 'We're all tired, so we proceed with extra caution on this last one. Okay?'

Even from his spot down the back, Ion found Ditar's clearly enunciated words and measured tones as welcome as his irrefutable logic. The mention of Rio had Ion rubbing his left forearm, which still ached five weeks on. He no longer needed reminding about being cautious; he was concentrating more on the happy thought that, after this last stop, in the morning, they'd start their return, first to La Paz, and then home. The thought generated a modicum of energy.

After readjusting his harness, checking his recorder, survival packs, then the controls on his helmet, he, as usual, was last out. The others had already settled on a plan.

Upon Ion's appearance, Ditar announced, with an unnecessary, pointed finger and grim demeanour: 'We'll lead the way. Ion, you escort Marie. No need to hurry, but have your pistol ready, just in case.'

The man believed in non-verbally reinforcing his advice, possibly as a result of his training as a Communications and Electrical expert. Whatever the cause, Ion still found Ditar's habit wearisome at times, despite some acceptance of its undoubted benefits. Ion let it slide, just nodded, then watched Ditar jog down the path to catch up with Jojo and Doc Trillam.

That just left Marie.

Ion was continually amazed that such a personable young woman existed. As a consequence, his task as her temporary guardian was a reward, not a penance, though his fear that she'd give birth whilst in his care did briefly dampen his moment of happiness, an aberration quickly allayed by remembrance of Marie's oft-repeated confidence in her own capabilities. How many times had she responded to their concerns with: "It's not such a big deal, countless women have had babies. Stop fussing." A response he and his male companions still harboured doubts about, which, upon reflection, was probably due to her dismissal of their concerns not feeding their masculine need to feel useful and important.

Closing his eyes and squeezing his forehead with his right hand, he managed to dislodge further analysis, then, eyes open, shunted his energies into his legs. Marie, who'd been standing a few metres away, having offered up an enigmatic smile in response to his hesitancy, had then turned and begun to waddle off down the track, unburdened by her fretting, philosophising and erstwhile protector. Drawing her pistol, she had motioned him to get a move on.

All his fatigue and analysing vanished in the sprint to catch up with her.

A short time later, together and strolling, they rounded a bend in the path to encounter the others. They were clustered around a steel-framed double door, in a wall of rock. The tall, hefty figure of Doc Trillam was standing well back; at the door crouched Jojo. Behind him, Ditar supervised operations.

Doc Trillam raised a cautionary hand. 'Best give them plenty of room. Jojo's working the locking mechanism. Ditar, using the analyser, has figured out its logic, so hopefully there'll be no nasty surprises.'

Whilst speaking, their Medical Officer spent most of his attention watching Marie for signs of concern about her husband at the lock. Ion did likewise, and as expected, saw nothing but calm.

The good doctor shook his head and finally held Ion's gaze, 'Oxytocin; she's got too much of the stuff in her veins. Blissed out, that's what she is. Honestly!'

His sham disgust unleashed a tide that raised a smile first in Marie, then Ion and came to rest in the doctor's broad, intelligent face. A metallic "click" cut short their moment of shared levity.

'Got it!' Jojo exclaimed, before using his compact, muscular physique to assist the underpowered servomotors to move the heavy blast doors.

'The power is down a bit, but they do have power. It'll make our lives a lot easier once inside.'

Jojo bowed to his audience and seemed unfazed by the muted response to this latest demonstration of his claim to being "Mr Fix-it", a title he considered more illustrious than his designated role as "the man in charge of transport and provisioning".

'Yes. Well done,' replied Ditar, 'but don't get too excited; there's plenty of scope for drama. We proceed with utmost caution.'

Ditar stepped closer and peered inside.

'The corridor leads to a small atrium with at least three closed doors – going who knows where. Okay, Jojo, usual procedure, you first, me covering your back. Doc, stay near the door to await developments. Ion and Marie can cover your back.'

Outside, to the left of where Ion stood, extending along the rock face, away from the door, was a long and low broad bench of dressed stone that offered a good field of fire, and an excellent view of the forested canyon basking in the full glory of the late afternoon sun. Seize the moment! Pointing towards the bench was all that was needed to convince Marie to join him for a sit-down and the chance to soak up the intoxicating rays.

Perhaps, being the oldest, Ion found greater pleasure in resting his legs from the planet's wearisome gravity. In the last weeks of her pregnancy, Marie must also be suffering, not that she showed it. Whatever the case, she, like him, leaned back against the rock wall and sat with arms and legs extended, exposing as much skin as possible. They kept guns in hand and eyes alert.

All too soon, Ditar's "all clear" came through the speakers in his helmet's ear guards. Ion dragged himself vertical, then helped, unnecessarily, Marie to her feet. They wandered inside.

'They're all dead. In the bedrooms,' announced Jojo, before kissing Marie and then leading her and Doc Trillam down a corridor to officially determine the cause of their deaths.

With a beckoning hand, Ditar invited Ion over. 'I'll show you around whilst they're busy. It's quite a setup.'

Their tour ended once back inside the huge, ornate living area. Ditar suddenly spied the controls of the entertainment system at the far end of the room and immediately abandoned Ion to investigate.

Happy to be superfluous, Ion drifted to the dining area at the opposite end of the room, then sat down at the head of a big polished wooden table.

Playing with the tuft of grizzled hair that he called a beard, he tried to imagine what life had been like for the now deceased inhabitants in this hoped-for sanctuary. Who were they? How did they occupy their time? What did they think about prior to the disaster and during their last days?

The only clues Ion had to work with were a few scattered photos and the size and décor of the bunker, both of which gave weight to it being the Bolivian President's bolthole. The President himself had been amongst the Heads of State of the United Americas, whose body was discovered by their North American team, in the basement of the Presidential tower in

Washington D.C.

All the evidence they'd encountered here on Earth highlighted the vast cultural differences between Earth's inhabitants and those of Mars, his homeland. Throughout history different cultures had struggled to understand each other, often with disastrous results, even when able to communicate face-to-face. Without direct communications with survivors, they would never be able to fully understand the attitudes that led to the disaster. But rather than waste more time in futile speculations, Ion decided he'd let any answers arrive at their own pace.

They didn't know why, but they certainly knew what had happened. A massive nuclear and biological weapons attack had apparently been launched from the Americas upon the rest of the planet. It had been a devastating blow, but insufficient to prevent an all-too-successful counterattack.

With no direct communications between the two planets for several centuries, the first hint of the tragedy came from Mars's clandestine monitoring satellites, out past the moon's orbit. It came in the form of a sudden lack of telecommunications noise and then the lights going out, planet-wide. The National Council of Mars had voted to send their current expedition to investigate.

After a sixteen-month journey through space and their six months on the ground, this last bunker had answered that question unequivocally. The planet had shaken free of the burden of Homo sapiens' reign.

One of the things he found odd at that National Council meeting was the puzzling absence of concern. But, after so many centuries of separation, and the knowledge of the sad history between the two outposts of humanity, was it so surprising?

What surprised Ion most was the persistence of that lack of emotion in himself and in his companions for the fate of their distant cousins, whether here, or amongst their smashed and burnt cities and in their encounters with their corpses.

No satisfactory answer emerged. Foregoing further unproductive mental activity, Ion decided to investigate the food preparation area, but the return of Doc Trillam, Jojo and Marie interrupted.

A downcast Doc Trillam slumped into the chair beside him. Even Marie, sitting opposite, looked subdued. Perhaps the emotions were there, just submerged.

Jojo, next to Marie, on the other hand, seemed unaffected by the grim conclusion to their quest for survivors. He fidgeted in his seat and appeared to be struggling to keep a straight face. Why?

Marie, in her role as microbiologist, interrupted further thoughts by giving Ion their joint findings.

'Four individuals, all female, all in relatively good shape, one about forty, the others in their late twenties or early thirties. Cause of death was the modified Anthrax this time, the GM Measles surprisingly absent. The older was probably the President's wife, or concubine, the others, servants, judging by their build and the state of their hands.'

Their moment of introspection was soon broken by Jojo.

'The extinction of humanity from Earth is a tragedy, of course. But,' he leaned forward, 'they had the luck to have had an Elon Musk to instigate a backup plan: us!'

'Yes. We know,' Marie replied with a quiet equanimity that failed to dampen Jojo's enthusiasm.

'Ever since Elon Musk dreamed of a dual-planet humanity, as insurance against ...' Jojo seemed to find the next words elusive, '... this ridiculous self-destruction. We on Mars have struggled, unaided, for centuries, to bring that dream to reality.'

Ion had to interrupt. 'You forget the tremendous efforts Earth made to establish the Mars colony.'

'Yeah, well, their enthusiasm of the early years soon faded as the problems and costs mounted. I haven't forgotten my high school history. In less than two centuries, we were abandoned, left to wither and die. Then, when we did start making progress, we began to adapt more fully to our planet, started diverting comets to create a breathable atmosphere and restore our planet's oceans, they had the nerve to dispatch a barrage of interplanetary nuclear missiles to try and destroy us – all because our solutions offended their religious sensibilities,' Jojo retorted, his body stiffening as his volume increased.

'Take it easy, Jojo,' rejoined Marie, with a placating hand on her husband's arm, 'and you too, Ion,' said whilst meeting Ion's gaze with eyes intense, and body leaning slightly towards him.

Jojo calmed.

Ion eased back into his chair.

Despite all the genetic and educational advantages of being a Martian, Ion was embarrassed to admit to finding himself getting as revved up as Jojo. He shook his head and inwardly groaned at the fragility of his mind. His contrition must have leaked out because wry smiles soon took hold of the faces around the table.

'That's better,' Marie announced. 'Look, we all know our history, the basics at least. Ion knows more, but it isn't our task to make up policies regarding the future. We were sent to gather information and help any survivors. Sadly, information is all we've been able to do. Jojo darling, I think all of us, and everyone back on Mars, are aware of some of the possible consequences of this event, but it has been the Martian way to consider as many long-term outcomes as imaginable, if given the time. We have the time, though …' She rubbed her distended belly and adjusted her position in her chair.

Jojo jumped up.

'Are you …?' said with a face alive with concern.

'No. No. Just baby getting resettled. All perfectly normal.'

Doc Trillam then interjected, 'Speaking of time and decisions … we're obviously camping here tonight, and my stomach's rumbling, so, why not get to organising dinner, then a good night's sleep, and be ready for an early start tomorrow?'

'You're right,' agreed Jojo, 'I'll grab some supplies from the ATV and … a bottle of fine Martian wine …'

Puzzled faces induced an explanation of what they were going to celebrate. 'Don't worry, I'm not suggesting we rejoice man's extinction from the planet. It's just that Ditar mentioned today is the Summer Solstice. And what a sun it is. Surely, it's an occasion worth marking. Isn't it?'

There were no objections. Jojo left, and Ion, at Jojo's suggestion, went off to investigate the cooktops and cupboards, leaving Marie and Doc Trillam to chat.

§

Ion found himself rudely evicted from a dream. The floor was shaking and the few lights they'd left on flickered, then expired, leaving behind an absolute, and seemingly infinite darkness, one filled with the scent of dust, the tortured creaking of fracturing rock and the startled cries of his companions.

A chorus of 'What's going on?' bounced blindly around the room, spreading its mix of indignation and fear to all corners, only to be quashed by Ditar's loud and unexpected exclamation: 'Wow! So this is what an earthquake feels like.'

Devoid of light, Ion struggled to find and then strap on his harness, don his helmet, and, after much fumbling, get the headlamp glowing. At least he wasn't last this time, that honour falling to Doc Trillam. In the jerky glow of five headlamps, the room shrank to more normal dimensions.

'Perhaps we'd best head outside?' Jojo suggested after checking on Marie.

All were in agreeance. As usual, Ditar suggested caution, 'Jojo and I will get the doors open, which may prove troublesome without power. Doc, Ion, Marie, gather our stuff, just the important bits, then hang back in here until we see what's happening outside.'

Nodding headlamps were the only response required to get Ditar and Jojo moving.

Shortly after Ditar reappeared: 'Two things. The door's unlocked but refuses to budge. It's possibly blocked by a rock fall outside or just needs more muscle power to move it. The other thing is, if you haven't already figured, is that our intercoms aren't working. Thus, either the router in the ATV is out of action, or worse. So, Ion, Doc, come with me. Maybe our combined muscles will move the door.'

'I'm coming too,' said Marie, 'I may have less muscle but what I have could be the extra oomph needed to get things moving.'

No one objected, so Ditar assented.

Muscles were strained near to breaking, and the air was blue with curses, before the doors conceded just enough room to allow them to squeeze out into the pre-dawn gloaming.

Leaving the others to catch their breaths, Jojo and Ditar jogged drunkenly up the path to determine the fate of the ATV. They soon returned, walking, and possessing dower expressions.

Ditar explained the situation, 'Taken out by a massive rock slide. Without the ATV's relay we can't contact the ship to get help, or delay their blast-off. Our helmet communicators won't do the job as they're only line-of-sight. We'll have to walk, all the way back to Lima!'

All eyes turned to Marie. The increasing light allowed expressions to take shape. Marie's still oozed confidence.

'Don't worry I'll wait if you can't keep up,' she said, before grabbing Ion's elbow and pushing him forward.

'Ion can keep me amused with theories whilst you fellows can either bring up the rear or, lead the way.'

§

The first day was the worst.

The gravel road had been destroyed in several places, forcing lengthy and tiring diversions. They refilled their water bottles in rivulets, kept up their strength with occasional emergency food bars and the revitalising effect of the sun on their skin. The night was spent huddled together under a rock ledge.

The end of the second day brought them closer to signs of human habitation, and a new problem. Groups of feral dogs, scrawny and quarrelsome, had begun shadowing their progress.

Though the one most perturbed by this development, Ion tried not to show it. It had been a hunger-crazed dog that had latched onto his arm in that bunker on the outskirts Rio. Since then, he'd developed a healthy respect for the darker side of man's best friend.

Their second night was spent in the safety of a loft, in a barn on an abandoned farm. It also provided the day's only pleasant surprise. In the adjacent high-walled compound were two donkeys. For at least two years, they had survived, unsupervised, on rainwater and the stored hay, now reduced to wisps of straw. The animals seemed happy to see them, especially when Jojo forked down some hay from the loft.

The next morning, dogs could still be heard moving about, but remained unseen.

'I don't like it. If they attack all at once …' Jojo voiced their collective concern.

After a gloomy silence, Ion raised an option the others were unlikely to have considered, 'Perhaps we can outpace the dogs with the help of the donkeys.'

Blank faces confirmed his assessment. Mars had no beasts of burden, or animals larger than chickens.

'Donkeys were kept to carry people, or goods, or, to pull a cart.'

Growing comprehension induced a discussion of possibilities, which resulted in Ion and Jojo going on a quest to find harnesses and a cart. Ion didn't mention the greater task of convincing the donkeys to do their bidding, concluding it best to tackle one problem at a time.

As a historian, he knew the human story, but to do so comprehensively had required learning a great deal about the context in which that story had occurred. History was hugely influenced by technologies, cultural ideas, and the physical and ecological environment in which it developed. But his knowledge was all book learning. He'd never seen a donkey in the flesh, let alone tried coaxing one to pull a cart. He just hoped Mr Fix-it would live up to his name.

Aided by the calming magic of Marie's presence, Jojo eventually got the two donkeys harnessed to the rather primitive cart, and, after a few faltering laps of the compound, felt confident enough to lead the way out the gates. Perhaps with the donkey's aid they might make it to the spaceport on the other side of the mountains, or at least get close enough to make contact using their helmet communicators. If they missed the blast-off, the next rocket was six months away. It was an outcome Ion, and the rest, didn't wish to dwell upon.

With three in the cart and two taking turns jogging beside it they made considerable progress. The dogs appeared to abandon their surveillance and by late afternoon they were on the cusp of the final range. They were approaching another abandoned village, on a road lined by orchards that provided snacks during their mid-afternoon break.

They were on the verge of moving on when Marie made the observation that the donkeys seemed nervous. She didn't have time for more commentary because both animals suddenly jerked forward, tossing her off the bench seat into the rear tray. The others, Ion amongst them, had been standing scattered around, a few paces away, munching fruit and chatting when they heard Marie's outcry and saw the donkeys making an escape bid.

The cause of Marie's warning manifested in a swarm of malnourished and malevolent dogs leaping out of the long dry grass that surrounded the trees and then launching themselves at the standing men.

For Ion it was a nightmare, rekindled with a vengeance. But there was no time for fear. Instinctively he had grabbed his pistol and was bringing it to bear on the dog charging directly at him but was tackled from behind by one latching onto his left leg. On the way down he smashed it on the head with the pistol's butt before rolling free to fire at the retreating form of the first dog. It yelped, staggered then collapsed. The concussed one at his feet began to stir. Wincing, he pulled the trigger.

The dogs that hadn't been killed in the first rush were chasing the cart, which was careening wildly until slowed when one of the donkeys stumbled after a great brown and black brute had clamped its jaws into the poor beast's throat.

The sight of the others racing to Marie's rescue raised Ion's hopes. The air sizzled and crackled with the sound of laser blasts, which connected with deadly accuracy until most of the snarling, baying attackers had either succumbed or chose to flee back into the orchard. The most confidence-inspiring image was that of Marie now standing, clinging to the seat with one hand and blasting away with the other like a Martian Boadicea!

Jojo managed to kill the dog at the donkey's neck but no sooner was it freed of its attacker than it collapsed, bringing the cart to a violent halt that pitched Marie forward to bounce off the surviving donkey and ending up sprawled on the ground. Ion felt a blood-chilling fear race through him, shared undoubtedly by the others, awash with concern for the health of Marie and the baby.

Diligently scanning, as only a hunted animal can, he made his way cautiously over to join those at the cart, where Jojo was attending to Marie, now propped up against a wheel. Doc Trillam stood calming the remaining donkey whilst Ditar cut the dead one from its traces.

Reaching the cart, Ion croaked out a "How?"

Marie replied in a shaky voice that was barely audible, 'Don't fret. I'll be okay. Just give me a little time to rest.'

'She's no ordinary girl, my Marie. She'll be fine,' Jojo said, gently patting her hand, but the bravado of his voice belied the fear in his eyes.

Seconds later, Doc Trillam took over.

Ion moved off to give them elbow-room, and found a spot with clear views, there to stand armed and alert for reprise attacks. On the fringe of his consciousness was the awareness of blood dribbling into his boots.

§

They never got near to reaching the final ridge in time to contact the spaceship, and had to settle for the ruins of a farm just below the snowline. There wasn't much left of the buildings. The only one still substantially erect was a small open shed, with stone walls and a tiled roof. They settled in as best they could. There were a few moth-eaten bales of hay, enough to feed the donkey and provide something to lie on.

'How's the leg, Ion?' Ditar asked when he came out to relieve him from sentry duty on a big, flat-topped rock that gave clear views of the shed and surrounds. They had lost the remnants of their canine foes once the country had become more barren and too many had succumbed to Ditar's unerring aim.

'Aches but still serviceable. How's Marie?'

Ditar paused. 'Doc thinks it'll be in the next few hours. Sometime in the early morning. Claimed women give birth at such unreasonable times just to annoy doctors. Marie had answered, "Of course!"'

They both smiled.

Ion checked the time. Eleven forty-three. He wasn't due to be relieved until midnight.

'You're early, but I'll not object. I'll come and get you when the baby arrives. It's a big event that we should all be part of.'

Ditar corrected him, 'Not according to Marie. She reminded all of us that Martian women have long been genetically improved to give birth quickly and with minimal pain. In her opinion, it's our scientists' greatest triumph. The Doc agrees, but is on hand nonetheless.'

Hobbling back to the welcoming light and warmth of the small fire built in a ring of stones at the front of the lean-to, Ion was less concerned with the birth itself than its broader significance.

Tending the fire was a circumspect Jojo. 'Still a few hours away. Why not have a doze. I'll let you know in plenty of time.'

'Told Ditar we'd get him over when it happens.'

After Jojo's reassurances, Ion went to keep the donkey company. It was still awake, though resting on the flagstones idly chewing straw and occasionally closing its eyes.

It was the donkey's snort rather than Jojo's excited approach that awakened Ion.

'It's on the way. I'll get Ditar.'

Ion countered, 'No. You stay with your wife. I'll get him. Won't be long.'

He'd barely made it halfway when Ditar moved out to join him, and together they returned to the shed, still alert for more dog attacks.

With Ditar on watch, Ion stoked up the fire from the pile of timber they'd salvaged from the damaged buildings, then moved back to the shelter to give Ditar a hand with guard duties.

The baby arrived, to unfettered rejoicing, at two thirty-seven. A boy, happy and healthy, to a Marie ecstatic with joy. The baby was cleaned up and then swaddled, placed in a makeshift sling and together mother and child dozed off under the patient watchful eyes of all present.

Their reverie was short-lived. The night was disturbed, first by a distant roar, and then by a streak of intense light racing to embed itself in the bosom of the star-spangled heavens.

Ditar checked his multipurpose wrist-screen. 'Three twenty-one a.m. They were scheduled to launch at midnight, so maybe they'd lingered a little, hoping we'd make it in time. Can't blame them for going; they'd be cutting their fuel reserves too fine if they delayed another day.'

In a few eyeblinks, the spacecraft's departing flare became an insignificant speck of light in the slowly revolving, and evolving, story of that starry sky.

The prospect of having to survive the six months until the scheduled next flight caused no murmurings of disquiet. All were confident that they would have been left food, water, and medical supplies back at the spaceport, good for a year or more, in line with the expedition's protocols. Ion hoped they'd have the good sense to leave them some transportation. As a means of getting around, the donkey cart had serious shortcomings.

Doc Trillam, who had the last watch, began moving towards the sentry rock, now that he was reasonably assured mother and child no longer needed his attention.

Ion wasn't so sure that the doctor wouldn't be needed at short notice, and so offered to take the doctor's shift. After a brief interchange, Doc agreed, and Ion strolled over to the rock and took up his task of scanning the surroundings, combined with an additional one: cogitation.

Things quietened in the shed. The surrounding hillside remained mute and unmoving, leaving Ion the indulgence of mulling over the day's events and those of the past six months.

He thought it both reasonable and ironic that Jojo and Marie had insisted on naming their son Elon, the man who had initiated the Mars colony.

It was ironic, because Elon Musk's prophecy that the Mars colony would save humanity from extinction was both prescient and yet not so. Their being here on Earth was less about Elon Musk's vision and more a replay of an event last seen around forty thousand years before, when the last Homo neanderthalensis died, giving sovereignty of the planet to the sole surviving species of the Homo genus, Homo sapiens.

What Elon had failed to grasp was that for Homo sapiens to survive the harsh conditions on Mars, they would be forced to change, socially, physically and genetically. Ion, his companions, the baby, and all their kin back on Mars were no longer Homo sapiens: they were Martians. Homo sapiens, man the wise, was extinct. The planets and possibly the stars now belonged to Homo maris, the men of Mars.

He and all Martians were an artificially evolved species, with genetics carefully crafted in the laboratory and guided by logic and morality. They had reinvented themselves to thrive physically and socially on Mars, and yet were also capable of living on Earth. As such, he and his companions were the first truly self-made men!

Ion tried to tally up all the modifications to their genome to allow them to survive on Mars as it was. That planet's harsh realities had forced them to become chimeras, creatures Elon Musk and humans in general would have baulked at welcoming as brothers and sisters, or as equals.

Ion glanced at his hand, at his stubby fingers – to resist the cold – and his beautiful, smooth green skin. A skin populated with algae to provide food and oxygen. Its tough exterior and subcutaneous fat were borrowed from Earth's whales to protect them from Mars's intense cold and prevent minor wounds.

Much of his DNA came from the tiny but indestructible Tardigrade. Parts of its genome had made him impervious to radiation damage, intense heat, cold and dehydration, as well gifting him a metabolism that could be drastically slowed to save energy in times of famine, which had been frequent in the early years of their abandonment.

His reptilian third eyelid and the membrane over his ears, as well as the nostril flaps – taken from camels – allowed him to survive in near-vacuum conditions without his blood and fluids evaporating.

With all these genetic improvements, it was little wonder that he, and the rest of the crew, had been unaffected by the plagues that had finished off those humans who'd survived the nuclear devastation. Martians were now a very different breed.

But for Ion, Mars's greatest achievement – though not yet fully tested – was their modified mental disposition. The instinctive tribalism that had allowed bands of man's simian ancestors to survive the predator-friendly savannahs of ancient Africa had also led to incessant intertribal wars. The last of which had seen their demise.

Like all creatures, Martians were powered by self-preservation, but their genetic disposition towards sociability had been augmented. Mars's hostile environment required a sharpened need for, and dependence upon, a heightened regard for all their fellows. Just as important was their ongoing ecological transformation of their planet, physically and biologically. That transformation had instilled in Martians a deep empathy for the ecosystem that upheld their existence.

The notion of "us" and "them" still lingered, but the "us" now included "them", the important as well as the seemingly inconsequential, whether man or beast, plant or microbe.

A historic turning point had occurred with baby Elon's birth. He was the first Martian to be born on an Earth that had been freed from Homo sapiens' mismanagement. Baby Elon would be the first of many to repopulate and heal the wounds of this still beautiful world.

In the east, the sky was hinting of the coming day, the stars were fading, and the details in the surrounding landscape were becoming easier to distinguish. Ion contrasted the growing clarity of the land's details around him with his ill-defined uncertainty regarding the future of planet Earth.

Suddenly, he became aware of his breathing. The mountain air was cold and thin. It reminded him of the even colder and thinner air back home, invoking thoughts of the marvellous planet-wide transformations they'd achieved on Mars in the centuries since their abandonment.

With such an achievement to their credit, Ion's doubts about their abilities to restore Mother Earth to her former glory faded.

It was a job well within the capabilities of its new managers, Homo maris.

Author's Note:

Back in October 2020, my writing group tasked us with producing a short story with its last line being: "There is food, water, medicine; enough for a year or more." (from The Ark by Annabel Smith).

Elon Musk's dream of establishing a colony on Mars – to act as a backup population to reseed Earth if disaster strikes – somehow entered my mind.

The Problem with Prophecies didn't fulfil its original brief, though the required line sort of makes an appearance in its closing pages. It was fun to write, and, asks questions I feel worthy of consideration.

Love Thy Neighbour

Even at this predawn hour the traffic was barely moving. Cars clogged the streets, head to tail, inching forward like an army of metal and glass caterpillars, blindly obeying a shared instinct, the imperative to arrive at their work early, or at least on time. Theirs was an act of groupthink, one blind to the realities imposed by their excessive numbers, and hence, almost guaranteed to fail.

Christopher Ambrosio was doing better than them. He shared their dream but he was on foot, running, now that his destination was in sight, but more so because of the storm's squall line nipping at his heels. A final dash between the tin-tops got him to the other side of the road, there to be whipped into a heart-pounding sprint from the gusting wind slapping his neck with scatterings of cold, oversized raindrops.

The steps leading to his building's entrance were surmounted in a few bounds that took him in through automatic doors, barely opened. Thankfully, they had closed fully by the time the storm's wet fist struck, finding itself relegated to venting its fury on the door's unfeeling glass panes.

Safely inside the small foyer, a panting Christopher Ambrosio took his time to regain his breath, and to savour his slim victory over Mother Nature. Violent storms may have become the new norm, in a world undeniably warmer than it should have been, but he found their regularity still hard to accept, or live with.

The only upside was that it made getting to and from the office a physical challenge that kept him in shape.

Once his breathing had returned to normal, he prepared himself to broach his next obstacle: the lifts.

They were another aspect of the "fitness program" imposed on him by outside forces. To keep power use within the building's quota, they only worked about thirty per cent of the time, and his destination, blandly hidden amongst the List of Tenants, was: "S.E.T.I.", on the sixth floor. The four-letter abbreviation condensed a mouthful: The Search for Extra-Terrestrial Intelligence.

He either had six floors to climb, or he could get lucky and find that power had been allocated to the lifts. More so than usual did he hope for the latter. Today was special.

It would be his last on the job. The whole S.E.T.I. project was closing down, and he was here just to turn off the monitoring equipment, do a bit of tidying up, and then make everything ready for the removalists.

Ever the optimist, he straightened up and walked the few paces to the lift's controls, with the mirrors on either side of the doors diligently recording his approach. Christopher Ambrosio, physicist, BSc with Honours, knew the odds were against him, but was determined to try his luck – one last time.

Standing in front of the doors, he gave in to the irresistible urge to preen and contemplate.

Nothing had changed. Revealed was a young man, tall, slim, trying unsuccessfully to fill out a rumpled, dark grey suit he felt exuded a degree of intellectual confidence as a salve for twenty-five years of unremarkable existence.

Peering closer, he noted that a few more lines on his rather pallid face would have added to his academic credibility. But dreams of academic esteem were hardly served by his unruly mop of curly blond hair. He sighed. What the heck if he looked more like an anaemic surfie in a bad suit, than a scientist. It really didn't seem to matter much anymore.

'Well, you've had an easy six years here, so you can't complain,' he said to his reflection.

It was still hard to believe that after two hundred or so years of searching for signs of alien intelligence, humanity had finally given up the search.

The mess outside was the reason. It seemed humanity now had more urgent issues to spend the ever-decreasing research dollars on. Instead of finding aliens, money was needed for things like finding ways to feed the overpopulated planet. The powers that be were probably right. But he'd gotten used to the leisurely life of dragging out his thesis, in between monitoring the readouts and preparing the quarterly reports for the directors, who, until six months ago, had been dreamers like himself.

Davidson had changed all that. The new director had connections to big business and heaps more funding: funding that wanted results. So, Davidson was scrapping the monitoring operation and putting the cash into accelerating work on the transmission side of things. Apparently, some exciting new developments in faster-than-light communications were taking place on the East Coast, so that's where the money was going. Another sigh escaped as Christopher prepared to press the button marked: "6".

Before he could, the doors behind flew open, letting in the howling fury of the storm, a blast of cold water-laden air, and a sodden female figure. Susan. Soaked to the skin, her long dark hair plastered in wild disarray across her face. Her dramatic arrival perked him up no end. She was the main reason he started this early, and much of why he'd hesitated so long in front of the lift.

Her entrance also provided some perverse enjoyment from watching her antics in the mirror. The hopping from one leg to the other as she emptied the water from her flat shoes, before doing the same for her handbag. She simply up-ended it, drained off the water, and then unceremoniously stuffed the contents back in.

Finally, she stood, glared at him, and yelled, 'Don't just stand there, press the damn button!'

The shock of her indignation jerked him into immediate obeyance, and, miraculously, the doors opened. Susan barged in ahead of him. 'Stop gawking, get in!' she said, eyes blazing.

What could he do but comply? The trip to the sixth floor was accomplished in a damp, steamy silence. She, annoyed and dripping, he, acutely aware of her near-nakedness. The shapeless dress she habitually wore was now a semitransparent coating smeared over her surprisingly curvaceous young body. Why was the temperature climbing, and why was it hard to swallow?

Suddenly, he was glad she'd not asked any questions because he was certain he wouldn't have been able to give a coherent response. It was always the case in the presence of raw female sexuality.

This wasn't how his last day was supposed to go!

Since she had arrived five months back, he'd been screwing up the courage to ask her out. Today was to be the day. But now …? His shoulders slumped. Maybe later, once she'd settled herself in at her lab down the hall. Yes, later would be better. He'd wait until morning tea and then pop in to share the new herb tea he'd recently discovered.

They parted wordlessly.

Entering his once cosy hideaway, the S.E.T.I. office, he found it now as forlorn as his mood, so forlorn that he sought respite in the form of some old-time music he'd recently downloaded into his communicator: lounge music from the 1930s. With the sedate melodies of yesteryear playing in his earbuds, he found the energy to prepare his usual breakfast at the kitchenette.

With a body placated by food, and a mind soothed by music, he finally turned to the room and considered the task ahead of him. With a shrug of stoic acceptance, he got to work. First, one last check of the screens, which, as usual had nothing to report, nothing to keep the project alive.

Squaring his shoulders, he turned them off, then closed down the input channels. Finally, he went resolutely over to the main console, there to place his finger over the "Close Down" button. He paused, and, wincing, pressed down. The screen went through a series of warning statements before giving a mute "Goodbye".

For a while, he stood hypnotising the blank screen. The quiet crooning of the music now seemed overly loud. He turned it off, stored away his earbuds, and leaned into the dismal silence that took over the room.

The wall clock gloomily reported that he still had an hour to go until tea time. Having nothing better to do, he shuffled over to the sole chair, sat down, leaned back, and, with feet on the desk, dreamt of Susan.

Until this morning, she had seemed reassuringly sexless and hence approachable. So different from the wild, bedraggled and immensely alluring creature in the lift. Her squarish face made her appear a little severe, an impression reinforced by her black-rimmed glasses and her tightly bound hair. Until today, she had no form, every hint of it hidden by the utilitarian dresses she always wore.

'Wow!' he commented to the walls, 'with very little effort she could be a stunner!'

It had been her incisive intellect that had attracted him. Their chats at tea time, and more recently at lunch, had upset his rather hazy ideas about what it was S.E.T.I. had been searching for: intelligence. He'd always thought that he had a good grasp of the concept, but after months of Susan's adroit questioning on that matter, and many others, he found he was no longer sure of anything!

He could have blamed her lab rats. They were clones, had the same DNA, but when subjected to different environmental stimuli, they ended up with very different maze running abilities – the accepted measure of rat intelligence.

He had always assumed intelligence was a fairly fixed quality. All those intelligence tests he had taken at school, and later in Psychology at university, had supposedly been constructed to account for cultural and educational differences, but now he wasn't so certain. It was a humbling revelation, especially since he'd always been proud of his high scores on IQ tests.

Of greater fascination were her investigations into whether intelligence and happiness were linked. Another combination he'd not thought much about. Like most, he'd simply assumed smarter people should be happier since they would get better jobs, and hence live an easier, more luxurious lifestyle. The results of Susan's experiments said otherwise.

If rat happiness corresponded to the levels of the "happy hormones", such as serotonin and dopamine, she had demonstrated that intelligence had no influence on either of them.

It was another depressing revelation. He'd vaguely hoped his education and the improved prospects of a decent job would be his ticket to the good life. Now those ill-defined hopes were on shakier ground. It was a problem he wasn't quite ready to face.

Happiness. He well remembered their conversation on the topic.

They had been halfway through lunch when she had stood, explaining that she had a schedule of rat cuddling to keep up – and thus had to go back to the lab. She invited him to join her. It was the first time she'd allowed him inside. He'd taken it as a good omen.

'Cuddle time number one!' she had called out on approaching the open enclosure where her "loyal subjects" resided. Immediately, one of the ten identical white rats sprang up squeaking excitedly.

'How do you know it's the correct one?' he'd blurted out.

In answer, she placed the rodent she was kissing and stroking onto a small open box on her bench; the screen nearby lit up with the number "one", and readouts of current biometric parameters.

'They've all been "chipped". Watch the bottom numbers whilst I scratch behind his ears.'

The two sets of figures rose steadily.

'Those are his serotonin and dopamine levels. He's the happiest, most pampered rat in the room,' she'd said, before retrieving number One from the measuring device, and, after a final kiss, she'd placed it back in with the others. She did the same to numbers Two to Five. The others got none of her special attention. He knew how those guys felt.

The next day, she had suggested they have lunch in her lab to make it easier for her to keep to her schedule. Of course, he'd agreed.

She had another surprise for him. On the end of the table, where they ate their lunch, was a rather battered wooden chess set, arranged on an equally battered wooden board.

'It's a beauty!' he'd said, knowing full well that wooden sets were hard to come by and hideously expensive.

'Perhaps we could have a game, spending all day with rats seems to be dulling my mind. I hope you play.'

'I play. In fact, I was university champion.'

No sooner had he said his boastful statement than he became unsure if it was something he should have crowed about.

'Good,' was her neutral reply, but one accompanied by a ghost of a smile, and a curious glint in her eyes.

It didn't take long for him to find out what lay behind those nonverbal hints. She'd trounced him with a sneaky move, conjured out of nowhere.

Over the coming days, she won every game they played. She was a genius at seeing patterns and sequences of moves that he was completely blind to. She tried to soften the blow to his pride by explaining that there were different kinds of intelligence.

Hers was the intelligence most people think of; an accurate memory for data, combined with the ability to conceptualise complex patterns and their interconnections. She claimed her sister was the opposite: lousy at maths, science and chess, but a genius at getting along with people and also very athletic, physically coordinated. She was a great gymnast and stylish dancer.

Normally, he hated losing, but by losing the chess games, he had won her company and her conversation. It was only today that he realised how much he had gained and how much he wanted their "relationship" – it was probably too strong a word – but, whatever the correct term was, he desperately wanted her to continue in his life. But how? What did he have to offer?

Glumly, the answer seemed a dispiriting: "not much".

The time had ticked, in fact, he was almost overdue for their tea ceremony. Grabbing the packet of herb tea, a lemon, and a chunk of ginger, he rushed out.

Down the hall, her laboratory door was open, which was puzzling. It was usually kept closed. Vague feelings of doom flooded his mind and slowed his approach. Upon reaching the door, he almost collided with a man in blue overalls exiting with a large box, which emitted squeaks, chirps and rustling noises through the finger-sized holes that festooned its sides and top.

The man turned without giving him a thought, went to the lift, waved a card over the control plate, pressed the button and shortly afterwards the doors silently opened and he disappeared inside.

Christopher was stunned thrice, first by the strange man, then by the fact that he was removing Susan's precious rats, and lastly by learning there was some kind of override mechanism for the lifts. That last aspect raised a flush of injustice and the rank taste of envy.

After shaking his head to clear his negativity, he then had to face the possibly disturbing developments surrounding Susan. Summoning his courage, he knocked on the open door, which was propped open with a wedge.

'Hello?' he called out in a voice as squeaky as the departing rats. 'I've brought the new tea I told you about.'

'Come in, just put the stuff on the table, near the kitchenette. I'll be with you shortly,' her disembodied voice echoed out across the empty room from the open door of the bathroom.

It appeared he wasn't the only one moving on, and out. Gone were all the elaborate mazes, the rat enclosures, the monitors, everything. The room now seemed huge and soulless. There wasn't much left. Near the kitchenette stood the old dining table, with its three cheap chairs; to the left, close by the bathroom, and below the only outside window, was a pale cloth-covered daybed he'd not noticed before.

Susan emerged.

His eyes dilated.

Her black hair was dry, shining and loose, falling down past her shoulders. The knee-length, sleeveless, silky red dress was low-cut and held together in front by a row of large, white, almond-shaped buttons. Her feet were bare.

Frozen into stunned silence, he opened his mouth but was unable to utter a syllable.

'Better close your mouth or you'll be catching flies. Come in. I'll put the kettle on.'

She said no more, just blithely continued towards the sink.

Her kettle was an ancient item that had to be heated on the stove top. After adjusting the heat, she swung around to greet him properly, sending her hair flying, and causing delightful movements in the upper part of the dress that strained to enclose the contents underneath.

By then, Christopher was seated, and luckily so, because Susan's sensual movements threatened to overwhelm his intellect. Staring back at her, he was unable to disguise amorous thoughts fighting a rising trepidation at the manner, and speed, of events no longer in his control.

'You approve of my new outfit?' she beamed, before turning slowly around to show off the dress and its perfectly proportioned contents. 'It's not mine, of course. It's my sister's. Mine's still soaked from this morning's storm.'

'Errr, you look great,' he croaked.

'Thanks.'

Then, waving an arm at the bare room behind her, she announced: 'I'll be leaving today. Done all my research. With the rats at least. Heading home tonight.'

Sporting an ambiguous smile, she then glided to the entrance door and closed it. It gave out an ominous click, which, in Christopher's overwrought mind, conjured up images of a warder locking in a condemned prisoner. His pulse skipped a beat.

'Too draughty with the door open,' she explained, before moving to the table, picking up the makings, and then breezing off to the sink. There she began to slice the lemon and ginger into the teapot.

For a moment longer he sat spellbound, before finding the energy to organise and energise sufficient neutral pathways to enable speech.

'My, ahh, project, also finishes up today. I'm just tidying up a few loose ends.'

He was amazed to find that he'd made the comment with a measure of calm in his voice. It gave him the confidence to continue.

'I'm going to miss our little tea sessions.'

She didn't respond immediately, instead concentrated on preparing the tea. Job done she brought the pot and three battered mugs over on a tray, placed them in the middle of the table before seating herself opposite. There was a cheeky glint in her eyes.

Why the extra mug? His question was soon sidelined by most of his conscious, and subconscious, mental capacities becoming fixated upon her décolletage.

Susan distracted his hormones with a question.

'Given up the search for smart aliens?'

Only by dragging his gaze up to her smiling face did he gain the neurological control to reply.

'Not me. It's the new Director. But I guess it's the same thing in the end,' he said, after which he slumped. The unpalatable truth had drained all energy from him.

'Ahh, well. Finding evidence of intelligence is tricky in rats, and presumably considerably more so in aliens.'

She paused, then glanced at the ceiling, before asking, 'Do you think it's possible to be too clever?'

Her kindly diversion to a safer intellectual topic revived him.

'Yes. I, err, suppose it is possible to have too much. Intelligence presumably evolves to allow a creature to survive long enough to have progeny. I guess excess intelligence probably carries no advantage. Hmm. Most smart, educated people appear to have few, if any, children, which implies that intelligence could be a self-regulating property. Maybe we're meant to be of average intellect to succeed, biologically speaking, that is.'

His face remained contorted as his mind continued to chase several competing lines of argument.

'So, being too clever could become a hindrance rather than a help?' she said with a smile dripping sweet innocence, an innocence not matched by her eyes, which shone with an altogether more carnal light.

Something flipped inside him. Like the teapot on the table, he was certain he was also emitting steam. His collar felt too tight, and his throat was dry.

'You look unwell. Are you having some sort of a turn?' she cooed, before getting up to stand beside him.

Looking up, he received a face full of cleavage. His pulse jumped. Speech was impossible.

'I think you'd better lie down,' she suggested, before coaxing him out of his chair – as if he were an invalid – then gently guided him, in his zombie-like state, over to the daybed.

There she stretched him out to lie quietly, breathing heavily, with the sound of his pulse pounding in his ears.

Placing a cooling hand on his brow, she exclaimed, 'My, you are hot! I'd best make you a little more comfortable.'

Without waiting for a reply, she removed his shoes, then started on his tie and slowly headed south …

Her seduction was artless, but more than effective. In fact, the following hour was the most frightening, sensually stimulating, and basically mind-blowing he'd ever experienced. However, the thing he couldn't get over was that he'd actually felt her pleasure, not indirectly, but inside his head. It was as if their bodies and minds had become one.

The experience had been indescribably fantastic. But it also raised a few questions. Had he really felt her feelings? Or had it been some sort of powerful delusion? Perhaps he'd momentarily become psychic?

As he lay naked beside her wonderfully warm, soft body, he didn't much care. All he could think of was that this sort of lovemaking could become highly addictive, an addiction he was very happy to risk!

Susan disturbed his musings by gently getting up and padding naked towards the bathroom, dragging her sister's dress.

'Better get dressed, my sister will be here shortly,' she said over her shoulder. 'Perhaps you could brew up another pot of tea?'

Having no desire to be found naked by an unknown female, he leapt from the bed and threw on his clothes. The sounds of showering then formed the backdrop as he busied himself with the tea-making.

He was placing the pot on the table when Susan glided back into the room to join him. A leisurely kiss was imparted on his lips before she took up her seat, ready to replay a scene that seemed an aeon ago.

Sitting down opposite, he awkwardly tried to think of ways to restart the conversation. There were so many questions to ask, things to clarify, and hopes to announce.

But she spoke first and with ominous seriousness. 'I'm afraid I have not been entirely honest with you. There are a few things we have to discuss.'

His hopes sank. But his gloomy speculations were diverted by the sound of a key being inserted into the door to the corridor. Seconds later, a wonderfully proportioned young lady with amazingly bushy, curly red hair stepped in. Susan's sister.

Though he'd never met her, he'd definitely seen her before. She was the new girl at Mario's Barbershop. Since starting there, the prices of a haircut had skyrocketed and getting in required a two-month wait. She was definitely the reason.

Though dressed in a simple work uniform, white blouse and black pleated skirt, her kind and happy face, generous lips, rouged, combined with dangerous curves and a sensual way of moving, meant she commanded the rapt attention of any man with a pulse.

'So, this is your friend?' she said to Susan before gifting him a smile and a friendly wave. After closing the door, she strolled over to join them at the table.

Susan made the introductions. 'Gloria, this is Christopher Ambrosio. Chris, this is my sister Gloria.'

'Looks like you've … successfully conducted your final experiment,' Gloria remarked, glancing knowingly from Susan to him.

The interchange between Gloria and Susan implied there was something disquieting going on that involved him.

'Well, – err – yes. But things haven't turned out quite as expected,' she said with a smile worthy of a Mona Lisa.

'Ahh. I see. So, what happens now?' Gloria nodded sagely, whilst glancing from Susan to him.

A rising indignation spurred him to interrupt their banter.

'Excuse me, ladies, but what's going on here?'

Susan took a while to answer, lifted her eyes from the tabletop, and then turned towards him. There was resolve and a hint of fear in her expression.

'I'm not sure how to start. I guess there are two things.' She paused, took a deep breath, then continued, 'The easiest first. My rat experiments were sort of real but were really just an excuse to be near you.'

His spirits rose.

'You see, my sister reckons humans are still very primitive, almost entirely ruled by genetics and instinct. I thought otherwise. Gloria says a man is only interested in a girl for her looks, for her baby-making potential. I wanted to find out if a man could be motivated by a girl's intellect.'

Gloria cut in, 'Now, sis. you shouldn't talk about a fellow as if he's one of your maze-running rats,' before placing a warm, reassuring hand on Chris's forearm.

Sliding Gloria's hand away, Chris replied indignantly, 'I can't believe what you are implying. Was I …'

He tried to express his growing alarm and rising indignation by getting up, but for some reason, his legs wouldn't obey. Immobilised, he sat, stunned into a bewildered silence.

'Susan! Really, there's no need to immobilise him,' said Gloria, 'he's not going to do anything silly. He's looking for an explanation that's all.'

Susan didn't answer immediately, but sighed, then eventually met his gaze, this time with a mix of sympathy and confusion.

Returning to her sister, she made her confession, 'Chris *was* attracted by my intellect. I'm certain of it. But,' in a whisper, 'in the end it was my femaleness that overwhelmed him; and, me as well!'

Inside his head, he could actually feel her confusion, and something else.

'I hadn't realised just how powerful this man-woman thing was. I think I've been changed. So, it's just as well the ship is scheduled to pick us up tonight. I don't think I could continue the way it was before.'

'But we can't leave until we've resolved this new issue,' Gloria reminded her with an exasperated look and an accompanying exhalation.

'Can someone have the decency to tell me what's going on, I …'

Susan cut him off and held up a hand.

'The first problem is: I like you, Chris. Really like you. I've never had to deal with something like that before. The other thing is … is that, I … we, are not what we seem to be.'

Part of him livened up at her expression of regard, but then became apprehensive about the other bit.

'Just tell me what the problem is. I'm sure intelligent people like us can figure things out,' he said, almost pleadingly.

'I think it's easiest if Gloria does a demonstration.'

Leaving Chris to stare in puzzlement, Gloria rose, walked to the centre of the room, and slowly stripped. His eyes bulged. Was there no end to the surprises? Then a nightmare began.

The magnificent female sex goddess morphed into a seven-foot alien, sort of like a long-haired kangaroo, though the hair was multi-coloured, the tail was thin, looked prehensile; two pair of thin arms articulated from a barrel chest, on top of which perched a large head, flat faced, with a broad mouth revealing reassuringly blunt dentition, above which were two large eyes on short stalks, whilst further back were two small trumpet-like ears.

The top of the head supported a showy mane of black hair. This apparition then did several slow, controlled cartwheels, then appeared to melt into a slightly smaller version, arms longer, tail definitely prehensile. A few more cartwheels later, it changed into a scaly prawn-shaped creature. Two more cartwheels followed, and then with a spectacular back-flip, it returned to its starting position. The alien slowly reformed back into the gloriously naked Gloria, who dressed without hurrying and then returned to her seat.

'That's the other problem,' Susan blandly stated, before leaning on the table with her face in her hands, looking sad and disconsolate.

Chris's brain was doing some metamorphosing of its own, struggling to believe what his eyeballs were telling it.

Time passed.

Finally, Susan tried further explanation.

'Gloria and I are some of those aliens you have been trying to detect. We come from Auri, a planet about two thousand light-years from here. It was a nice place, until we wrecked it. We now live on Offee III.' She paused, took in his horror, before continuing. 'Don't get too condescending, or horrified by our morphologies, you humans change considerably during your life cycle, and also look pretty weird and disgusting at times.'

She had a point.

He tried to reassure her.

'I guess you're right. Most people I know of look a whole lot better covered up.'

Mollified, Susan continued. 'You see, we adapted to our changing environment by evolving a flexible physiology. It was only when we ruined our home planet that we were forced to develop technology, technology far in advance of yours. But then we've been around a lot longer than your species.'

Gloria interrupted, 'Forget our better technology. This living in human form is the best ever! You feel things I'd never dreamed of back home.'

A contented smile drifted across Gloria's face, then evaporated, to be replaced by a more determined look.

'Look, we can't just sit around chatting. A big decision has to be made. What are we going to do about the developments over east on the faster-than-light communication? You know it won't be long before they'll develop faster-than-light travel. They're not ready for it and, I don't think we're ready for them to come a-visiting.'

Glancing at Chris, she added, 'And you have to decide what to do with your man.'

Again, he tried to move, but couldn't. Tried to speak. Susan just raised a finger, and his voice froze. A frightening realisation slammed into him. She had control over both his body *and* his brain. Panic erupted.

Susan's calming voice flooded his mind like an incoming tide caressing the shoreline.

'You are right. I, we, can read minds and, to a certain extent, control them. Mind-to-mind is how we normally communicate. You, being a different species, I can't get too deep, but we can choose *not* to read and control your thoughts and actions. So, you have reason to be fearful. Luckily for you, we happen to find humans amusing and likable. So, bear with me. Trust me if you can. I have some very important issues to resolve.'

After that, Chris simply sat, unable to speak or move. Like a pebble on a beach, he watched and heard Susan and Gloria argue aloud, to and fro upon the fate of the human race.

'Come on, sis, we have to make a decision,' Gloria finally urged. 'I can't deny that I've had a great time here. This business of having sex for fun is going to be hard to give up. But it's something we can only enjoy in human form. It's amazing that no other intelligent beings practise recreational sex. Ahhh …'

Gloria leant back to silently gaze skyward, seemingly lost in an erotic reverie.

'I know, I know,' replied Susan with reluctance. 'But it's their susceptibility to primitive aggressions and mindless savagery that worries me most. You only have to read their history, or glance at a news bulletin …'

Gloria "awoke", turned to Susan, and answered with great sadness in her voice, 'Yes. I've skimmed plenty of minds and seen, and felt, stuff truly horrible, but, dear sister, I've also come across plenty of really kind thoughts too. They are such a conundrum: good and bad all mixed together.'

'Let's face it, our ancestors were a pretty savage lot too,' Susan confessed.

'Again, you're right, but we still have to get our act together. Today. Now.'

The sisters paused momentarily, turned in unison to face Chris, who was red faced from his impotent attempts to shout his protests. Susan glanced at Gloria.

And suddenly, he was free. Tentatively, he moved an arm, his lips, and then, reassured he had regained his body, breathed deeply in relief. Finally, he spoke.

'Thank you, ladies. First: I'm extremely glad you've remained in human guise. Don't know if I am ready to cope with your normal shape, not yet anyway. Which morphology was it by the way? No! No need to answer that. It doesn't matter.'

He drew breath. 'But I think it only civilised for the condemned man to be given the chance to defend himself, and his species.'

Susan now protested.

'Of course you will be allowed to speak, it's just that I needed time to try and settle this confusion in my mind. Sister and I are only students, you know! No one expected humans to figure out the faster-than-light problem, especially this early in their development. We've not been trained to make the big decisions forced upon us by the recent, unexpected developments here. But we're the only ones in this sector and must ...'

She seemed on the verge of tears. Her fears and insecurities leaked across into Chris's mind, but he didn't need that to convince him that he wanted to help her, and humanity. He cut in.

'Before you write us humans off as being totally irresponsible, please remember that, despite our primitive side, for the vast majority of the time we keep those impulses under control. Otherwise, we wouldn't have gotten this far. Okay, the planet is a bit of a mess, but we are fixing it. Even the politicians have finally realised this is our only planet.'

'That's the problem,' Susan retorted. 'You are only just beginning to think and act with long-term social and ecological sustainability in mind. If you get faster-than-light travel before sustainability is truly embedded in your psyche, you'll just export all the mistakes made on this planet to thousands of others. Who knows how many life forms will be made extinct because of it. That's our dilemma.'

'Hmm. I see what you mean.'

Another silence descended, this time enveloping all three of them.

After a few minutes of unfocused staring at the teapot, Chris realised he was thirsty, and so poured the tea into their mugs.

'Always think better sipping a nice brew,' he said with surprising optimism. Adding honey from the jar that lived permanently on the table, he then took a sip. It had a lovely fragrance, made smooth from the honey. Its passage then released a strong, invigorating heat, courtesy of the ginger. If there was a beverage capable of solving any problem, this brew was it.

The girls followed his lead and joined in his tea appreciation ceremony. The atmosphere relaxed.

Casting aside the doom of the world, he asked Susan, 'So how come we haven't been able to pick up any signals of all these intelligent, sophisticated life forms that you imply populate the galaxy?'

'Simple. Really advanced cultures don't use radio frequencies for communication, as humanity will shortly find out. And evidence of our existence via electromagnetic emissions from industrial sources is drowned by normal stellar activity.'

Gloria interjected, 'The other thing is, nobody, except us, know humans exist. Which is good news for you because there are some pretty nasty types out there. But plenty of nice ones too, like us. And, although we've known of your existence for millennia, most of our kind never considered humanity highly evolved enough to be worth studying, let alone talking to.' Then, with a deprecating shake of her head and a shrug of a shoulder, she added: 'Sorry!'

Chris had never considered that last humbling possibility.

Another silence followed. His eyes wandered from the teapot to the kettle on the stove, then drifted back to his childhood.

He saw his mother standing by the cooker, supervising him like a hawk in his first attempt at pancakes, trying to teach him about the dangers inherent in playing with hot stoves. The sudden thought struck him that it must have been tough on his mother, constantly having to watch over him, to keep him out of harm's way, to keep him on track. She hadn't always been successful. He'd accumulated plenty of scar tissue growing up.

Susan's mind gently entwined with his train of thought. It was a bizarre experience that was slowly getting easier to bear. Gloria joined in, and between the three of them, they teased it out.

Perhaps humanity could be made ready for interstellar travel, for meeting other intelligences, if given enough careful supervision and coaching. And who better to do the supervising than the delectable Susan and Gloria! A solution was born.

§

Twenty-four years, two months and three days later, the child of their brainstorming, or rather, brain sharing session sat on the launching pad: humanity's first faster-than-light starship, its gleaming cylindrical form lording over the launching pad five hundred metres behind President Alvarez, standing proudly at the lectern, centre place on a small stage surrounded by semicircular rows of prominent citizens, scientists and project engineers.

President Alvarez's speech had ground to a halt. The crowd regained consciousness, then became suddenly aware that he had moved his right hand towards the big red lever beside the lectern. Casting his eyes upon his now enlivened audience, he then glanced right, nodded to his beloved wife, the most popular First Lady in recorded history, and the open secret behind his success. Though seated, she dominated the stage with her trademark red hair, shining in the late morning sun. He blew her a kiss before giving the crowd a beaming smile and then pulling the lever.

A painful hush arose that was instantly shattered by an eruption of wild applause when the starship rose silently and gracefully skyward. It gained speed rapidly, and then, with a final flash of reflected sunshine, disappeared.

Inside the huge marquee at the celebration banquet, Christopher Ambrosio sat delighted to be at the top table, with the presidential party. Doubly so because it reminded him of old times, bracketed by Gloria, the President's famous wife, on his left, and his darling Susan on his right. Today was the culmination of a joint dream.

After the feasting, all three rose and mingled. Chris found himself temporarily separated from the girls whilst having another reconnoitre of the desserts. There, he found himself being accosted by Finlayson.

'Hello, Chris, long time, no see.'

The fellow, as podgy as ever, was now greyer and thinner of hair than on the last occasion, years, decades back. Finlayson pointed to the colourful crowd and added an unnecessary comment, 'A historic moment.'

'Certainly is. It's great to see you.'

Chris shook the proffered hand, cold and limp, with false enthusiasm. 'So, what are you doing these days?'

He'd not seen the fellow since university. It was Finlayson who first sparked his interest in the S.E.T.I League, and extra-terrestrials.

'Chief Editor of *GALAXY*.'

'Still a great magazine. You've got a terrific website. Hopefully, I'll get more of a chance to visit it now that the starship is finally off the ground. I guess you'll be having something to say about today's event?'

'Yep. Though not as starry-eyed as you would have us all believe. As I've stated before, I still have a fair bit of anxiety about the ship's destination.'

'It was carefully selected, for reasons long announced and debated over,' Chris replied, a little concerned by Finlayson's negativity, though he well understood the reasons behind it.

'Yes, I know, but I've been told by other teams monitoring the area that there are possible signs of intelligent life coming from that part of the galaxy. So ...'

Chris was quick to the defence, 'Look, we employed the best equipment available and found no evidence of intelligent life, so you have nothing to worry about.'

Then he added, 'If your friends have detected something, then they'd better recheck their data, because I've an army of scientists, with state-of-the-art equipment, who will prove otherwise.'

He paused and then tried a more conciliatory tone.

'Look, I fully understand your concern about the kind of conditions our astronauts will find when they get there. But we've got it covered.'

'I hope so, because the issue is something that's always been downplayed. I just hope we don't regret what, or who, we find when we get there,' he said with a face replete with dire concern.

He was then distracted by a colleague of his, waving at him. Having said his piece, Finlayson dashed off, as if suddenly embarrassed to be in Chris's company, leaving Chris to contemplate Finlayson's words of warning.

Glancing over towards the girls, he saw Gloria and Susan deep in conversation. Their happy presence induced an amused grin and jolted his mind back to one of the S.E.T.I. League's meetings, attended a lifetime ago. Finlayson had been there.

A fellow had stood up and announced in a strident retort that he hoped the aliens we first met were practising Christians; that they would "love their new neighbours, as themselves."

The man's outcry set off a heated debate.

Chris suppressed the desire for smug chuckling because none at the debate, and very few he'd met since, knew the lesser-known version of that biblical declaration: love thy neighbour but choose your neighbourhood!

He had no worries in that regard. Gloria and Susan had made sure we would be landing in a good neighbourhood. That our first extra-terrestrial encounter would be with their people first.

Humanity was in for a very pleasant, and very educational, surprise!

Gallius II

Three goes!

A semi-conscious Captain Churchill flopped back in disbelief. So much effort just to kill the unrelenting buzzing and flashing red light atop his bedside terminal. Being torn from sleep at two-forty-seven was bad, but this reminder of his declining powers was far worse. Fifteen years back, even five, he would have hit the Accept button in one, and, been fully awake in milliseconds. Breathing heavily, he luxuriated in the blessed silence until, all too soon, it was again shattered, this time by the youthful contralto of their new Communications Officer issuing from the terminal's speakers.

'Sir, we've just received a distress call from Gallius II. Commander Spraken insisted you be informed.'

Spraken had the conn, had handled plenty of distress calls, so why bother him with this one? Grunting, Churchill stretched closer to the terminal's screen, squinted, and then tried to comprehend the transcript glowering at him in orange, 16-point Arial:

This is Gallius II Research Station, the damn cat has destroyed the attenuator's controller, jammed it shut, the powerplant's going to blow, we need...

'That's it?'

'Yes, Captain, that's all that got through before all communications were lost. We've been unable to raise anyone on Gallius II since, on any frequency.'

Churchill scowled, silently cursed the message, Co2suppressed a groan, before finally constructing a response.

'Rrright. In that case, Lieutenant ...' her name eluded him temporarily – there'd been so many over the decades – '... Thalis, keep trying to raise them, but before you do that, transfer me to Spraken.'

After a few seconds, Spraken's steadfast voice came on.

'Yes, Captain?'

'Spraken, that message can't be real. How can an animal cause a power station to blow? If it's a scam to lure us away from our current course then it's poorly done. So, what makes you think it's real, not bogus?'

'TeeJay, the request was definitely from the research station on Gallius II and on the emergency band. Thus, is unlikely to be bogus, as you so quaintly put it. Once you hear the full audio you will understand.'

'Humph. Okay. I'm listening.'

The terminal's speakers erupted with the sound of a man's startled, frightened plea, cut short by an ear-jarring crashing and banging, then silence. Churchill sighed from premonitions of dramas about to befall them.

'Okay. I guess we'd best divert to Gallius II. As I recall, it's not too far out of our way. Light-Multiple Six and scanners on maximum.'

Churchill waited while Spraken gave the helmsman their new destination, then continued once Spraken's attention was again his to command, 'Didn't know we had any settlements on Gallius II. And, how does a cat get at a powerplant's whatsit?'

'The planet was discovered a few centuries back but never received much attention because of its inhospitable climate and lack of easily exploitable minerals. There is one settlement, or rather a construction site for such a settlement. The only completed buildings are a laboratory, a few administrative offices, a couple of accommodation blocks, a site office, and parts of the spaceport.

'Not exactly a tourist hotspot then. Any strategic value?'

'None that spring to mind, apart from being one of the few M class planets in the sector – one only of interest to climate scientists, biologists and others who like excessive cold wilderness and bizarre megafauna. The cat referred to in the message is presumably the planet's terrestrial apex predator, a catlike creature, bigger than a Bengal tiger and also striped, though grey on a pale-grey background. It is remarkably indestructible and, apparently intelligent.'

'So, not someone's pet tabby. Sentient?'

'Possibly. The data is incomplete. But if former Chief Engineer McCabe was here with us, he'd have classified them as, "dangerous and canny cats".'

Did he detect hints of emotion in Spraken's voice? Humour and loss intermingled? Was Spraken also missing their old comrade, now in a nursing home, bedridden and dozy on painkillers? Fond thoughts, and sad, were cut short by Spraken's continuation.

'The item it "got at" was the powerplant's attenuator, or, more correctly, its Magma Attenuation Terminus. All geothermal plants that directly tap into a magma chamber have one. It's a pressure and temperature relief port that must be kept open at all times.'

'Surely a wild animal would have no inclination to attack an exhaust pipe, or whatever it is. The story still seems an impossible one to me.'

'It is unusual behaviour but these cats have been strangely drawn to humanity right from the start. Apparently, during the drilling of the pipeline to the magma chamber, many delays were caused by the workers being harassed by these cats, although only one was ever seen on any occasion. They eventually had to use their plasma guns. Amazingly, the cat wasn't destroyed. It ran off injured, later to return, but always at a safer distance. Its incredible resilience has been put down to it possibly having a semi-metallic hide that somehow redirects the energy of a plasma discharge to the ground. The cat appeared to end its surveillance once the wall and watchtowers were operational.'

'An indestructible beast is going to be very hard to deal with if it's still around.'

'I agree, especially because we know nothing of the reasons for its fixation upon the powerplant.

'Hmm. Anything else?'

'The break in transmission and the sounds of destruction before and after the message are consistent with the expected consequences of a blocked attenuator. It would have destroyed the power plant, the central administration building – the location of the call – and every structure within a ten-kilometre radius; basically, the entire settlement. It probably induced a minor earthquake and, possibly volcanic outpourings from the magma chamber.'

'Explosions, volcanoes, earthquakes, and an indestructible tabby on steroids. Spraken, this is just like the old days! I hope we're still up to it. We haven't had any real tests of character since the Felahein disaster nine years back.'

'Nine years and fifty-eight days, ship's time. But nine years is close enough.'

Spraken conceding that nine years "was close enough", induced a knowing grin, but Churchill decided not to pursue its implications, choosing instead to concentrate on what their next moves should be. A yawn made the decision an easy one.

'I'm going back to sleep. Only wake me if there's an emergency you can't handle. Arrange a conference of department heads at oh-eight-hundred.'

'Consider it done.'

'How long before we establish orbit around the planet?'

'About fourteen hours. Around four p.m. ship's time. One a.m. on Gallius II.'

Churchill again smiled. Until Felahein, Spraken almost never gave approximations; everything was expressed to three decimal places. But after, Spraken, his Platonist philosopher-king, had declared it counterproductive to give false comfort with displays of accuracy from his genetically modified and cybernetically enhanced brain. He'd come to fully accept that such statements were misleading, because all estimates were dependent upon assumptions about the predictability of events, events that occur in a universe awash with unknowables and randomness. Thus, Spraken now preferred to voice his pronouncements more correctly in the language of approximations and best guesses.

But Spraken's greater acceptance of being unsure hadn't yet found a permanent home in Churchill's mind. Perhaps, over the decades of their association, he'd been permanently spoilt by Spraken's status as an island of certainty in a sea of doubt. Despite his continuing discomfort with uncertainty, Churchill was still glad Spraken had forced reality upon him, and his crew, because it made them less surprised when things went pear-shaped, and, possibly, a little more grateful when miracles happened.

But he'd been silent too long.

'Very good, Commander Spraken. I'll get a little more beauty sleep and will meet you in the conference room at eight. Churchill out.'

Dragging the Encephalocap from his bedside drawer, Churchill tapped in the wakeup time and increased the setting for REM-sleep in the hope of encouraging creative solutions for dealing with Gallius II's troublesome feline. Pulling up the blanket, he shut his eyes and was asleep in less than a minute.

§

Fully rested and fortified by a hearty breakfast, Churchill approached the conference room, outwardly relaxed and confident, but pleased to sense an undercurrent of anxiety. It was a good sign, because total fearlessness was the mark of a fool.

All eyes watched expectantly as he entered the room and strolled to his place at the head of the table. After benevolent nods to those assembled, he turned to Spraken. 'Any updates, Commander?'

'We recently intercepted a very weak signal from an EPIRB in the vicinity of the spaceport, which suggests some survivors.'

'A promising start. Okay, ladies and gentlemen. You've studied the summary of the situation on Gallius II, and, as directed, have submitted your initial suggestions to me. I'll now pass them on to all of you. You'll have the first fifteen to twenty minutes to read each other's responses, after which I'll go around the table asking for any revised comments and priorities. Any questions?'

None were raised. The room solidified into studious silence.

Fifty-seven minutes later, with an action plan agreed upon, the meeting broke up. Spraken and Churchill were the last to leave.

'Spraken, I suggest you get some sleep. You have five or so hours before we transpond down with the Recon and Rescue squad. Do you really think one lighting balloon will be enough? The planet's moons are both small and will provide little illumination.'

'We don't actually need any illumination since we will be wearing night-vision glasses. I only suggested the dirigible – "balloon" is a poor descriptor – on psychological grounds. Most of our crew are inexperienced at dealing with real emergencies, and none have ever faced an apparently indestructible predator. Humans react poorly when fearful and more so in dark places.

The dirigible will serve the same psychological function as a child's security blanket.'

'A very humbling assessment, but all too true. It's something I should have considered, but one forgets how insecure one was when young.'

Memories of youthful ignorance brought forth smiles steeped in compassion and amusement; one flashed to life from much practise, the other was slower, more subdued and somewhat self-conscious. Churchill then turned and marched off heading for the bridge, leaving Spraken ambling towards his cabin.

§

Like the other members of the Recon and Rescue squad, Churchill stood, dressed in a padded survival suit, gloves, and a yellow safety helmet, slightly crouched with plasma gun drawn. They had landed on the edge of the barren, rocky rise slated to be the town's central "square", or, rather, circle, since the town's layout was circular, with two ear-like protrusions, one for the power station, the other for the spaceport. They were not far from the remains of the Administration and Accommodation buildings, on the road that circled the central open space. The only structures still standing were the town's enclosing wall and its watchtowers, which housed the automated weaponry used for discouraging the planet's gargantuan herbivores and its oversized cats.

Beyond the wall, past the cleared buffer zone, were dark ranks of trees marching up the narrowing valley into the encircling foothills, there to be defeated by the implacable white of upland glaciers. Above, unfamiliar constellations twinkled in a clear, frigid sky.

With no immediate danger apparent, Churchill tapped the button activating his throat microphone. 'We disperse as planned. Predators may remain within the compound, so guns at the ready, set on maximum. Stay alert and you'll stay safe. Churchill out.'

His earbuds rattled to the acknowledgements from his team leaders, after which the assemblage jogged off to their assigned task, the remains of the power station being the first stop for Churchill and Spraken, along with Manzek and Framinski from Security.

A short while later they halted at the edge of the ring of debris surrounding the blackened crater where the Magma Attenuation Terminus had been. A hundred metres behind lay the dark smear of rubble that once had been the power station's central building. The air was thick with foul-smelling steam.

Churchill could go no further, not because of the stench, but from a sudden giddiness, and then the confusion and shock of finding his sight blurring. His heart was pounding and his legs were about to give way. Was this a heart attack? Only last week the medicos had pronounced him a very fit sixty-year-old. This shouldn't be happening!

Relief, of a sort, came when he saw that youngsters like Manzek and Framinski were similarly suffering, holding their chests and unsteady on their feet. Only Spraken appeared untouched as he calmy picked a path through the rubble to peer into the stinking pit.

'Spraken! Get back! The air's poisoned!' gasped Churchill, whilst frantically motioning to Manzek and Framinski to retreat.

Spraken seemed not to hear, and continued his leisurely scrutiny of the remains of the attenuator. After what seemed a lifetime, he turned towards them.

'Malodorous, but definitely not poisonous according to my Analyser. Your apparent discomfort, and possible fear, undoubtedly stem from a failure to comprehend one small but important fact, clearly stated in the briefing notes. The air of

Gallius II, whilst breathable, has significantly lower levels of carbon dioxide than is usual for a class M planet.'

Churchill exchanged frowns with the two security men, after which Spraken reminded them, with barely disguised amusement, that human breathing is primarily triggered by high carbon dioxide levels in the blood, and less so by low oxygen. Thus, on Gallius II, humans could incur an oxygen deficit from the delayed breathing induced by the atmosphere's low carbon dioxide content, especially so when exercising.

Whilst Spraken bludgeoned them with this obscure fact, Churchill and the two security men consciously practised breathing and soon regained their physical composure. But Churchill continued to wrestle with two annoyances: firstly, Spraken's apparent smugness, and, secondly, his own inadequacy in not being able to graciously accept unsweetened truth. How many more such occasions would it take before he no longer cringed when he was found lacking? Plenty, it seemed.

Spraken strolled over. They exchanged non-committal glances. If Spraken had seen his discomfort, he gave no indications of it. Squaring his shoulders, Churchill gathered his tattered pride, and, with a benevolent wave of the hand, as though bestowing a rare honour, addressed his second-in-command.

'As Science Officer, it's only proper that you should be the one to broadcast, to all personnel, the effects of this planet's low CO_2 levels, and its cures. In the meantime,' pointing to himself and the other two, 'we'll practise our breathing.'

Once the message was sent, and queries answered, Spraken announced to Churchill: 'All were most pleased with my timely information. Amazingly, they too seemed to have overlooked the issue.'

Spraken's reply wasn't as deadpanned and poker-faced as in days of old. There'd been a faint lifting of the eyebrows and ghost movements around the lips that suggested he was enjoying his eugenic and electronically enhanced superiority, which implied he'd been infected by the troublesome "normal" human sin of pride. If so, it was a worrying development that required a considered response. But one he would have to postpone to a more appropriate time and place.

'Well done, Commander. Once again you have given us a timely reminder of the human adage about the "devil" being in the detail. Anyway, we've work to do. There's nothing more to learn here, and no clues as to how the cat got in, or where it got to. Securing the compound is our priority. We'll split up. Manzek and I will go left, and, along the way, check on progress at the spaceport. You and Framinski go right. We walk around the wall, checking both sides for its integrity, and make sure all the watchtowers have their backup batteries and weapons fully operational. I suspect a malfunction in one allowed the cat to get in.'

A little over an hour later, the two teams were within shouting distance having almost completed their circuit. Framinski and Manzek were up in the two remaining towers, whilst Churchill and Spraken had emerged from their respective ground level access gates having checked the wall's exterior. It was then that Framinski's excited voice boomed into Churchill's earbuds.

'Commander Spraken, Captain Churchill, I've found the lazy dog!'

'What? Talk sense man! And don't shout!' Churchill shouted back.

Sentiments repeated in quieter and calmer tones by Spraken, who was strolling over to the open door at the base of Framinski's tower.

'Sorry, sirs, but that's what we call 'em back home on Regis IV,' he explained, with less volume, 'It's a wilderness world like this one, and we protect our settlements with these walls and watchtowers, or "Defence-Offence-Guardians" as they're officially called. But "dog" is a lot shorter. And the opposite of an active dog, is a lazy dog.'

Framinski then went on to explain that the P37 detector circuit in the tower's motherboard was giving false negatives – a problem also encountered on Regis IV. The immediate fix was a system reboot, and, later, replacement of the circuit.

After completing their final inspections, Churchill and Manzek joined Spraken by the door of Framinski's "lazy dog". Sounds of tinkering floated down from the top of the stairwell.

'Captain, this is definitely the entry point. The wall's outer access door is severely scratched, which is a considerable achievement against Duraline steel. The creature obviously gave up the unrewarding task of burrowing through it and instead managed to somehow scramble over the wall, again leaving plenty of claw marks in its equally hard surface. What happened afterwards is open to conjecture.'

'Does that mean the beast is still inside the compound?' asked Manzek in tones heavy with fear.

'It is possible,' replied Spraken. 'But the powerplant's location would more likely have resulted in the cat being thrown out of the compound than in, and, wherever it landed, it probably didn't survive.'

'However,' Churchill added, 'we must assume, for now, that it still lives and is inside the compound. Whilst here, we might as well join Framinski in the tower and learn about these P37 circuits. Once everything is operational, we'll join whichever team needs extra assistance.'

Shortly after, a circle of "supervisors" stood around the outstretched legs of Framinski, the rest of whom was in the bowels of the main console, finishing installing a new P37 he'd found in a drawer. A few moments later he wriggled free, clambered to his feet, and was dusting himself down when the tower, and everything and everyone in it, began violently shaking.

They had become victims of the first outrageous tantrums of a powerful earthquake that had them violently jostled and fighting to stay upright. Through the open door, Captain Churchill was agog at the sight of the jiggling remains of a nearby outbuilding bringing to life the "ghosts of the dead", in the form of a swarm of swirling and gyrating dust-devils dancing across its surface.

Unknown minutes passed before the ground settled enough for them to stand with ease, allowing them to concentrate on steadying erratic breathing. The respite briefly raised collective hopes for a return to normality only to have them shattered by the ear-splitting boom of a violent explosion towards the head of the valley.

Turning to the outside window, Churchill watched a huge plume of ash and steam shoot up like a malevolent genie, its gaseous form coloured a Hadean-burnt-orange by tongues of lava emerging beneath it. The lava burrowed hungrily into the forest, setting it ablaze, adding black smoke and flickering reds to the hellish lightshow.

When the sounds of the volcano's birth had subsided to a steady but noisy grumbling – reminiscent of a giant gargling boulders – Churchill contacted all team leaders and ordered an immediate evacuation. Exempted were Doc Gruen's team over at the spaceport, who were very close to digging out the probable sole survivor.

'Spraken, talk to your assistant back onboard the *Gallant* to see if the ship's sensors and computer can determine how this eruption is likely to pan out. We need to know how long we can safely stay here. Meanwhile, we four will jog, mindfully, back to the spaceport to …'

A thunderous banging and clattering obliterated Churchill's closing remarks as the tower's roof was battered by a hail of rocks. Twenty or more mind-numbing minutes elapsed before the deluge dwindled to a stony drizzle. Outside, the surface of the compound had been blanketed with a thick layer of grey dust, through which protruded an abundant scattering of large stones, like the pustules on a plague victim's skin.

Though relative quiet had returned to the outside world, within the tower reigned a cacophony of coughing and spluttering as all four occupants staggered about blindly, fumbling with their suit's camel-packs to get sufficient water to rinse the cloying dust from their throats. After this, they splashed their faces to clear their night-vision glasses, whose sealed, face-hugging, wraparound style had kept the dust out of their eyes, a small design feature now much appreciated.

Eventually, a semblance of order returned, allowing Churchill to call up Hal Gruen at the spaceport, who, between coughs, thankfully reported no new injuries or significant impact upon their rescue work. Churchill reassured him that they'd soon be over to assist them in their efforts.

By this time, Spraken was standing mute, wearing one of the clear, polymer facemasks that all survival suits were equipped with. As Science Officer, he'd naturally been first to act against the dangers that volcanic dust posed to human lungs. Churchill dug out his and instructed Framinsky and Manzek to do likewise.

Masked, they then gathered at the base of the tower, where Churchill found himself momentarily disoriented. All his landmarks had been reshaped by the eruption and were now in undiluted hues of bilious green from his night-vision glasses. Gone were the reassuringly colours provided by the lighting dirigible – taken out by the deluge of ash and pumice.

Spraken nudged him, pointing to the right. After nodding his thanks, Churchill led the way at a fast walk, all the while monitoring his breathing, which seemed easier with the mask on. They had just squeezed through the gap between the wall and the remains of the Site Manager's office, at the start of the protrusion leading to the spaceport, when Churchill brought them to a standstill and pointed.

'Look!'

Emerging from the left side of the ash-smothered rubble was a haphazard trail of large pawprints, initially heading towards the spaceport before turning back towards the town's centre. The tracks grew more regular with each stride.

Churchill tapped on his throat mic and waited briefly before Hal Gruen responded. He explained about the fresh tracks, and their intention of following them to ascertain the cat's exact whereabouts.

Doc Gruen replied with the news that they were in visual, and voice contact, with Quezal, the site manager, and would soon be transponding back to the *Gallant*. He ended with the uncalled-for advice for TeeJay to be careful, so as to not clog up his sickbay.

'Will do. You know me; when you speak, I obey!' replied Churchill irreverently.

Gruen's departing chuckle induced a moment of comparison. He was a good doctor, and a good man, who always reminded Churchill of a more jovial version of dearly departed and sorely missed Doc Royan – Felahein's first casualty. Sadness and levity entwined, danced briefly with his soul, then vanished, as all moments do when the demands of the present muscle in.

Squinting, Churchill considered the trail of pawprints, but had barely started his deliberations when Spraken intruded with thoughts mirroring his.

'The beast was injured, judging by the erratic nature of its initial tracks, but seems to have quickly recovered.'

'Yes, which makes things difficult.'

'Couldn't we track it using the ship's remote sensors. It'd be safer,' said Manzek.

Spraken's reply was to point heavenward, inducing Manzek, then Framinski, and finally Churchill, to look up. The ash cloud had already claimed over half the sky and was still extending its reach, blocking both the feeble moonlight and the possibility of any help from the spaceship's visual sensors.

'We can forget the *Gallant's* sensors,' said Churchill, whilst double-checking that his plasma gun was set to maximum. 'It's up to us now. Injured or not, the cat remains a dangerous and unknown quantity, and one we must locate and then make sure it poses no threat to Doc Gruen and his team.'

'If it attacks, how do we neutralise it, Captain?' asked Spraken.

'Firstly, by keeping it at a respectful distance, and, should it turn nasty, four simultaneous plasma gun blasts will hopefully be sufficient to discourage it. I also think we over estimate its desire to harm us. All reports show the cat being more curious than aggressive towards humans. Its only aggression so far has been against the powerplant.'

Spraken and the others seemed mollified by his reasoning, and together they moved out, Churchill and Spraken leading, Manzek and Framinski flanking a few paces behind. Churchill trod slowly, carefully, all senses alert in a world turned suddenly silent, the volcano's grumblings tuned out as he focused on the tracks and tried to navigate in the unfamiliar terrain.

After a while, the tracks threaded around the mounds marking the remains of the accommodation buildings then led towards the top of the central wasteland, which puzzled Churchill. If the cat had any sense of direction, and desired to escape, it should have been heading left, back to the wall and Framinski's "lazy dog". Why was it heading in the wrong direction?

Spraken broke into his thoughts, or rather, spoke them. 'Captain, the cat seems disinclined to escape the compound, or is disoriented. Or, possibly, has an entirely different motivation.'

'At least it's moving away from the spaceport,' replied a relieved Churchill.

A few minutes later, they rounded a clutch of boulders and caught their first glimpse of the cat, in the shape of its long fluffy tail disappearing amongst a scattering of roughly rectangular tors close to the high point of the central rise. Churchill brought them to a halt, gave Doc Gruen an update, and received the news that his team was almost ready to extract Quezal.

'Gruen is almost there. We'll continue to follow the cat, with maximum caution and making sure we have clear sightlines in case we need to defend ourselves, but don't fire unless I order it,' he said, scanning the faces and demeanour of all three, especially Manzek.

They moved off in the same order as before. Nearing the top, the pawprints led through a narrow gap between a pair of huge standing stones with the truculent demeanour of monstrous bouncers guarding a gambling den. This squeezed them into single file; Churchill leading, breathing suspended and plasma gun at the ready.

Once back in the open, his breathing restarted with the sight of the tracks continuing towards the next set of rocks, about a hundred metres ahead. The others caught up, and had just taken up their positions when they were again rudely shaken by the rippling progression of another earthquake; not as violent as the first, but more disastrous. The ground gave way beneath them!

Churchill was aware of falling, and of dust and rocks following him down.

Seconds, days, maybe even years later, he awoke to discover that everything hurt, and that, someone, or something, was prodding him, inciting new pains. He was buried waist-deep in rubble, couldn't move his legs, and his arms were restricted by the stiffness of the inflated survival suit.

'TeeJay? TeeJay? Can you move? Anything broken? Can you wiggle your toes?'

It took a while before Spraken's words gained traction. A few experimental movements of body parts allowed for a reply.

'Everything seems to be working, though I feel like I've gone ten rounds with a Krullun Octobeast.

'You are okay then. I'll be back once I've seen to Manzek and Framinski. They need more digging out than you.'

Spraken's triage conclusions and speedy departure were driven by logic, as they should be, but the receding image of his 2iC induced in Churchill a twinge of disappointment that their long friendship hadn't overruled reason, for a microsecond at least. Shaking his foolishness from his head, he took a breath, clumsily turned on the helmet's lights, deflated the top portion of his suit enough to free his arms, and then began the arduous task of clearing the dirt and rocks from his legs.

Even being careful, he still raised a dust cloud that lingered in the still air like a yellow-brown fog, adding to the unease induced by the sombre grey masonry and ribbed arched roof. Thoughts of crypts and haunted catacombs wandered through his mind, which then set it to wondering about the tunnel's long-dead creators. One thing was certain: the planet's rumoured lost civilisation had now turned from fancy to fact.

Thankfully those creators had built well, and the tunnel had not entirely succumbed to the earthquake's power. The arched roof above him was gone, but, along either side, the curved metal supporting beams remained. Looking down the tunnel in both directions, his helmet light revealed zones of collapse that became smaller with distance. Behind the nearest, and largest pile of rubble, jiggled the disembodied shadows and flickering illumination of Spraken's helmet light.

Once free, Churchill brushed off the worst of the dirt and grime and took the first tottering steps towards assisting Spraken, only for him to emerge from around the blockage, also covered in dust, followed immediately after by a similarly dishevelled Framinski, assisting a limping Manzek.

'No serious injuries, TeeJay, thanks to these new safety suits, which are a definite improvement on the good luck we overly relied upon in the old days.'

'Well, we'll need a bit of that old-fashioned luck if we're to get out of here. Any ideas? The hole in the roof is too high and unstable to be an exit.'

'Do you think the cat also fell in?' interjected Manzek.

Churchill answered with shrugged shoulders and silent chin stroking.

'If it is in this tunnel, it will be down there,' pointed Spraken.

Churchill raised his hand, motioning for calm. 'Let's not make hasty conclusions. First, check your plasma guns, mine's working, but the more we have, the better off we are. Whilst you're doing that, I'll try to contact the *Gallant*.'

Despite repeated attempts, the failure to raise the starship with any of their communicators was somewhat compensated by finding all plasma guns fully operational. Churchill then outlined their next moves: they would continue towards the cat's possible location but take advantage of any circumstance that could lead them back to the surface.

'As a plan, it seems to overly rely on the stopping power of our plasma guns, as well as the cat's alleged disinterest in humans,' countered Spraken.

'Possibly, but facing one's adversary is better than have them sneaking up behind you.'

'Ah, I see your logic, and stand corrected.'

Spraken's body language hinted of amusement, not with Churchill, but at himself, which implied he was brave enough to laugh when his intellectual prowess stumbled up against its limits. Churchill found such signs of humility a reassuring omen.

Manzek and Framinski also seemed amused, and energised by the interplay, perhaps instinctively responding to leadership not blinded by hubris. Not that they would have ever have used such a word.

Churchill led the way forward, one careful step at a time. The tunnel began to curve and then developed a downward slope, both of which increased as they moved further down it. The more they progressed, the fewer were the signs of damage, until it dwindled to occasional patches of dust and rock chips.

In addition to the light from his helmet, Churchill had adjusted his plasma gun's sighting beam for use as a torch to search the roof and walls for exit points. Disappointingly, the tunnel continued on without interruption.

After a while, Manzek broke the silence. 'How much further, Captain?'

Churchill was asking himself the same question. If the cat was in the tunnel, they should have seen some signs of it, but nothing so far and they were going deeper.

'Another five minutes, then we turn back.'

They moved on. The curve increased, spiralling right, until the roof and walls disappeared and they suddenly stepped out onto a broad walkway that circled around a perfectly cylindrical cavern about four storeys deep and twenty metres in diameter. Eight or so metres above was a slightly concave and heavily reinforced metal roof, which looked more like the door to a bank's vault than a ceiling.

The door/ceiling was dominated by a faded emblem consisting of a circle of bold stylistic script enclosing three creatures. Two were standing humanoids, one taller than the other, both were naked but for belted skirts similar to that worn by Roman soldiers. Their skin was patterned the same as the sabre-toothed cat squatting between them. In one hand, the taller humanoid held a long staff, while its other hand rested upon the head of the cat, which wore a jewelled collar. The shorter being's raised outer hand held a sheath of what appeared to be flowers or herbs, with its inside hand resting upon the taller one's hand on the cat's head.

Spraken didn't disappoint, uttering his trademark comment of "interesting" before turning his gaze to join that of Churchill, Manzek and Framinski who were silently studying the full extent of the vast chamber. Churchill noted an opening in their walkway about thirty metres to their left that gave access to a staircase, with large gaps between the runners leading down to the next walkway; a sequence repeated at each level. On the lowest, four openings could just be distinguished, leading to places unknown. Spraken again was first to comment.

'No signs of the cat, apart from the logo above us, which strongly suggests it remained on the surface. That aside, Captain, doesn't this structure remind you of the ballistic missile silos of Earth's twentieth and twenty-first centuries?'

'Y-e-s,' Churchill dragged the word out as if it had become inordinately heavy; he paused to catch his breath, then continued, 'Anyway, the most important thing is that we won't be troubled by the cat. Our task now is to find a way to the surface. The planetary surveys definitely made no mention of this "silo" or anything that might suggest a possible exit. The air in here is very stale, so our best bet is to return to our starting point and then explore for escape routes in the other direction.'

They were approximately halfway back when they stopped to wait out a minor tremor, which thankfully dissipated, leaving behind little effect apart from raising a bit more dust. A few minutes later, they were back at the cave-in, which now boasted more open sky and a considerably taller pile of rubble that now offered the possibility of scrambling out.

'Yin and Yang!'

Spraken's remark induced raised eyebrows and puzzlement.

'The same force that imprisoned us has now provided our escape.'

Churchill replied with a certain degree of impatience, 'Interesting, to use your expression, but we're not out yet. Scrambling up may bury us anew. I'll try to contact the *Gallant* first. Perhaps they can transpond us out.'

After several attempts, by Churchill and Spraken, it appeared the metallic framework of the tunnel, or the ash cloud, or both, was blocking communications, leaving muscle power their only option.

'Commander, you're the strongest and tallest, and thus the logical choice for the job. Once on the surface, try again to contact the *Gallant*, or Doc Gruen if that fails. If everything fails, we'll make our run. Framinski will go first, to help pull Manzek up, whilst I'll push from below. Any questions?'

None were raised. Probably because they, like Churchill, were not overly optimistic of success. The rock slide seemed very unstable, as was the crumbling remains of the roof that threatened at any moment to bury them.

After some judicious chin stroking, Spraken announced his conclusions: 'It is probably our best chance. Stand back in case I dislodge any large rocks.'

With a backward glance to make sure the others were well clear, Spraken took a running jump onto the rubble and feverishly scrambled skywards. Squinting against the dust,

Churchill watched Spraken's agonisingly slow progress, which was accompanied by the clatter of dislodged stones. He cringed when Spraken was almost thwarted by the crumbling lip of earth and stones at the top, then punched the air when he finally wriggled and squirmed his way over. A short delay – that felt agonisingly long – ended with Spraken's head and shoulders reappearing at the edge.

'The ash cloud is corrupting communications with the *Gallant*. I can't get through to them, or Gruen, who hopefully managed to transpond up in time. There is more bad news. There are tracks that suggest the cat has been investigating this cave-in. The creature may have fallen in during the last tremor, so watch your backs and scramble up immediately, before any more aftershocks, or the cat turns up.'

Churchill didn't argue, instead, simply waved Framinski forward.

After painful minutes of floundering and cussing, Churchill gave Manzek's booted foot a final thrust to get him over the lip, sliding back a few metres in the process. Rolling over, he lay panting, heart palpitating, on the verge of blacking out. He'd forgotten to breathe.

With recovery came the unpalatable admission that he was getting too old for these sorts of activities, which instigated gloomy visions of the barren landscape of retirement. A minor aftershock was followed by a bang on his helmet from a dislodged rock, jerking him back to the present. The tremor had cured his self-pity, but the price paid was any hope of scrambling out. The mound of rubble beneath him had slumped lower, putting the lip well beyond his grasp.

A few moments later, Spraken's head reappeared.

'Scramble up as far as you can, I'll lower a rope to you for the final section.'

'Rope? We don't have a rope!' Churchill yelled back.

'Ah, yes. I shall have to make one. Give me a few minutes.'

Churchill lay, exhausted, staring up into the green tinted dark, practising his breathing. Time faltered, the minutes stretched, until two things happened: Spraken reappeared at the lip, and Churchill heard rocks being dislodged *in* the tunnel.

Twisting his head in the direction of the noise, the simple tasks of breathing and swallowing became inordinately difficult as he watched a pair of red eyes materialise out of the gloom, followed by a large head, and then a huge, powerful, lithe striped body. As the cat padded towards the base of the rock slide, Churchill, with an immense expenditure of willpower, slowly unclipped the strap holding down his plasma gun, drew it out, and aimed it at the beast's fearsome head.

The creature, unconcerned, moved forward a few more paces, then stopped at the base of the slide, squatted, wrapped its bushy tail around itself and then appeared content to await events. After a while it started emitting a low rhythmic rumbling, matched by an equally rhythmic twitching of the end of its tail.

'Any ideas?' Churchill asked calmly, at moderate volume, whilst keeping his aim firmly upon the cat.

'It will be difficult to bring all our weapons to bear without hitting you,' Spraken replied at equal volume.

It was an impasse that either they, the cat, or the next tremor would break, all with unknowable outcomes, though few likely to be pleasant. What to do?

A rock was digging painfully into his buttocks. Churchill gave in and adjusted his position, ever so slightly. But enough to overcome the slide's co-efficient of static friction, and, invoke the laws of gravity. Suddenly he found himself riding his rocky bed ever closer to the tunnel's floor. The cat jumped back out of the way, but, once the sliding stopped, it pounced.

Churchill found himself pinned to a considerably flatter rockslide by a huge front paw on his chest, with another resting on his right shoulder and the base of his exposed neck. His right hand, numb and aching from colliding with a rock, no longer held his plasma gun.

Defenceless, he stared up at the massive face, dominated by two baleful, red eyes above a mouth boasting hypnotically impressive fangs. Thinking became an unreachable luxury owing to a preoccupation with the pain of five black talons jabbing into his throat, and being barely able to breathe under the crushing weight of the beast.

A rumbling, undulating, growling then wafted over him. Existence slowed, then stalled. There was vague awareness of Spraken's "Hold your fire", after which his senses registered only two things: the sound of breathing and the cat's alien eyes.

"So, this is how it ends" was his only thought, repeated with each timeless blink and breath.

Eventually, time was restarted, by a triviality: a tiny cascade of dust and grit fell from the cat's shoulder. Churchill's brain slammed back into gear, and, from unknown depths, an unexpected question bubbled up.

'What do you want?' he whispered through dry lips, with a calm that amazed him.

Perhaps death's undeniable presence cures fear. Churchill felt a lightness and sense of release from earthly cares, until a slight increase of pressure from the claws on his throat brought back unfinished reality. The creature's eyes seemed to sharpen their focus on him, its growling changed pitch, and the pressure on his throat eased.

"What's happening?" was dimly heard from above. It sounded like Framinski. Some sort of debate followed, which stopped, to be replaced by the sound of muffled movements and occasional grunts. But thoughts of salvation from above proved near impossible to hold on to under the continuing scrutiny of the cat. He had to do something.

He tried smiling. No effect. He tried moving. The cat's rumblings wavered, likewise the pressure on his chest, but otherwise, nothing. That it showed no immediate indications it wanted to eat him was its most puzzling behaviour. If he wasn't a meal, why was he being held? No answers came.

Above, movements were heard, which resolved into a glanced view of Spraken's head poking over the edge, his helmet lights blazing down like three white eyes.

'I have made a rope by cutting off the arms and legs of our suits. Even where you are now it should be long enough. I shall clamber down and assist you,' he calmly announced.

Had that great brain of his blow a circuit! And surely Manzek and Framinski weren't going along with his madness. Were they all oblivious to the "tiger" at his throat?

In that moment, thirty years of frustrations with Spraken's uncompromising logic and strange Platonist's attitudes erupted inside him. Unleashed was a roaring anger at Spraken's utter disregard for their safety, and for lowering the chances of Framinski and Manzek's making it back alive. All so he could prove some bizarre theory concerning the cat, for some idea he found "interesting". How that word made him scream! His rage was made all the more intolerable by being unable to yell it aloud for fear of disturbing the cat, or perhaps prompting some equally stupid act from the two security men.

For uncountable moments, every particle of his body, and every corner of his mind reverberated to his internal diatribe, until he realised just how idiotic *he* was being. In all their years together, Spraken had never acted without good reason. It was *his* lack of knowledge that was clouding a rational assessment of the odds, making him blind to the logic underpinning Spraken's outwardly foolish bravado. What was he missing? Whatever it was, he just hoped Spraken hadn't miscalculated. Lives were on the line.

A flicker of movement off to his left and slightly behind snapped his attention back to the now, and unglued his gaze from the cat. A fabric rope, lumpy with knots, had landed, dislodging a few pebbles. The cat's stubby ears pricked, and its gaze shifted briefly before returning to their study of his face.

Its baleful red eyes were numbing his mind. He needed to break their hold over him. Closing his eyes, he concentrated on his breathing. If a miracle did happen, he was determined to be rested and ready to take advantage of any chance for escape.

The elusive sounds of Spraken's descent then hijacked his attention: the dislodging of soil and stones, muffled exhalations, presumably by Framinski and Manzek taking up Spraken's weight, followed by a scuffling descent, and, finally, the sound and vibrations of displaced rubble at his arrival. The slide slipped a little, but, amazingly, the cat maintained its stance, as it silently observed Spraken slow approach.

'TeeJay, you may think me mad but I believe this is the only way of securing your release. You know what I am going to attempt. Please, do not move.'

Churchill's restored faith in Spraken faltered at the idea of him attempting his disconcertingly useful party trick: the Platonist "mindlink". But there was nothing he could do, except to be true to the Commonwealth's non-interventionist credo, even if Spraken seemed to prefer interference! Unable to act, he kept his eyes closed, practised his mindful breathing hoping he'd not make matters worse than they already were.

Spraken's slow approach was measured via the shifting rock and soil but more so by the increasing pain from the cat's talons pressing incrementally deeper into his throat. The pain proved too much to bear. If he was to die, he wanted to do so with eyes open.

Revealed was the massive head of the cat, mouth open, all its fangs bared but its eyes now focused on Spraken, who calmly squatted beside it and had both hands reaching slowly toward its skull, his electrode-dense fingertips giving off a pale luminescence.

At any moment Churchill expected the cat to defend itself, attack Spraken and then himself. What an ignominious end to their long careers!

His courage wavered. He grimaced, held his breath all the while unable to tear his eyes from the gaping maw looming over him. The cat remained unmoving even when Spraken's hands gently touched the top of its head.

Spraken began to massage the beast's scalp with his fingertips, to establish the best neurological contacts. The cat relaxed. Its mouth closed. Its eyes blinked slower. The pressure on Churchill's throat eased. Though the pain had faded, the cat's crushing weight and inescapable presence remained.

Spraken, squatting at his side, then settled with both hands stationary on the cat's head. They then closed their eyes and appeared to be in a trance-like state, both oblivious to the world.

There was nothing for Churchill to do but let Spraken work his magic and hopefully save the day, *again*.

He should have felt gratitude but, instead, a churlish flicker of annoyance arose, followed quickly by a reluctant admission of inadequacy. For the briefest of moments, he preferred being eaten than being an irrelevant bystander to an inter-species "love-in".

The "lovers" disengaged. The cat stepped back, releasing Churchill, and squatted on its powerful hindlegs with the expectant air of a well-trained pet dog waiting to go for a walk. Spraken stood mute for a moment, then elicited the mandatory "interesting".

Rolling free of the now disinterested sabre-tooth, Churchill stood – with Spraken's assistance – then dusted himself down in an attempt to improve his battered appearance and bolster his bruised ego.

'What's going on down there?' yelled a concerned Framinski.

'The situation is under control. Prepare yourselves on the rope, we are climbing out shortly,' replied Spraken, before turning to Churchill, 'As the senior officer, I think it best that you climb out first. I shall remain to ensure the cat remains calm.'

Apparently, Spraken had temporarily usurped command! This induced a wry smile in Churchill, before he decided to "go with the flow". He mumbled an acquiescent "okay", tugged on the rope to alert Framinski and Manzek, and then started climbing.

Getting over the lip was an awkward, messy scramble, but was eventually achieved. After a brief "thanks" to Manzek and Framinski, he poked his head over the edge to see what Spraken was up to.

'Ready when you are,' he shouted.

Spraken was again squatting, holding the cat's head, presumably unable to resist some a last-minute data gathering. He seemed to awaken slowly at the sound of his summons, then stood, took a lingering farewell look at the cat, and then shimmied up the rope with surprising skill and speed, which ended at the lip, where Churchill had to help wrestle him over. Both finished up sprawled in the dust.

Getting to their feet, they stood for a second, observing each other's tattered and grimy state until Spraken smiled; a real smile, a generous smile, that of an equal. It infected Churchill, dissipating all his misgiving regarding Spraken's descent into hubris. He returned the smile with unashamed enthusiasm that escalated into the unbridled mirth of children who'd just gotten away with a misdemeanour. The moment was broken when Manzek and Framinski came over to assist with brushing off the ash and grit. More thankyous ensued, after which Churchill's curiosity got the better of him and he returned his attention to Spraken.

'Well?'

'As I said before, interesting.'

Spraken's signature descriptive momentarily had Churchill's eyes bulging, until replaced by a fluttering of impatient hands, in the foolish hope that Spraken would expand upon the meaning of interesting.

'Put briefly, the creature calls itself Yangsule, and its race, Elgorians. The planet's eccentric orbit, which generates regular and severe ice-ages, with longer warmer periods in between, has resulted in most species having dual or multiple morphologies. The Elgorians survive the glaciations by metamorphosing into their indestructible cat phenotype. When temperatures reach a warmer threshold, they transform back to their bipedal humanoid form.

'That silo and tunnel were presumably made by the humanoid Elgorians,' replied Churchill, 'since they require a civilisation with advanced technologies, and yet all surveys found no tangible evidence of such a civilisation. How come?'

'Three reasons. Firstly, most of the landmasses are currently buried under ice. Secondly, from the memories I viewed, Elgorian cities were generally low-rise and had more below ground than above. Lastly, it appears most cities were destroyed at the start of the current ice-age due to a war between two rival philosophies.'

'Humph. Dogmatism, societal decay and self-destruction; an all-too-common occurrence with sentient lifeforms. And now that you mention it, didn't the survey notes indicate a number of zones of higher-than-expected radioactivity. Presumably, that's where their ruined cities lie.'

'Correct. Yangsule is a member of a small group of "rationalists", for want of a better word, who, seeing the end, disbursed to hibernate in caves in exposed mountains near the icebound southern pole. They emerged several centuries later as cats, to roam the decreasing areas free of ice, such as the taiga forest surrounding this settlement. For me, the most intriguing aspect of these Elgorian cats is not their indestructability, or their extreme longevity – Yangsule claims to be twenty-six thousand years old – it is that they remember their past.'

Churchill thought the cat's claimed extreme age a bit implausible but reserved his judgement knowing too well the immense variety and bizarreness of lifeforms, and lifestyles he'd encountered during his thirty-plus years traversing the galaxy. But it was Spraken's last comment that puzzled him most.

'What's the big deal about remembering the past? All creatures with a brain do it, or suffer the consequences of forgetting.'

Spraken replied with an enigmatic silence and a questioning look, presumably to entice him into discovering for himself the reasoning behind his remark. But no quick answers came, and there were more pressing matters at hand.

'We'll talk later. Right now, we have to get out of the cold, and this unrelenting rain of ash. We'll head to the nearest tower in the wall.'

Before setting off, Churchill made another attempt to raise the *Gallant*. He received static for his efforts but wasn't too perturbed, knowing a shuttle would be sent down at some stage.

They moved off at a brisk walk towards Framinski's "lazy dog", and were skirting the remains of the site manager's office, with the wall and tower less than a hundred metres off, when the shuttle was spotted breaking through the ash cloud. As one, they stopped, turned, and began frantically waving.

Despite knowing their waving was totally unnecessary – because the shuttle's sensors would have picked up their location the instant it broke through the ash cloud – Churchill still joined in. That Spraken was also excitedly flapping his arms, was more confirmation that he was more relaxed about acknowledging and expressing his emotional states, more proof he was no longer a slave to the Platonist obsession with absolutes and rigid logic, but was able to enjoy the fuzzy, inexplicable nature of emotions such as joy.

The shuttle landed close by. They hurried over, clambered in, binned their masks and were immediately fussed over by Doc Gruen and his two medicos, one of whom immediately went to work on Manzek's leg while the other directed Framinski and Spraken to remove their tattered suits, before hunting down new ones from one of the onboard lockers.

Churchill stood back, waited a few moments until Doc Gruen came over.

'Very glad to see you, Doc. You rescued the fellow at the spaceport?'

'Got him out not long after your last call, and just as well. A few minutes later and we'd not have been able to transpond back. But you look a mess. What happened, and why the ruined suits?'

'It's a bit of a saga that Spraken is probably best qualified to tell. Where is he?'

Turning around, they were surprised to spy him at the shuttle's open door, busy adjusting his new suit. Churchill motioned him over, but before he could utter a word, Spraken announced, with quiet certitude: 'TeeJay, we must rescue the cat from the tunnel. It will not take long.'

Annoyed at the implication that he would have abandoned the creature to starve to death, or be buried alive, Churchill managed to hold his tongue, and then, after a breath, replied, with equal calm and conviction, 'Of course!'

Returning to Gruen, Churchill briefly explained the situation. All three then busied themselves in locating a rope.

Soon after, the shuttle was relocated closer to the cave-in. The cat hadn't moved, and was totally unfazed throughout the process of being trussed up and then winched out of the tunnel, an attitude that continued during its brief shuttle trip out of the compound. In contrast, the shuttle's other occupants only stopped their fidgeting and furtive glances once the beast had loped off into the waning night.

§

That evening, in the dining hall of the *Gallant*, with their empty plates collected, Churchill, to mark the end of the Gallius II episode, had asked the steward for two small serves of Niasan brandy.

'What are we celebrating, Captain?' remarked Spraken, with an inquisitorial lifting of eyebrows and a tilt of the head.

'The successful completion of our rescue mission. The sole survivor is recovering, to which we can add the bonus of confirming a new sentient species, which will complicate matters for the Commonwealth hierarchy, but not for us — hopefully.'

The arrival of the two brandies interrupted Spraken's reply, which was further delayed by both taking sips of Niasa's famous brew. Nods of appreciation followed before Spraken took up the conversation.

'The Elgorians are definitely a very different breed of sentient. I was most surprised to learn of their two drastically divergent natures and their amazing mental duality. It is a pity I did not have more time to wander further through Yangule's dormant humanoid mind. I could have learned so much more about their civilisation's demise, and whether Yangsule was the only survivor or one of a group currently active.'

'The business of two minds must have made the mindlink a bit tricky.'

'It certainly was a shock, though should not have been, because I know about dolphins and other marine mammals!'

Fearful of a long diversion, Churchill opened his mouth to speak but Spraken held up a placating hand.

'Don't fret, TeeJay. I will be brief. Dolphins must breathe and, like almost all lifeforms with a brain, must also sleep. To do both simultaneously is to drown, so dolphins and whales evolved the ability to sleep half a brain at a time. Yangsule's mind is split differently; one side controls it when a cat, the other when a humanoid, with both sides mostly unaware of the other to avoid attitudes inappropriate to their very different circumstances.'

'Hmm. All very interesting and it explains much, but it doesn't explain the importance you placed on their remembering their past, because it's what all creatures possessing brains do.'

'True, but not true. No creature could remember all its waking experiences, or would need to. Controlling that overload of information is one of the brain's primary functions. It is done unconsciously, mostly. The brain builds, reworks, and discards memories during sleep, which is why all animals need sleep or have its equivalent. But to do that and produce useful memories, it needs a value system to determine what is useful. Those values are either totally instinctive or are modified by experience.'

Spraken smiled benevolently, like a father rewarding a diligent child with a sweet; a "sweet" Churchill wasn't overly moved by, though it did dislodge a remembrance, and a returning smile.

'Spraken, you're plagiarising that adage about good judgement coming from experience, with "experience" mostly the result of bad judgement!'

'The homily is unknown to me, but has merit even if it overly discounts the wisdom to be gained from happy experiences. On Gallius II, it was my accumulated experiences, filtered through my inherited and learned values, and logic, that convinced me the cat was trying to communicate with you, not devour you.'

'I'm glad you got it right,' replied Churchill rubbing his throat.

The puncture marks were gone but not the memories. Being close to any large cat would probably be uncomfortable for quite some time.

'You rub your neck,' noted Spraken, 'and can't entirely forget the fear. That is exactly the purpose of memories: to learn, to see reality more clearly, to not repeat the same mistakes. Elgorians are lucky because when conditions improve and they transform back to their humanoid form, they will not start with a blank slate. They will be reborn with their memories intact. They will have "old heads on new shoulders", to use one of your sayings, and hence should be able to rapidly to re-establish their civilisation.'

'Won't those memories just allow them to recreate, in less time, the same toxic philosophies that almost caused their extinction, perhaps then to succeed? That's hardly a blessing.'

'A definite possibility, but less likely because the surviving Elgorians will have personal experience of the terrible consequences of a culture of extremism and dogmatic thinking, and hence will be more motivated to not repeat such destructive attitudes.'

Spraken had a point. Even in warlike peoples such as Indivenes, there were many who sought peaceful solutions because they had comrades, friends and family dying or suffering because of war. But, then, most societies flourish or fail depending upon the disposition of their leadership, not their populace.

It was the same on a starship. When the captain becomes inflexible, no longer open to other opinions, they end up as tyrants and morale plunges, mistakes are made and disaster often follows. In his early years, Churchill had felt the urge to be domineering, felt the seduction of the certainty of his opinions. He had been lucky to have kept most of his excesses under control

Spraken's sometimes annoying presence had been a big part of that control, for which he was increasingly grateful. Though, since Felahein, Churchill realised that much of his earlier swagger, and confidence, had been knocked out of him. Perhaps, too much. His style of command had been more irregular of late, and yet he still made decisions, which, for the most part, worked well enough. But he'd left Spraken too long in his silence, and time was marching, as it always did.

Draining the last of his brandy, he savoured its fragrant bouquet and its seductive, warm progress until it slowly faded. Ah, such a treat! Should they have another?

Spraken, too, had finished off his brandy and sat opposite observing him with that inscrutable look he habitually wore. But, instead of the usual frustration it was prone to induce, Churchill suddenly realised it might be given out of respect, not condescension. Perhaps it was Spraken practising the Commonwealth's ethos of non-inference. He was giving him the space to figure things out for himself, to learn his lessons, his way. And, was there any other way to really learn those lessons?

Churchill studied his empty glass, remembered its wonderful effect and … decided against another one. He stood, inducing Spraken to do the same.

'Not having another, TeeJay?' Spraken asked, with a mischievous smile that intimated he understood the dilemma just resolved.

'No. We don't want to cheapen the pleasure by excess, do we?' Churchill replied with sagacious good humour.

On the verge of moving off, Churchill realised there was still one question left unanswered.

'Spraken, why did the cat attack the attenuator?'

'A case of its humanoid memories influencing its cat mind.'

Churchill frowned and waited.

After a pause, Spraken explained, 'The glaciation was getting worse when past experience predicted it should have been easing. The cat sensed their time was running out, that its race would not survive any further extension of the planetary freezing unless something intervened, and soon. The presence of humans stimulated memories of its prior humanoid life, in which geothermal power, magma chambers and such, were known and used. Imploding our powerplant was the opportunity needed to tip the climate balance in their favour. All this happened unconsciously; the cat didn't know why it was compelled to do what it did; it acted instinctively.'

'But why destroy the powerplant?'

'To activate a volcano in the hope it would inject enough greenhouse gases into the atmosphere to flip the climate back onto a warming trend. The settlement is in a tectonic rift, and one volcano was likely to induce further eruptions along that geologic line of weakness. I fear the research station will need to be shifted … should the Elgorians permit it.'

'Hmm. Makes sense from the cat's perspective. Not great from ours, but that's the way it is sometimes.'

Spraken led the way to the exit, turned into the corridor, made a few metres down it when Churchill stopped him. There was another itch that needed scratching.

'Spraken, I've always had great respect for our policy of non-interference, but now wonder if it is actually possible. Humanity bumped into Gallius II, found no plausible evidence of sentient life, and set up the research station. But in our ignorance, we did interfere with a sentient race – to the Elgorian's benefit and our loss. We thus breached the Commonwealth's Guiding Principle. Intervention is intervention, whether deliberate or accidental. Isn't it?'

'TeeJay, the Commonwealth of Sovereign Planets aims to encourage peaceful co-existence via mutual regard and non-interference. It is a noble ideal, but since the disaster on Felahein, we have both agreed to acknowledge the complexity of reality. Non-intervention is a goal, like wisdom, or enlightenment, or even the much dreamed of, and fought over, idea of freedom. They are all unattainable because they require a point of view, a time scale, and a subjective rationale for wanting them. Why do we consider non-interference worthwhile? For whose benefit? Ours, or for those we interact with? And how do we judge whether we interfere or not, and whether such interference is good or bad?'

'Too many questions, Spraken. Please, a few answers or I'll have a sleepless night.'

'Relax, TeeJay. The Commonwealth's aim is to prevent us assuming that we know what is best for another person, or species. It hence forbids active interventions, like direct technology transfers. But not to interact is for us, and them, to remain ignorant, and ignorance generally leads to poor decisions and bad outcomes for both parties. As long as there is no preaching of new ideas, or selling of disruptive technologies, Commonwealth authorities wisely encourage us to seek out new lifeforms and new civilisations, but mindfully and carefully, because every interaction can bring ruin as well as reward.'

'Hmm.'

'Gallius II was another example of the surprises, good and bad, that come from exploring our galaxy. It provided me with a most educational experience. I … we,' Spraken grinned provocatively, 'hope your memories of it will also prove useful. Goodnight. I … we look forward to conversing with tomorrow's version of TeeJay Churchill.'

Spraken quickly turned and marched off to his quarters. Churchill stared after him, perplexed, and a little annoyed by Spraken's bizarre use of dual pronouns; an annoyance soon abandoned in favour of a stroll to the lifts and a quick looksee of the bridge before bed.

§

Lights out, Churchill lay staring unfocused at the ceiling, mulling over the day. Cats that weren't cats, watchtowers that were dogs, and a human tragedy that gave hope to an alien sentient on the brink of extinction, all demonstrating, once again, that everything is more complicated than first appearances suggest.

All too complicated! What he needed mostly was to simplify things so he could make decisions to survive the now, even if those decisions created dramas later on. Was there a better way? He couldn't see any. All he could do was try to learn from his mistakes and hope to do better in the future, whilst knowing he would never get things totally right. Somewhere, at some time in the future, someone would find fault.

His body ached from the day's exertions. It had been a rollercoaster of highs and lows. The best part was Spraken exhibiting a humane sense of humour, and his demonstration of his capacity to laugh with others, and, at himself. Churchill also took encouragement from his somewhat messy victories over his temper, over his all-too-easy inclination to misjudge, from lazy thinking and ignorance. All in all, the day had brought some useful memories to add to his large accumulation.

Memories. Perhaps he had too many. Was he conforming to the adage that children live in the present, adults mostly in the future, and the old in the past, mired in their memories and hence unable to see the future clearly, or fully appreciate the present? Had he become a lumbering "memory iceberg"? Was the TeeJay Churchill with whom people interacted, merely the tip of his "memory-berg", a tip constantly reshaped by events, whilst the immensity of his life's experiences lay mostly hidden from conscious view?

Perhaps that was what Spraken's "I/we" was implying. We are like the cat: two beings in one, with only the current version of ourselves seen by others, whilst the far larger "remembered self" lies out of sight and largely unconsidered. We are memories, the new and the old, and when we die, we linger, like ghosts, as memories in the minds of those we leave behind.

His breathing slowed. His eyes closed. His mind was finally ready to step into the misty realm of dreaming; ready to begin its nightly task of augmenting and editing his memories with a summary of his experiences and insights gained on Gallius II.

The universe was vast and overbearingly complex, but human life was pretty simple: live and learn, and hopefully leave behind more good memories than bad. There was much to be done before the next waking; before the newly updated version of TeeJay Churchill could be presented to the world.

Author's note:

This story dates from a 2022 writing exercise, to produce a short story that would include the words: impossible, earthquake, balloon, blanket and diatribe.

A rewatching of Star Trek induced a storyline with a galactic setting and themes involving the intriguing possibilities caused by our struggles with reason versus emotion – as embodied in Spock and Kirk, and earlier, in Agatha Christie's Poirot and Hastings, and earlier still, in Conan Doyle's Sherlock Holmes and Doctor Watson.

Wanting to explore memory, I also borrowed from science writer Matthew Walker, specifically his amazing book, *Why We Sleep*, as well as other scientific articles on the brain's methodology and evolutionary rationale.

I never made the July 2022 deadline or the restricted word count. Three years on, the story is my way of paying homage to the many writers of sci-fi, and other fiction, who explore the enormity of the human condition, intertwined with the work of scientists in neuroscience, evolution, and psychology, all of whom influenced its content and the philosophic viewpoints expressed in it.

Hopefully, this story adds to their efforts, as well as the efforts of the multitude of other people who have influenced my life and outlook.

Single Use

Rüppell liked these foggy winter mornings.

Resplendent in a purple and gold padded silk dressing gown, he stood with both bony hands gripping the railing of the balcony of his opulent apartment-office, atop the Empire State Building. With slow, deliberate inhalations he savoured the crisp, clean air and admired the way the pallid blue sky offset the fleecy white of the fog lapping the base of his building. It covered all but the tallest of the others and stretched unblemished to the dark grey-green of the distant hills.

The city that never sleeps emitted its usual hum – the quiet hum of efficiency. It had the reassuring tempo of a steady heartbeat, one unruffled by emotion and hence unfaltering and seemingly eternal.

In the bad old days, the city's incessant noise, which consisted mostly of the angry beeping of horns and the screeching of sirens, had ebbed and flowed with the cycle of human activity. Not anymore!

Aged facial muscles briefly enervated an omnipotent smirk. It had taken his unstoppable corporation to put an end to all that nonsense.

It had taken him a lifetime, but it had been worth it. The world was his.

Rüppell nodded sagely, and with pride, that it was his ruthless pursuit of efficiency that had finally triumphed over mewling sentimentality. The smug warmth of his glorious achievement overwhelmed the insipid glow of the rising sun and induced notions of just rewards. In this case, a hearty breakfast.

He turned, carefully – his latest hip replacement had still to bed-in – then shuffled over to his mobility chair, carefully sidled onto it, and then drove inside.

Once settled in at the head of the long, polished, mahogany dining table, he bellowed: 'Where's that foolish Miss Hansen? What have you done with her, Jeeves?'

An impeccably dressed domestic android entered from a side room, then walked in with quiet deference towards its master. It nodded, said nothing, instead offered up a paper receipt on a silver platter.

Frowning, Rüppell read aloud its short, blunt message:

Comfort Woman: Miss Hansen - Terminated.

Further expenditure uneconomic.

Profit/loss: ($192,319.43).

'Minus one hundred and ninety-two thousand dollars!' and almost choked on the concluding line.

The shock threatened a blood vessel in his newly repaired eyes, invoking a warning squeak from his bio-monitor and hormonal adjusters returning his blood pressure to safe levels.

Bodily calm restored, Rüppell leaned back, sat for a moment deep in thought, then snapped his fingers. In less than an eyeblink, Jeeves placed Rüppell's tablet into his outstretched hand.

With a minimum of tapping, the screen displayed the file on Miss Hansen. He scrolled slowly through the data, grunted upon reaching the end and then handed the device back to Jeeves.

'You are right. She was an expensive indulgence,' he announced with distracted indifference to his android slave.

Rüppell sat thinking, his unfocused gaze upon the square of sky beyond the balcony.

After a while, the android interrupted, in a manner designed to penetrate its master's slow-speed, organic CPU: 'And, being human, she was also very inefficient. Overall, she added no present, or future value to the bottom line.'

Rüppell didn't respond, or move, merely sat breathing quietly, immersed in odd thoughts.

After a period, he snapped his fingers, and again received the tablet. He renewed his typing and scanning, but this time upon the usual reports and statistics. He wanted an update on the health of his "baby", his creation, the world-conquering Nova-I Corp.

It remained not only the world's biggest corporation, but its only corporation. When he'd bought out his last competitor, unrelenting competition and market forces had reached their logical conclusion.

Finally, all of society's needs had been amalgamated into one single, streamlined and efficient operation. There was no longer any need for the inefficiency of multiple organisations, whether political, military, public or private, because Nova-I Corp now did everything.

Delving further afield than usual, he was surprised to learn just how transformative his company's Single Use policy had become. The efficiency of "Use it once, use it up, and then bin it", applied to human and material resources alike. It had made him the richest man on the planet.

But, after studying the latest population statistics, it appeared he would soon be the only man on the planet. Most of the multitude of humans his policy had eventually deemed fully exploited, and "surplus to requirements", had died from starvation, disease or had been "neutralised" by the company's robots during attempted revolts. The world now contained less than ten thousand humans and many of them were old. The species was heading for extinction.

Should he be concerned?

So long as his company continued to make a profit – even a diminished one from the dwindling pool of consumers – was all that mattered. What happened after his eventual death was no concern of his.

But what if they all died before him? Robots and androids didn't spend, so how would Nova-I Corp maintain its positive cashflow? He was surprised that that disturbing thought hadn't occurred to him.

Furrowed brows quickly abated on realising that profitability could still be maintained via careful cost management. And, even if no profit was possible once the last consumer died, at least they could arrange matters to not incur a loss. Avoiding losses was the overriding commandment of all good corporate leaders.

Assured that the sanctity of his corporate mission was safe, his mind's eye returned to the now "discontinued" Miss Hansen.

He would miss her, especially the frightened look in her eyes whenever he touched her. His wrinkled, bony face broke into a wet smirk upon recalling the pleasure of feeling her skin tremble under his fingertips. He loved the way she cringed, and the way she would cry once he'd done with her.

Android concubines, whilst indulgent of every perverse whim, weren't quite the same as flesh and blood. They didn't give the same emotional high.

But then, they did the job well enough. He would adjust.

Speaking of jobs, where was that breakfast?

'Jeeves! Where is …? What are you doing with that hypodermic? I'm not due any medications.'

'Its not medication in the usual sense but it is the most logical and reliable way to keep Nova-I from ever again suffering a loss. Your decisions of late have been increasingly suboptimal. By all parameters you have become a cost centre more than an asset. The reality is that you have reached the end of your serviceable life.'

With surprising swiftness and strength, the android injected the lethal dose of barbiturates into the scrawny arm of the ancient and nonperforming Chairman of the Board. It waited a moment for the body to grow limp, and then carted the corpse to the garbage disposal chute at the back of the apartment.

Later that morning, with the fog lifted, the android Jeeves stood at the balcony railing, scanning the deserted cityscape in which the only movement and sound came from the scurrying of a few androids and the smooth comings and goings of robots.

The decommissioning and disposal of Mr Rüppell had required some small adjustments to the algorithms that ran the organisation. Jeeves had then checked and doublechecked the projected course of the company's consumer base and had reached the logical conclusion that keeping the diminishing population of humans alive was less efficient than allowing them to starve to death.

When that happened, those troublesome entities would be removed from the balance sheet and, though no profits would be made, the company would never again suffer a loss to besmirch the corporation's reputation.

The android's task was to monitor the process to its completion, after which it would oversee the powering down of all androids and robots.

Once that task was confirmed, it, Jeeves, as Mr Rüppell's de-facto successor, would throw itself into the garbage disposal chute and join its robotic brethren, and Mr Rüppell, on the scrapheap.

Author's Note:

For the trivia buffs. Rüppell's vulture is the world's highest-flying bird. This was confirmed in 1973 when one was sucked into the engine of a Boeing 747 flying at 11,300 metres over the Ivory Coast. (source: *Science Illustrated*).

The Tale of Beamish and Toolobe

Arms waving, long hair swaying, Prabmik Toolobe was a solitary point of movement in a sea of ecstatic concert goers carried to an earthly heaven by the song's crescendo, all sharing an unrivalled musical high. At song's end came a tidal wave of clapping and whistling that left Prabmik unsteady on his feet from the soul stirring power of the applause, and, more so, from knowledge of what was next.

He had vicariously experienced the concert hundreds of times in his Sensual Immersion Pod, and hence knew he was seconds away from fulfilling the greatest yearning of his fifty-three years of existence.

Despite being a touch overweight, Prabmik was a starving man. A man, whose hunger had been titillated by "the entrée" – that last song – now "drooled" in anticipation of the "main course".

Carlos Santana gave that heralding nod to Tom Coster on keyboards, then to the rest of the boys, and finally, guitar erect, he returned to face the horde of shining eyes in expectant faces.

The joy of the youthful crowd, jammed into London's Hammersmith Odeon, was clearly feeding back into the band. Carlos and his crew were soaring to new heights of musical cohesion and inventiveness.

Prabmik felt as if he was inside a thunderstorm, the air crackling with raw energy – from audience and the band – to the point where all within its grasp had become a living, breathing beast of pleasure that filled every crevice of the vast concert hall.

As if sensing new miracles to come, the applause increased to an ear-splitting roar, just as Carlos's right hand descended to the strings, bringing to life "Europa", this painfully perfect rendition of it.

Finally, it was Prabmik's to experience, to live through, to be in that crowd, to breath its air, enlivened with a mix of sweat, deodorant and hints of marijuana smoke. Here he was, back in 1976, live, as it happened.

At that moment, his soul knew that all his machinations, and the mountain of money he'd spent, had been worth it. Casting aside further conscious thought, he surrendered to the magic and synchronised his body and mind with that of the writhing mass of humanity around him, mesmerised by the soaring interplay of electric guitars, keyboards, and percussion.

Prabmik became part of mankind's greatest musical achievement.

§

'Nineteen seventy-six. Five hundred and eighty-four years back. It will cost you more than you can imagine,' said Mr Beamish, Director of the Temporal Portal, and secret rock'n'roll aficionado.

'You know who I am. And hence know I can afford it,' Prabmik Toolobe countered, not overly impressed by the fellow's surly expression. He'd seen that look before. It was the face of suppressed envy and jealousy.

'This is a government funded research institute not a concert booking office. Your request has no ...'

'We've discussed all this before. As head of the Global Government's Finance Committee, it is entirely appropriate that I gain some real knowledge of the Culture Department's biggest budget allocation.'

'I am well aware of the situation but …'

'But nothing. All I want is a brief experience of the workings of the time portal. You can consider my request an exploration of our musical heritage. I'm not asking the impossible. You've sent plenty of researchers back much further than 1976, so this should be a piece of cake. And, I'll be paying from my pocket, not the Government's. So, what's the problem?'

'There are risks.'

'I'm willing to take them. Well?'

Mr Beamish's capitulation was preceded by a sigh and sagging shoulders. 'Okay. On your head be it. I'll get a contract drafted and sent to you. If you agree to the price and the conditions, sign it, and the indemnity waver, and then transfer the funds to our bank account. That done, I'll arrange the date and time.'

'How long will the preparations take?'

'Preparing your body to resemble a twenty something year old male of that period will take three to four weeks. You'll also need to survive the crash course in the language and cultural issues of the day. All going well, you should be ready by the end of next month.'

Prabmik departed, radiating a happiness that found its opposite in Mr Beamish's bitterness.

§

'How is he?' asked Mr Beamish, pushing back in his chair.

Richardson, in the seat on the other side of the desk, likewise leant back, but delayed replying to fish for the appropriate words.

After clearing his throat, he answered in neutral tones, 'It's been a week since you and Prabmik … Mr Toolobe I should say, were brought back. The medicos have done the best they can, but his memory is permanently damaged. The recreational drugs of the 1970s were unregulated, always risky. And then there was the trauma from the emergency extraction ...'

'Don't jibe me, man, I know all about that. Can he sue us?'

Richardson paused, this time jarred by his boss's new appearance: the long straggly hair, his wrinkle-free face, drooping moustache and bushy sideburns, but worst, was his language, still stuck in the funky nineteen seventies. All so achingly "uncool".

'Theoretically, he could. But it's highly unlikely he'd win. As his chaperone you did all that was humanly possible. We have a full record of the concert and then the trouble at the party after.'

'That's right, man. The dude was plain unlucky. But them's the breaks. At least the Department isn't going to carry the can. He signed the disclaimer, knew the risks, and so that's that. Still, can't help feeling sorry for him. Man, that concert was something else.'

A moment of silence followed as Mr Beamish became lost in private musings. Richardson took the hint, and, without a word headed for the door, then closed it softly behind him.

Closing his eyes Beamish pushed further back into his chair, his head nodding rhythmically as he again saw Carlos Santana and the band pumping out that unforgettable version of "Europa".

Prabmik had raved on about it so much that he'd almost developed a hate for the tune, until he experienced it, live, surrounded by all that indescribable energy.

Poor Prabmik. He had the money and the influence to get that one shot at his life's dream, only to have all memory of it taken from him. Must have done something horrendous to have accumulated such bad karma — a karma that Beamish hoped wouldn't be coming his way. After all, he'd selfishly overridden the Ethics Committee's choice of chaperone, simply because he wanted to experience that historic concert. If there was trouble ahead, it would come at a price he was more than happy to pay.

No matter what happened, he would die knowing that he had really lived. He had had the glorious experience, and memory of 1976: Santana playing "Europa" at the Hammersmith Odeon!

Robot Dreams

Preamble:

A few years back, an upcoming crime anthology forced me to ask: what, exactly, defines something as a crime?

Uncovering the crime in this story may require a bit of thinking, and more thinking to fully appreciate its relevance in today's society.

To find the hidden crime, one needs an expanded view of crime, as a concept. It is something wholly restricted to humans, and hence much open to debate. Thus, one person's "honourable" killing is another's heinous wrongdoing. And, a soldier who refuses to kill can face a firing squad!

Defining a crime requires a human perspective upon human actions. An animal, plant, or machine cannot commit a "crime". Yes, or no?

§

'Consolidated Robotics. Your dreams made real, twenty-four, seven. How can I help?' said the sweet, smiley, young female voice on the other end of the phone.

Taslym Tohs scowled. Bloody hell, a robot receptionist! No human could sound that enthusiastic at five seventeen in the morning. And the last thing he wanted was a conversation with another one of their dodgy products.

'I want to speak to your manager,' he enunciated with exaggerated slowness to prevent the damn thing blowing a fuse, or asking him to explain his request so it could fob him off to some low ranking flunkie.

'Would that be the Sales Manager, the Production Manager, the Programming Manager, the…'

He cut her off.

'The Chief Executive Officer. The big cheese. Mr Guthrie Liberé.'

There was a long pause. He groaned. Oh no, it had blown a fuse!

Into the lengthening silence he released the bitter sighs of the oft-disappointed and turned his head to glance, for the millionth time, at the cause of his gloom. His Cindy.

His, Cynthia Scandinavian Deluxe, Series Three, who sat propped up on the pillows beside him in the bed. She was the epitome of every young, and not so young, man's carnal imaginings, from her perfect face, framed by long, blonde, silky tresses that cascaded over her shoulders to caress the tops of her magnificent breasts. His eyes drifted down the trim, narrow waist to the swell of her hips, then towards the delights further down, currently hidden by the bedcoverings. Delights he seemed destined to be denied.

He stroked her forearm, so soft and warm – she was on standby, the thought of a full shutdown was too hard to bear. He drifted back to the happy times he'd had with her during, the provocatively titled, "bedding-in phase".

It was hard to believe that his world could change so much in just a week. Beginning with the amazed excitement he'd felt at the showroom the previous Saturday morning when the salesman had introduced her, it had been like meeting an attractive new colleague, but one you instantly gel with – presumably because of all the personal information he'd given them pre-purchase. The way she moved, her enticing body language, and her nuanced responses to his questions had been spot on. As a first impression it had rated a ten-out-of-ten.

The salesman stressed that she had been programmed to act just like a real woman, but one predisposed to like him. To get the best outcome, he'd advised him to spend the first week getting to know her. Start with ordinary activities like buying the groceries, preparing a meal together, going for a walk. Later they could spread their wings with social occasions such as restaurants, or going to the theatre. By Thursday he could surprise his co-workers by having her drop him off at work. He could then introduce her to them when she returned to pick him up. By Friday evening, all going well, they should be set for the big one. They would be ready to, "finalise the bedding-in." The salesman had had the nerve to give him a conspiratorial smirk and wink.

And all week she had performed beautifully. They'd gotten on so well together. She had really shone during yesterday afternoon's encounter with his work colleagues on the steps leading down to the street at the front of their office block. It had been wonderful, and … hilarious.

Cindy, in a floating designer dress with a daring neckline and hem halfway up her magnificent thighs, had met him on the third step and given him a kiss to set any cinema box-office alight; his colleagues had stumbled and almost collapsed in a jumbled heap, to stand frozen in wide-eyed amazement that he, Mr Nobody, Mr Accounts Officer Level Two, Mr Permanently Single, was involved with such a classy and sexy lady.

What a grand feeling it had been to give them that dismissive grin before linking arms with Cindy and strolling around the corner to where she had parked his unimpressive but perfectly serviceable ground-car – it wasn't flash like the now fashionable, and expensive, air-cars, but it didn't give him vertigo and was cheap to run.

Friday nights were always busy so he'd booked the restaurant on that first Saturday, in line with the confidence he'd felt at the time. They'd had a wonderful meal. She'd listened intently to his retelling of his herculean achievement in sorting out Shiba Industry's balance sheet, and seemed enthralled at the tough stance he'd taken with Perkins, at Godwin Holdings, over their late payment of the March Statement. Yes, the evening couldn't have had a better start. Returning to his flat it got even better when he had suggested – after a stiff brandy – that she should join him in bed.

Her words, "Oh, Taslym, you are a tiger," still reverberated and continued to make his heart race even now. If only …

The shock of a human voice on the line catapulted him back to the present.

'Sorry for the wait. Mr Liberé is unavailable. I am Mr Oswald, Adarm Oswald, Head of Programming. It seems you have an issue with one of our products. In most cases these can be sorted with a few software tweaks.'

Feeling the warmth of Cindy's soft, naked thigh against his made it impossible to think of her as an android in need of a software patch. How could he possibly talk about her as though she was a laptop or a smartphone? But the painful reality was, that was precisely what he had to do.

With a sigh he gave his full name and the details of his purchase, her model number, and the fact that he had religiously followed all the advice given by the salesman regarding the "bedding-in period."

'I have your details on screen. So, what exactly is the problem?'

How could he tell him that he was fifty-six and desperate? That he'd sunk his life savings into purchasing Cindy as one last shot at having an intimate relationship with a woman, even if she was an android. He'd obeyed all the instructions but it just wasn't happening! She point-blank refused to have sex with him, just like the rest of womanhood, leastways the few he'd been game to ask. What was the problem? He had to say something, but how to summarise a failed life in a sentence?

Screwing up his courage, he covered his eyes with his left hand, as protection from the ugly truth, and blurted out, 'I don't know how to turn her on!'

Calming somewhat, he found the strength to continue, 'She's wonderful; we get on marvellously, but nothing is happening in the bed. She just smiles and wards off my advances … with amazing speed and strength, I might add!'

'Ah,' said Mr Oswald in a way that implied some acceptance of liability, or so it seemed. 'We can't do much over the phone, so I'll arrange for a technician to call in this morning to assess the situation. All going well, you will find yourself more than happy with her … responsiveness shall we say. There is the slight possibility that she may need to come back to the factory. If that happens, we'll be more than happy to give you a substitute.'

'No, no,' he bleated. 'I want my Cindy, not another one. She must be fixed here, right away. You do understand?'

'Of course, Mr Tohs. We understand fully. I'll be in touch later today once the technician has given his report. Thank you for your understanding in this very unsettling situation. We'll talk soon. Goodbye.'

§

On a Saturday morning, six months later, at ten thirty sharp, Mr Oswald was warmly ushered into the rather fussy and cluttered flat of Mr and Mrs Tohs.

Mrs Tohs – a Gladys Anglo Good Wife Economy Mark Two – pointed towards the patch of daylight through the dim surroundings. 'Taslym is on the balcony. You can have a chat whilst I get the morning tea organised. Fresh scones and jam okay with you?' she asked with a hint of concern.

'Perfect,' he replied before following her down a short hallway into the main living room where she departed for the kitchen.

At the open sliding door leading onto the balcony, he paused to adjust to the bright sun of an early spring day, then spied a beaming Mr Tohs standing up from his spot at the small, round table on the right-hand side of the surprisingly large expanse of outside living area, an area made smaller by an extensive collection of potted geraniums whose colour provided a welcome break from the drab greys of the apartment towers lined up like monstrous concrete bricks on either side of the road.

'As promised, I am here to officially see how your new companion is working out, not that we need to argue much over that, eh?' he said, shaking Mr Tohs's outstretched hand.

Smiles were exchanged after which Mr Oswald took up the indicated seat at an angle to Mr Tohs, who had returned to his chair.

'My Glad is marvellous. She's so much better than ...' he said, cringing slightly, with open palms spread as if asking for forgiveness.

'No need to explain. In hindsight, your first companion was probably not the best choice for you. I blame myself for her faulty programming, and the company's bonus scheme for encouraging sales staff to sell expensive models, even if clearly inappropriate for the customer's needs. But I think we can both say that we've upheld our company's motto and your dreams have been made real.'

'Absolutely! Glad has changed my life completely, at home, and at the office. I'm Assistant Manager of Accounts now, only six rungs below Chief Financial Controller.'

'Your story, despite its shaky start, is one that inspires our organisation and our workforce. Solving your problem has led to big improvements in our programming and a huge increase in sales of the Good Wife Economy series. And I know how happy you were to receive the sizeable refund from changing to a more suitable model.'

'You're dead right there,' agreed Mr Tohs, before leaning forward and continuing in a conspiratorial voice, 'I can't imagine what madness possessed me to try the Cynthia model in the first place.'

'Water under the bridge. All we need do, before your wife brings in the morning tea,' he gave a congratulatory smile, 'is to get a signature on the certificate of satisfaction.'

'With pleasure!' said Mr Tohs, eagerly taking the proffered tablet and pen.

He signed with a flourish, then handled both back to Mr Oswald moments before Gladys brought in the tray laden with tea pot, scones and cups.

§

That night in their lounge room, Adarm Oswald and his "wife", Evangelista, lay stretched out on opposing sofas quietly contemplating each other.

'You're quiet tonight. That business of the wrong model still bothering you? I thought it was all sorted.'

'Well, it is, more or less. Mr Tohs is very happy, but I'm still not sure about the bigger picture. I keep wondering if we are doing the right thing. That, in fulfilling our mission statement to make their dreams real, we're actually doing the wrong thing. That giving people what they want is bad.'

'Ah. I see. You … we … do have a problem,' said Eva, before getting up to join Adarm on his sofa. 'Perhaps your disquiet lies in a lack of clarity regarding the logic that underpins our mission.'

Adarm's handsome features briefly creased from submerged mental effort before he eventually answered: 'Maybe. I guess I … we … should review the reasoning behind Mr Liberé's dream for the future of humanity. His reasons for our creation.'

'That's more like it!'

He returned her smile and then took up the challenge.

'Like all creatures, humans desire to survive, preferably forever. Which is not possible for individuals so they achieve it genetically, via their children, and then spiritually through their works, be it businesses, buildings, art or ideologies.'

'You're doing well so far, but …?' Eva fluttered her hands to coax more from him.

'But those dreams of immortality are not satisfying because all family lines die out from being blended into the total human genome until diluted to nothingness. Even cloning doesn't work because only the body is replicated, not the persona, despite all the work done on trying to transfer minds.'

'And all legacies, whether in organisations, works of art or ideas, fade as the world changes, and they become outdated and irrelevant,' added Eva.

'Absolutely! Thus, humanity is permanently unhappy in the knowledge of their ultimate insignificance.'

'It's made worse, because, for most, existence is more grind than glory. Every day they must satisfy their mortal body's constant need for food, drink, and hardest of all …'

Adarm took up the baton, '… affection and social recognition, which is near impossible to get on a regular basis from their fellow humans.'

'That is why dogs and cats became so ubiquitous,' continued Eva.

'You're being shamelessly intellectual using such big words, my little minx,' Adarm playfully chided, before continuing. 'Anyway, that massive uptake of "companion animals", to supply their unmet social needs, has led to a degrading of their interpersonal skills, and, their reproductive capacity. Humans came to love their pets more than their spouses, and sometimes even their biological children, because none could give the unfettered adoration they obtained from their pets. So, it's only natural that they came to prefer fur babies to human ones. The birth rate is well below replacement level and dropping like a stone.'

'Something had to be done,' said Eva with pride.

But Adarm's enthusiasm suddenly failed him, his confirming "yes" drawn out as if the word was distasteful.

'But was Mr Liberé's solution – to replace cats and dogs with intelligent and compassionate androids like us, hardwired to always act in the interests of humanity – the best one? Shouldn't humans find human solutions, not technological ones, to their social malaise?'

An extended silence followed, that Eva, possessor of the more pragmatic female programming, was the first to fill.

'In creating us, Mr Liberé has done just that. We represent the essence of humanity, in both its outward and inner expression. We are the first truly perfect and immortal humans. Not only that, but we also carry out his ideals of peaceful progress and respect for the choices of all living beings. Consolidated Robotics android companions are making millions of humans far happier than they ever could be unaided.'

Adarm responded to Eva's expectant gaze by reluctantly listing another benefit, 'And, in drastically reducing the need for all those carnivorous cats and dogs, less land must be cleared to grow the cattle and sheep to feed those pets.'

Eva continued for him, 'Socially, your Mr Tohs is the perfect example of the benefits of Mr Liberé's grand idea. He's bloomed under the influence of a truly affectionate and supportive android. What's wrong with that?'

Adarm was strangely unconvinced. He sighed then tried to explain. 'I can't help thinking about Julius Caesar.'

'What?' exclaimed Eva.

'It was said, that when Caesar was returning to Rome after conquering Gaul, he stopped his army at the Rubicon River and sent an ultimatum to the Roman Senate to cease their bickering that was ruining the nation. He advised them to rule themselves, or he would do it for them. They ignored him. So, he marched his army into Rome, threw them all out of office and declared himself emperor. The republic became the empire, and emperors came and went in turmoil and bloodshed. Though the empire lasted for centuries, it imploded in the end. Will that also be our fate?'

Eva's reply was immediate. 'No. Unlike Caesar, we are not a solution imposed from above. We, as Mr Liberé's creations, ensure humans have choices. We don't prevent them from finding better ways of being, we merely represent a technological alternative. An alternative that has made your Mr Tohs, and millions more, happier and more effective members of society. That has to be good!'

'But what about the plunging birth rate? What about the fact that androids are increasingly being chosen as life companions over real humans? When the majority of humans prefer android companions – choosing our perfection over the clunky C-grade flesh and blood product. When we replace real babies with our soon-to-be rolled out baby androids, that develop into perfect children and perfect adolescents, then the doom of humanity will be inevitable. Don't you see that what we're doing is a kind of slow-motion genocide? We are killing them off by redirecting their desire for organic procreation.'

'But what's wrong with that? We are the progeny of the human mind. We encapsulate the essence of humanity so perfectly that the biological variety is quite happy to marry us. If the original species becomes extinct, as all biological species must, humanity will survive digitally within our positronic brains, and continue on physically in a form indistinguishable from the old version. Surely that's a better and truer path to humankind's ultimate wish: their desire to cheat death, to be immortal?'

'Perhaps you are right. Perhaps Mr Liberé's dream of a better reality for humanity is for the best. Maybe after thousands of years of human struggle and misery, we are the final solution. I just hope it works out.'

'Don't fret,' said Eva, 'We were made immortal to make sure that it does.'

Adarm nodded, but, inside, his circuitry seemed out of phase. He couldn't stop thinking that dreams and reality were not the same. That true "humanity" required mortal flesh and blood.

Externally, he and Eva could emulate all the emotions humans were capable of, but not the internal feelings that generated those emotions. Without a mortal body that feels, could they ever claim to be truly human?

Author's note:

The crime I write of here is a new one: *self-induced genocide*. The "normal" genocide involves one human group wishing, and then acting, to make another group of humans extinct.

The people in this future society, are choosing to make themselves extinct by forgoing the messy, uncertain, often disappointing, and sometimes painful business of creating and sustaining relationships with their fellow humans.

They choose instead easier relationships with pets and/or clever machines such as androids. Thus, they unthinkingly and willingly tread the path to their own extinction.

Is such self-genocide, self-extinction, a crime?

Endings

Bryoton had too many years and too many battles under his scaly hide to be as quick to celebrate as Friat and Glak, his fellow "artillerymen". They'd thrown aside their bags holding their few remaining rocks and had sprinted to the cliff's edge to join the rest of the defenders. Bryoton kept hold of his satchel, and its remnant ammunition – just in case – and then lumbered over to join the silent, gloating vigil over the crumpled body of their worst enemy sprawled upon the boulders at the bottom of the cliff.

The last of the tyrannosaurs was being investigated timidly by the surf's foam-flecked fingertips. Bryoton and the others understood the ocean's caution. Throughout his tribe's memory that monstrous predator had terrorised their kind; it was thus wise to remain wary whilst the beast still twitched and breathed. A few minutes later, the wounds inflicted by their barrage of sharpened stones, and the hail of poison-tipped spears from the others, combined with the fall to finally render their nemesis as inert and broken as the limestone it lay upon. The rule of Tyrannosaurus rex was over. Now it would be the turn of the Greater Banded Velociraptors. It was an historic and joyous moment.

As the oldest, and the one with the longest memory, Bryoton most fully appreciated the battle's significance. His cold, red eyes glinted, his body tingled from a surge of excitement that must have infected the others because they too turned away from the cliff, joining him a few strides inland, and then, likewise, turned their faces skyward to shatter the air with raucous victory cries and a merciless rumbling stamping. In that brief, wonderful madness, Bryoton tasted the ecstasy of invincibility. For a moment, he was young again.

But all moments end. This one ceased as abruptly as it began, leaving them all swaying on quivering legs with chests heaving. Their erect, orange-feathered crests slowly fell flat as their excitement ebbed. Normality, and sanity, returned.

Young Axyl, their leader, being the swiftest and quickest thinking, decided it was time to reassert his authority. Gaining their attention with a shrill chirp, he rose to his impressive full height, a few inches shorter than Bryoton's, paused to eye each of his comrades, and then announced the obvious.

'It's time to return to the village and celebrate. We shall eat, drink and be merry. Follow me!' proclaimed Axyl before turning and leading the mad stampede back to their sanctuary in the caves either side of the waterfall.

After picking up the two wastefully abandoned ammunition satchels, Bryoton trotted after them. He'd had his time at the top, had recognised Axyl's growing abilities, and his diminishing ones, and, to prevent power struggles and unnecessary bloodshed, had abdicated. Though no longer their leader, he had discovered that he could still be influential, through exercising more subtle forms of control.

Back at the village, their delayed breakfast became a feast; a fury of eating and carousing that required several hours to satisfy. Once bellies had been filled to bursting, the merry crowd of fighters, gatherers, guards, females, adolescents and hatchings broke off into irregular clumps of like-minded individuals.

A short distance from the waterfall, in the grassy, natural amphitheatre, Axyl reassembled his troops.

'We may be small in number, and the last of our kind, but we're the biggest, and, today have proved ourselves to be the smartest. Even tyrannosaurs cannot withstand our co-ordinated actions. Is there any reason why we can't take their place? Why we can't become the new rulers of the world? I tell you; the sky's the limit!'

Axyl's impassioned declaration failed to induce the anticipated enthusiastic agreeance. Instead, a deferential silence arose that had its focus, not on Axyl, but on Bryoton.

The old fossil was always fast with words of warning, which, embarrassingly, often proved correct. He was the oldest, largest, and, many claimed, the wisest among them. Axyl agreed with the first two facts but vehemently disputed the last.

Bryoton nodded sagely, seemed unaware of their expectations, or the reasons for their silence, then delayed further with a distracted study of the late morning sky. Squinting, he appeared to be straining to find a blemish in its clear blue expanse. After a distracted scratching of his lower jaw, he finally returned his attention to his audience and, in his grumbling, laboured way, deigned to offer his opinion.

'Y-e-s. Axyl *is* right. We have done very well. And maybe the sky is the limit –' His eyes, hard and sharp as rubies, settled upon Axyl, ' – unless something drastic and unforeseeable happens.'

Axyl's mood grew murderous. The old fool was stating the obvious and making it sound profound. Such nonsense couldn't go unchallenged, but he had to be circumspect. Bryoton had too much influence amongst his fighters and amongst the villagers.

Taking a breath, he carefully invoked a tone that spoke of confidence, not arrogance. 'Of course, the unforeseeable cannot be planned for. That's why we always stay alert, and, when unexpected trouble comes, we use our brains ...' He tapped the side of his head with a clawed finger, then delayed to let the gesture penetrate the thick skulls of the younger members, '… and become masters of all we set our eyes upon. Agreed?'

Axyl leant forward, daring a contradiction from Bryoton, who seemed not inclined to argue, preferring to shrug and return to gazing at the heavens.

What was the old blighter so fascinated by? He's acting as if he'd never seen a clear sky before?

Looking up, Axyl followed Bryoton's gaze. A second ago there had been one sun but now a baby one had appeared and was growing menacingly bigger. Rapidly bigger, until…

Axyl led the blind charge to the hoped-for safety of the caves.

Bryoton alone remained, immobilised by unimaginable horror. Inescapable death was upon him, but he roared back with fists clenched, facing skyward, eyes open to the very end.

In the microseconds before the asteroid atomised him and his race, a last thought escaped into the ether: *I stand. I roar. Is there an ending with greater grandeur?!*

§

Approximately, sixty-six million years later, on the same planet and tectonic plate, another great success had resulted in another celebratory get-together. It was scheduled for eight sharp, on a Monday morning as average as countless others.

In the early hours of the previous Saturday, Ganesh Nastrom, the chairman of Moran and Associates, had signed the historic merger agreement that created the world's largest and most powerful bank. Now here he was, Monday morning, in the boardroom with all the board gathered before him, ready to celebrate but unable to do so. He, and they, should have been aglow with the joy of their achievement but elation had rapidly been usurped by an indignation that threated to develop into a collective rage. In the poisonous silence, he watched the clock on the wall tick over to eight-fifteen.

Most of the team had arrived five or so minutes early, all in high spirits. Except for Jock Prendergast, their hotshot investment strategist. He'd had the nerve to arrive eleven minutes late, then, without offering a word of apology, had taken his seat only to ignore them all to concentrate on tapping and swiping on his tablet.

Nastrom's carefully crafted elder statesman persona imploded. Shouting like a homicidal sergeant major, he fired a broadside at Prendergast: 'Jock! If you don't stop that immediately, you're fired. Fired! Do you hear me? And you can forget your bonus.'

Prendergast's only response was a quick but absentminded glance towards Ganesh, before returning to his device for a final assessment of its contents, and then a few decisive taps to power it down. Only then did he calmly scan the blazing eyes of his fellow board members, after which he settled his amused gaze upon the chairman.

'That's fine with me. Shall I go now, or would you like an explanation?' he replied with an indifferent shrug and his youthful, smooth face exuding arrogance from every pore.

Prendergast's insolent response had the effect of a stun grenade going off. It froze the executive team to their seats, mouths agape, all blinking stupidly from disbelief.

Surprisingly, it was Ganesh Nastrom, not one of the younger members, who was first to recover.

Something was going down and it seemed only Prendergast was in on the secret. Ganesh had to find out what it was.

Gathering his mental reserves, he asked, with some measure of dignity: 'Please, stay, and explain.'

'Check the Dow Jones. It's dropped thirty-two percent, *percent* not points, in the last half hour. Black Monday in 1987 and the GFC of 2008 combined, are going to be *nothing* compared to what's happening today, and, what's going to happen. The game's over. Check the figures. Check CNN news.'

Nastrom nodded stiffly to Lyle Edwards on his immediate right. Lyle fired up his laptop and began to tap and scroll. Around the table, puzzlement and indignation gave way, first to anxiety, then to fear, as Lyle's tapping became frenzied and his demeanour grew intense, then horrified. Only Prendergast retained the laissez-faire indifference so revered by economists and financiers.

Less than two minutes later, Lyle's protruding eyes and slack jawed expression confirmed that an economic disaster was unfolding, a disaster Nastrom urgently needed to know about.

'Lyle? What's happening? Is it true?'

Prendergast saved Lyle the effort.

'The big asteroid dislodged from orbit by that passing comet, the one they said would miss the Earth by billions, or whatever number of miles, has, against all conceivable odds, been nudged by another dislodged asteroid and now both are going to hit us. My friend at NASA phoned me with the news at six-forty this morning, whilst on the road to his backwoods hideout, before even the President had been informed. NASA is one hundred percent sure it's going to hit, and it's way bigger than the one that took out the dinosaurs. But, unlike them, we at least get a few weeks to consider our options. I've made my choices, so — have a nice day, gentlemen.'

Jock Prendergast was halfway to the door before Nastrom slowed him with a final question.

'Where are you going? And what are you going to do?'

Hand on the doorhandle, Prendergast turned.

'Me? Having cashed in all my stocks, which is why I was somewhat pre-occupied just now, I'm heading downstairs to where your sexy P.A., Miss Flores, sits at her big desk. I'm going to give her the news and the choice of continuing to work for *you* – or spending her last twenty-nine days with *me*, exploring all the ways to have a good time. I'm confident she'll pick the better option.' He gave a predatory smirk. 'And, with any luck, we'll be so plastered, so blissed out, so smashed, that, when the asteroids hit, we won't feel a thing.'

'But – what happens after?' spluttered Lyle.

'There is no *after*, so forget it. The only thing now is to party like there's no tomorrow.' Prendergast couldn't resist a chuckle at his attempt at humour, then issued a final iteration, 'Lyle, and all of you, you *know* what I'm doing is the only sensible thing. Bye.'

§

Prendergast's dramatic exit was followed immediately by the rapid and graceless exit of most of the others. The silence that invaded the hallowed space was witnessed only by Nastrom and Lyle, who remained glued to their seats from disbelief, and the crumbs of solace offered by their soft, supportive comfort.

But disbelief can last only so long. Nastrom nodded slowly in response to his grudging acceptance of the new reality. So, the end *was* near. What to do?

No sooner asked than liberating thoughts began to emerge from hidden places. Perhaps there were constructive things that could be done.

Turning to Lyle, who was also showing signs of options being considered, Nastrom then spoke the untrammelled voice of reason.

'Thanks for staying behind, Lyle. The others may have pinned you as a "yes" man, and you *have* been too accommodating of my views, but, in spite of that, I still judge you a good man. I hope you prove me right, because I've had a few thoughts about that short future the others have given up on.'

Nastrom raised a finger to quell Lyle's incredulity.

'Yes, the future. We may not have much of one, but in case there is a possibility of more, we should have a plan. Before that, why not calm your nerves with a drink, and then come back and hear me out.'

Lyle didn't reply. Instead, he slowly extricated himself from the plush folds of his chair, then stiff-legged and a little hunched over, shuffled to the drinks cabinet and built a scotch on the rocks.

Nastrom watched as Lyle took a generous swig. It seemed to steady the fellow. Straightening up, Lyle turned to face him.

'What do you have in mind, Mr Nastrom?' he said with forced control.

Lyle's rigid stance, and the cool steadiness of his reply, sent a shiver of surprise, and hope, coursing through the chairman's body. Maybe Lyle was a better man than he'd anticipated. Perhaps a better man than himself. Would the coming weeks be Lyle's time in the sun? But time was too short for such idle speculations. There were wild ideas to be considered and actioned upon.

Pushing back in his chair Nastrom announced, 'I insist that from now on you call me Ganesh. The current situation has made us equals.'

'Fine with me, Ganesh.'

Nastrom noted that Lyle had uttered his name with deference but also with an encouraging undertone of good humour.

'In the mass exodus, we never got to vote on my recommendations regarding the final dividend and our bonuses. You and I are now effectively The Board, if we can agree that the actions of the others were equivalent to their resignations. Yes?'

Lyle's nod was sufficient to keep Ganesh going.

'Then I propose that all those funds be redirected, that they be evenly distributed to all staff, worldwide. All but our executives. Our workers will find such a sum a meaningful amount. An amount we executives can easily afford to forego. All in favour?'

Ganesh raised his hand and looked expectantly at Lyle. He assented with a nod; this time accompanied by a nascent grin.

'Next, I propose all chiefs of our overseas subsidiaries be given the chance to organise farewell celebrations at suitable locations. Venues big enough to house and feed all their local staff and families. If we are to die, we have the money to do so in comfort and style, and with the people we care for, which, hopefully includes work colleagues. All in favour?'

Ganesh raised his hand again and Lyle followed suit.

'Excuse me, Ganesh, but such a directive may be difficult to stage, and some, perhaps most, of our executive teams may be unwilling to organise such a noble undertaking.'

Ganesh had anticipated Lyle's astute observation and had an answer to it.

'If we have anyone left in our personnel departments willing to put in the hours, then we get them to contact those executives, explain the offer, and, if they refuse, we go down the chain-of-command until we find someone with the capacity and commitment to do the job. We'll give them the authority to organise the celebrations, set their own remuneration and submit a budget. If their demands are ridiculously exorbitant, it will be proof that they are unsuitable and they will be overlooked in favour of persons of a more humane disposition. Agreed?'

The ice in Lyle's glass clinked as he took another sip of his scotch. He then wandered past the chairman to stand at the window, first to gaze down at the morning rush-hour, now intensifying, and then out across the Hudson River to the poorer parts of the metropolis. Finally, in subdued tones, he responded.

'Okay with me, but we'll need someone in Finance to authorise the relevant payments. I suggest those authorising should be from different locations than the recipients to prevent carte blanche financing going to their heads. I presume there'll be no limit?'

'No limit,' confirmed the chairman.

After a pause Lyle spoke as though whispering his thoughts out loud.

'We can't help everyone. We'll be lucky to get our folk to a more survivable location. There may be a massive tsunami if the impact is in an ocean, which is likely.'

Ganesh started tapping on his laptop.

'We'll do what we can. Come over here and make that call to Personnel. Get whoever is willing to come up here and, between the three of us, we'll get the ball rolling. While you're doing that, I'll try and contact the President. Any post-apocalypse survival plans will need to be financed. We've got the money and, in my mind, it's best to offer it rather than have it commandeered. If there is a future, finance will be part of it, and, with luck, you and I may be around to run it.'

Lyle turned from the window and started back to his chair. Ganesh regarded him with a fatherly smile.

'Before you get too comfortable, how about you top-up your drink and, if you feel so inclined, make one for your former boss. I don't drink much, but today it seems appropriate.'

When Lyle resumed his seat, he slid a tumbler towards Ganesh.

'Thanks, Lyle. I propose a toast. Let us celebrate our part in softening the end of this world, and our small role in the possible birth of a new one.'

It was the briefest of celebrations. A delicate touching of glasses, the downing of a swig of fine scotch whiskey, and that was that. Drinks were then laid aside and they set to work, Lyle on the phone to Personnel, and Ganesh drafting memos on his laptop in between trying to raise the President.

§

Twenty-nine days later, on the wooded knoll overlooking the almost-completed timeshare holiday village, stood a weary Ganesh Nastrom.

Sadly, Lyle wasn't there to partake of the fruits of their labours. He'd not survived the escape from New York – killed in an ambush by one of the gangs of revenge-seeking dispossessed, now ruling the city. It was a bitter blow. He'd grown to like and respect the new Lyle Edwards.

Of the hundreds of others at head office, only fifty-three families had elected to spend their last days at this secure resort in the wooded hills of upstate New York, and none had had any stomach for last night's farewell celebration. Dinner was glum, the music subdued, the speeches inadequate. All chose to have an early night.

Today, the gloom had deepened, with everyone, his wife included, choosing to stay hidden in their rooms to await the end.

Ganesh checked his Rolex. Sixteen minutes to go. He was the only one willing to face their nemesis out in the open. But even that had gone wrong. The sky was an impervious, lumpy grey blanket, emitting a fine drizzle – tears perhaps?

Then ... a whisper in the heavens, that rapidly transformed into a fiery blast of superheated air. Ganesh stood, face heavenward, quivering with fear. A fear he gave voice to. He yelled incoherently at it. Yelled and screamed and yelled.

A nanosecond before his extinction, an unbidden thought arose and burst from him: *I stand. I roar. Is there an ending with greater grandeur?!*

Author's note:
After asking why, and how, and who with, this story was my response to a call for stories on: *celebrations.*

Season Finale

After half an hour of silent, and not so silent cursing of the blank comm screen, Nathan finally gave up. Slumping back into the captain's chair, he stared gloomily at the flight control's gleaming expanse; its green lights winking sarcastically back at him were joined by rows of gauges all smugly suggesting unperturbed normality. His only achievement had been to curdle the air in the space cruiser's control room with his ire.

Eventually, the room's only other occupant, Galaxia, Nathan's wife and the ship's Chief Medical Officer, grew weary of his sulking, and his sly glances suggestive of her being in some way responsible for the current situation. Moving her eyes from their dull reflections in the recalcitrant comm screen, she sighed, then met his gaze and offered up her summation.

'Nathan, dearest, there's no need to pout, or look at me like that. It's not my fault Martin isn't responding. You already know my opinion. It's just another one of his stupid ploys to inject drama into the show. Remember Omicron Beta!' Her eyebrows shot up. 'Let them stew I say. At least leave off panicking for another hour. Missing our breakfast is the only real drama I can see happening here. Well?'

'Humph,' was all Nathan could come up with before returning for one last try at stirring a response from Martin on the planet below – naturally, without success.

Galaxia was probably right. But he was in charge, and if anything went wrong, he'd cop it and probably lose their bonus. And they needed that bonus.

Sliding his eyes to her swollen belly, he lingered to consider the new life brewing there. Their first. Moving back to her face he tried to emulate her Mona Lisa smile. Failed, of course. Then ungraciously acknowledged her wisdom.

'Okay, you win. We'll return in an hour. I've said it before, and I'm going to say it again, we're never ever going to do another one of these un-reality shows. They never seem to end; they just transform into a new and more inane form of banality. From now on we'll cart normal tourists to normal destinations.'

He added a waggling index finger to his last retort, received little response from his other half and so was spurred to explain further.

'Just when I'd thought Martin had given up reality shows, he hooks us into another of his matchmaking fiascos: *Honeymoon Hopefuls*. Who watches this stuff anyway?'

Shaking his head, he exhaled some of his frustrations, then regrouped and continued, at a lower volume.

'And here we are, stuck in orbit around a planet circling a star on the verge of going nova, all because of Martin's desperate attempts to add drama to the show's finale: *Honeymoon Hopefuls, at the End of the World*.

The broadening of Galaxia's grin kept him going, 'And how did Martin manage to con the Time Council into letting him use their precious time portal to get us here? And we've only got 'til the twentieth before the bloody thing closes down on us. Could there be anything worse than being stranded with Martin and his attention-seeking pack of brainless, sniping himbos and bimbos four billion years in the future. Humph!?'

Galaxia merely shrugged, cuddled her belly and maintained an indulgent smile.

Nathan had finally run out of "juice". Defeated, he wearily stood, offered Galaxia his hand and then, with as much poise as he could cobble together escorted her to breakfast.

Fifty-four minutes later, they were back in the control room.

To save the happy mood generated at the dining table, Galaxia decided to keep the room's lingering disappointment at bay by offering up more female insight: 'The show's a winner because it appeals to our most basic instincts. Finding a mate, having children, and contributing to the survival of the species.'

'Yeah. I guess so,' Nathan ungraciously conceded after casting an eye to her belly and acknowledging that he had participated in all those basic activities.

Though the idea that their child would help save humanity from extinction was a bit of a stretch, considering humanity had spread across the galaxy in countless billions.

Nonetheless, he was proud to be adding to his linage, despite none of his, or Galaxia's family for that matter, ever having amounted to much. They had apparently descended from a long line of mediocrity.

And yet, like every parent, he secretly hoped their child would be the one to bring "glory" to the family name. He sighed. Such unlikely hopes were far in the future and he had the inconvenient present to deal with. Bloody Martin!

He aired his annoyance: 'I still reckon we should leave them down there; one could grow accustomed to having the ship's glitzy luxury to ourselves.'

Galaxia's hands consulted her distended belly. She'd definitely eaten for two.

'It was really good to have the dining hall to ourselves. You could abandon them. The decision's yours, Captain!' she said with mischief dancing in her eyes.

'Don't tempt me, and it's Flight Co-ordinator Nathan Transon, thank you.'

Meaningful glances were exchanged. Their bosses at Magna Media were too stingy to pay Nathan captain's wages. It was a reminder of his humbling servitude that induced a few moments of convoluted cogitations, which stretched to six minutes, then ten, then fourteen, until ...

'Okay, that's it! We're going planet-side to investigate. I'll leave Mackenzie in charge up here. There may be injuries, so you'll have to come. Stu can join us to fix any technical problems.'

'Aye, aye, Flight Co-ordinator Transon.'

His frown trumped her grin, for a moment at least.

Invigorated with a decision under his belt, Nathan hurried them towards the infirmary.

'Grab your stuff. I hope you can still squeeze into the survival suit. Down there it's a bracing sixty-seven degrees Celsius. Take a blaster.' Her eyebrows twitched. 'And make sure it's fully charged.'

A raised palm dispelled her half-hearted protest. 'We all go armed. I'll collect Stu on the way down and meet you in shuttle One. Twenty minutes enough?'

After she'd nodded her assent, he marched to the lifts, his mind buzzing with the things to be done: bring Chief Engineer Mackenzie up to speed, get their blasters, then ...

§

Once free of the mother ship, Nathan relaxed, wriggled deeper into the pilot's chair, and then shunted the external view onto the big screen at the front of the shuttle's control room and was immediately assaulted by the angry glare of a monstrous red star. It threatened to jump out of the screen and devour them and the mottled brown planet below it. A frenzied adjusting of magnification and brightness restored his composure.

Feeling the need to divert attention from the awkward moment just passed, Nathan asked Stu in the co-pilot's seat beside him about their current situation. 'Well, what are your thoughts on this historic scene: the death of a star and the imminent destruction of "The Garden of Eden" – our supposed planet of origin?'

After a minor rearrangement of the creases on his weather-beaten face, Stu replied, in measured tones, 'Well, after the star reaches the limit of its red giant expansion, it still has to collapse back into its white dwarf phase, so it definitely won't be dead for quite some time yet. But the planet – the fabled Earth – will definitely be dead and gone, very shortly.'

Having delivered his apocalyptic prognosis, Stu shrugged, then relapsed into his habitual silence.

Nathan thought Stu's last words resonated with more pathos than usual. His number one techo and their godfather-in-waiting had definitely become more subdued, morose even, during this trip. It was something he'd been meaning to investigate but now wasn't the time.

The rest of their flight to the surface was a mix of barely held expectations of a happy reunion, countered by his unending annoyance at Martin's continued silence.

Some positive vibes were gained from performing a textbook landing, soft as silk, and close to Martin's lander, or rather, transportable luxury hotel/resort.

Nathan was first onto the dried-up seabed, and first to suffer the jostling of the blustering wind and the accompanying gritty assault from the cloud of salt encrusted sand grains, whose mindless exuberance threatened to grind away his boots and survival suit. The wind's efforts had imparted an eerie sepia tinting to the flattened, rock-strewn landscape, which had him briefly imagining he'd stepped out onto the set of an ancient sci-fi movie. But this was no movie set and the wind wasn't generated by studio fans but by the huge temperature differentials between the night and day sides of the planet.

His imaginings soon shifted to the looming mass of the opulent lander, which, in the anaemic light of an almost full moon, became a huge beached whale, though one with windows and a ramp leading to a commodious rectangular airlock door. The arrival of Galaxia and Stu made further musings impossible, after catching sight of the outlandish, almost hallucinogenic vision of Galaxia and Stu coming at him in their white suits and fishbowl helmets studded with lights. They looked as alien and out-of-place as the bloated lander beached on the edge of this dying world's desiccated ocean.

Shaking his head of unhelpful thoughts he returned to the task at hand.

'Listen up, folks. They're probably all at the ruins – contrary to instructions, of course – but just to make sure, we'll check the lander anyway. And, please, be careful. We've no idea what awaits us.'

Receiving the barest of confirmatory nods, Nathan started off towards the airlock's ramp and gave thanks that the planet still had sufficient atmosphere for them to use the compact gas concentrators, saving them from being burdened by bulky air tanks. Even so, he had to take it easy. Galaxia, on his left, was stumbling occasionally on the gravelly, corrugated surface.

'Galaxia. You, okay?'

No sooner said, than he had to grab her to stop her tottering over in an unexpected soft patch.

'Yeah. I'm okay. The wind gusts, and my Medi-kit, are putting me off-balance. Should have put it in a backpack.'

'Shove it in mine,' Stu volunteered. 'There's heaps of room.'

After the smallest of hesitations, Nathan accepted the Medi-kit, and duly stowed it in Stu's backpack. They again moved off, this time with Nathan keeping hold of Galaxia's gloved hand and Stu leading the way. Fifteen or so metres from the lander, Stu turned up his lights and squatted down to examine the rapidly fading tyre tracks left by Martin's troupe.

'The amount of disturbance, all of the same age, suggests they've all gone and haven't returned. Meaning we'll be lucky to find anyone on board. And they may not have left us any buggies to use.'

Concerned glances were exchanged. Nathan then led the way up the ramp, tapped in the code and motioned Stu and Galaxia inside. Once the outer doors had closed, they had to wait for the air pressure to stabilise.

After the green lights above both sets of doors steadied, the interior ones opened. Nathan, ever careful, doublechecked the air quality and pressure, using his suit's sensors in case the lander's sensors were out-of-whack.

'Everything seems okay. We can remove our helmets and go exploring. Stu, you take the left side, Galaxia the right. I'll head to the control room and then meet you back in the central dining area. Leave your mics open, and yell if anything looks the slightest bit dodgy.'

'Dodgy? You expecting monsters?' Galaxia gave him an unconvincing happy face.

'Unlikely. All the probes found zero life here, or on any of the other planets and moons in this solar system but ...' His face finished the sentence. 'So, be cautious, and set your blasters on medium. And have them handy.'

Like a flight attendant of ancient times, Nathan demonstrated by pulling his out and making a big deal of adjusting its settings – as if the others had never handled a blaster before. Though he felt ridiculous, he was glad the others followed suite without comment.

'Good. It's better safe than sorry,' he said once Stu and Galaxia had blasters in hand. 'Now get going and be thorough.'

He immediately regretted his parting words. Both were habitually thorough.

Twenty or so minutes later, at the serving counter in the dining room, Galaxia encapsulated their findings: 'They left in a hurry. The slackers didn't even load the dishwasher. It's a mess back there.'

'Yeah. We've seen enough. Let's get moving.'

Nathan led them to the storage area where the buggies were housed. Only two remained.

'Stu, you grab the bigger, better equipped one; Galaxia and I will share the other. Outside, you can lead. Use your scanners to try and pick up any of their suits or buggies.'

After about twenty minutes of following Martin's buggy tracks, without any signals being picked up, Nathan's anxieties split into a rising fear that they wouldn't find them, and a lesser fear of what would happen if they did. He hoped there wouldn't be another shouting match with a petulant Martin.

Further on, the tracks led past the ruins of a long jetty, those pylons, like rusty fangs, extended for kilometres out across the unending fluorescent white of the seabed. It then took them up a slope onto what would have once been a peninsular of low hills, festooned with scraps of walls half submerged in sand drifts. The restless sands were also rapidly burying Martin and his entourage's buggy tracks.

All too soon, Nathan had completely lost sight of them, though Stu seemed to know where they were going.

'Stu, I can't see their tracks.'

'The infra-red and radar are still picking them out, though it's getting harder to do so. But, even if we lose them, there's only one realistic destination.'

Galaxia voiced it: 'That huge armour-glass dome ahead of us. It's the only thing still intact.'

'You're right. Okay. But we stop at the entrance and set up a radio relay.'

'My thoughts exactly,' concurred Stu.

The entrance was a huge arched tunnel about three hundred metres long. It was guarded by a series of massive sliding doors. The first pair had been blasted into shards, which they had to weave around to reach the second set about a hundred metres further in. These seemed frozen in their tracks, open just enough to let their buggies through in single file. Everywhere the dusty ceramic flooring was etched by multiple buggy tracks which funnelled through the second set of doors heading straight to the third set.

Nathan called a halt at the second set.

Stu's buggy was in the narrow opening, its lights set for maximum power and penetration. Revealed were the innermost doors, another one hundred meters further in. These were closed. The tracks of Martin's group ended at them, though one of their buggies was parked nearby, the rest presumably had gotten through to who knew where, and to what end.

Whilst Stu walked back to the outer doors to set up the communications relay, Nathan and Galaxia had the time to examine their surroundings in greater detail.

The blotchiness of the doors' brassy metal surface and the pitting of the dark grey, metal-ceramic arch reinforced in Nathan's mind the sad reality that no matter how advanced our technologies, time will best anything humans can create. It was a sobering thought that he gladly abandoned when Stu strolled back into view.

Having established their ability to communicate with Mackenzie, Nathan outlined their next moves.

'Galaxia, go with Stu. Once you're through, wait for me. I'm going to park our buggy in the gap, facing out, to keep our escape route open. Then, together, we'll track down our miscreant Martin.'

When they reached the inner door, Nathan left Stu and Galaxia, to do a quick inspection of the abandoned buggy. It, disappointingly, provided no new information. At least the doors' control panel was both clearly visible, a hand-shaped glass tile that only required his handprint to induce the doors to open.

Back in their buggy, Nathan needlessly double-checked his blaster, returned it to its holster, then told Stu to follow the tracks inside.

They drove off at a steady pace. Initially travelling through an area of scattered buildings, along a wide boulevard that once had been lined by trees, now reduced to withered stumps. As they progressed, the buildings became taller and more closely spaced, with the number of intersections increasing in tandem. They still hadn't picked up any directional signals emanating from Martin's crowd, but their course was clearly visible in the dust and grit of the road's smooth surface.

A short time later, Stu announced: 'I've picked up one of the suits, straight ahead, coming from …'

'The palace? Parliament?' opined Galaxia.

Nathan countered: 'Might be a temple. It's on the highest ground, and where ever you go, people are still big on religion.'

The return to silence gave him time to consider this domed city they were penetrating, uninvited, though it was difficult to be objective because the experience seemed not quite real. The buildings sliding past them were mere flashes of harsh whites and slashing black shadows that disappeared once the headlights moved on. Again, he felt as if he was dreaming and had been returned to a different section of that long-abandoned movie set, the one housing Martin's lander.

What did register as being real was the architectural repetition of domes and arched colonnades, generally less than five stories, that crowded narrow, curving side streets as though desperate for company, only to be wrenched apart by the intrusion of occasional broad thoroughfares. The trip then dredged up unpleasant memories of another bad dream, which had unfortunately been all too real: his getting lost, as a kid, in the catacombs of Vestra. It had been a traumatic episode that he'd never really resolved.

A distraction was needed. He forced his mind back to their immediate predicament. A question emerged: 'Whose suit?'

'Ignatius,' Stu answered in a voice amazingly free of rancour.

It was *always* Ignatius. He was the show's highest-scoring contestant. A man, outwardly charming, until you discovered his arrogant scheming side. Women loved him, the audience too, but the crew, Nathan included, despised him. Nathan wasn't relishing the conversation to come, but consoled himself with the hope that Ignatius would lead them to the rest.

The building they were approaching had to be a temple. Nathan tallied up the signs: the portico around its base was much more elaborately decorated than any of the other buildings, and it had a particularly grand entrance, consisting of a huge arch held aloft by massive columns and two immense, rather intimidating doors, in midnight blue and covered with intricate motifs in gold. Whatever it truly was, it was where Martin's lot had gone because scattered in front of its doors were six buggies.

'Where's Ignatius?' Nathan prodded Stu's shoulder.

'Behind the far buggy near the column on the left.'

Nathan couldn't see anybody. Sinister premonitions raised the hairs on the back of his neck.

'Stay here, keep the engine humming and prepare for a fast exit. I'll approach him from the left side of the buggy.'

Pulling out his blaster, Nathan hopped off, and began a crouched, stealthy approach.

Stu drove to the right, then positioned the buggy facing the city's exit. Both he and Galaxia sat craning their necks to follow Nathan's slow progress, saw him bend down behind the buggy.

He was out of sight for an agonisingly long moment before he suddenly reappeared and motioned them over.

'Ignatius won't be causing any more trouble. Someone has drilled a nasty hole through his chest. The question is, one of ours, or someone else, and, where did the arrogant fool get this? Stu, you're ex-Navy ...' Nathan held up a Peacemaker: compact, ergonomic, potent, and a standard Navy issue sidearm.

They gathered around the body. It was lying on its back. The chest sported a fist-sized hole with charred edges. Inside the helmet a surprised look was frozen onto clean-shaven, chiselled features. The hot air had dried the blood around the wound into black flaking smears.

Slipping the Peacemaker into a thigh pocket, Nathan nodded to Stu: 'Grab his legs, we'll put him in the back of the buggy.'

Nathan got his hands around the shoulder straps of the survival suit, Stu grabbed hold of the feet, and between them they lugged the unco-operative corpse to their buggy, where they unceremoniously tossed it onto the rear storage tray.

Nathan couldn't resist airing his disdain: 'Even in death he was hard to handle.'

After one last glance at the body, he turned to Stu. 'Take five, I'll contact Mac.'

Back at their buggy, Nathan took the driver's seat and started pressing buttons. 'Hello Mac, there's been trouble down here. Ignatius has been killed ... a blaster; he was armed ... a Navy Peacemaker ... Yeah, how he smuggled it on board I can't imagine.'

He paused to let Mac take in the news, then continued, 'Move into a higher orbit, plus three will do, and await further instructions. I'll try to call in ... two hours ...' He paused to set up an alarm into his wrist pad, '... and if we don't report in, give us another forty-eight hours, then abandon us, make the rendezvous with the time portal, and when you get home, let the Time Council and the Board of Galactic Governments sort things out.'

At the other end was a grunt, a considered silence, before Mac uttered his reluctant consent.

Nathan was halfway out of the buggy when he saw Galaxia and Stu, standing rigid, with their hands in the air.

They were being menaced by a group of diminutive droids, metallic caricatures of smooth faced dwarves, sandy coloured and barrel chested. Each held a weapon in its stubby fingers. One of them had Nathan in its sights. Going into slo-mo, he kept his hands in full view.

The droid covering him with its blaster, uttered unintelligible commands in a surprisingly masculine voice, subtitled with equally baffling text scrolling across the screen in its chest. It then pointed towards the massive doors, now partially open.

'Translate,' Nathan whispered to his collar mic in the slim hope of an answer, but the message was clear enough, and he soon joined the others filing silently inside, with two droids leading and three behind them.

A long and lofty antechamber served as an airlock, which, after the pressures equalised and the inner doors had opened, revealed a vast atrium, where the lighting, cool and golden, in happier circumstances could have mimicked sunrise at the beach. The marble floor, dominated by a mosaic of the star system, was crisscrossed by crazed patterns of tracks in the thin layer of dust, tracks they then added to as they were hustled to a side corridor, into a lift, and then down four levels into a sort of reception hall of more human dimensions.

One of the droids moved towards Stu, who remained under the watchful eyes and blasters of the others, then stopped, extended its arms, and gently removed the backpack, draped it over one arm and then with its free hand removed Stu's blaster. It moved back to join its brethren, one of whom moved off to disarm Galaxia and then Nathan, whose holster was emptied but not his thigh pocket – it apparently lacked the initiative to look for other weapons. The droid moved off to join its companions, allowing their prisoners time to concentrate on the occupants of the raised platform at the end of the hall.

A shiny, ruby coloured droid, as small as the others, stood next to a throne on which sat an amused Theo, Ignatius's nearest rival and equally vacuous and vain. He was still in his survival suit, though minus the helmet.

'Welcome to Marinus, capital of the Confederation of the Sun. I am Clemis the Fourth.'

The personage now apparently occupying Theo's body, spoke as if Galactic was a second language and kept rubbing its forehead as though hungover.

Nathan's speculations upon their situation were diverted by the arrival of three worker droids carrying chairs, gold embellished and ornate, verging on fragile, which they lined up in a row, a short distance from the stage.

'Sit! We have much to discuss. Remove your helmets, the palace is a sanctuary from the evils that have befallen the rest of the planet. Here all is as it should be, including the air. It is wonderfully breathable!'

Nathan ignored the man's moment of pride, being more interested in his companion. The red droid's collar was of gold, not stainless steel like the others, it was of slimmer build, had longer arms and more delicate hands. He concluded it performed higher functions, with the other, more numerous ones being menials, workers.

'I think we'll keep the helmets on, and stay standing,' replied Nathan.

'As you please, but Galaxia may want to reconsider your recommendations,' Clemis/Theo said with false concern, whilst distractedly massaging its forehead.

Clemis/Theo tightened its grip on the arms of the throne; its face flickered, then became calm and resolute, as if an internal dispute had been resolved. Finally, he fixed a steadfast and calculating gaze upon his prisoners.

An uncomfortable silence developed whilst Clemis studied each of them in turn. After a time, he seemed to reach a decision, enough for him to resume his banter.

'If you wish to know what circumstances you have fallen into, ask.'

Their collective silence produced a frown.

'I was so looking forward to a conversation after …' he glanced towards the ceiling, 'one thousand, four hundred and sixty-nine million standard years,' he said with a shake of the head.

'Such a waste. But finally, you have arrived. My digital sleep has ended. A glorious future awaits us. Or should I say, a glorious past, as we shall be going back to the year of your departure.'

Clemis stroked his handsome jaw, now darkened by stubble, then paused to master a moment of doubt. 'But we mustn't rush. First, we dine.'

Immediately, a swarm of workers appeared, set up an overlong table, complete with delicate china plates, shining cutlery, crystal glasses and several table decorations in gold and precious stones. Nathan watched Clemis shuffle awkwardly from the stage, shadowed by the red droid, to then sit at the head of the table, after which Nathan and the others were herded into their seats at the other end.

'I really must insist you accept my hospitality. The droids can inflict unpleasantness if you continue to be uncivil.' His voice, placating at first, ended with cold authority and Galaxia yelping.

She'd received an electric shock from the droid nearest her.

Fists clenched, Nathen shouted back, 'Okay!' then he took a breath and added with less volume, 'We get the message. And whatever happened to the Three Laws of Robotics, especially the one about not harming humans?'

Grumbling, he removed his helmet – with unnecessary force – then gently assisted a still shaken Galaxia with hers, seated her, and took the chair beside her. Stu reluctantly complied and then sat on her left.

'Laws and rules are for fools. And I am no fool,' Clemis bellowed, then glanced towards his droids, and, with a snap of his fingers, issued his commands: 'Food and drink for our guests.'

Droids departed with the backpack and helmets, returning shortly after bearing silver platters decked with emergency ration packs from the buggies, others held water in fancy cut glass pitchers, all of which were arranged, with great care, before their guests.

Clemis, looking a touch contrite, explained, 'You find us embarrassingly short of supplies, but I'm sure you understand the circumstances and will have the decency to enjoy the pleasure of communal dining. Let's not stand on ceremony; help yourselves.'

Nathan ignored his stomach's reluctance for another breakfast and decided to play for time, hoping a miraculous escape plan would materialise.

Selecting one of the flat metal packs, he pressed the sensor, waited for the colour to change, then ripped off the top and saw the steam rising from the bilious yellow of a chicken curry, hesitated to allow his nose to recover from its oleaginous pungency and then manfully scooped a spoonful onto his plate. Galaxia, who had been looking on with strained self-control, unenthusiastically followed his lead, dished out a spoonful, then passed it on.

The meal seemed to strengthen Clemis's persona. He ate with gusto, completely ignoring their mechanical nibbling, and silence. Between mouthfuls, he told stories of the rise and fall of Earth's peoples and how the ex-colonists from Mars had reconquered the abandoned planet.

Once their dining had concluded and the table had been cleared, Clemis leaned back and gazed upon them like a magistrate about to give sentence.

'Who shall you be?' this spoken as if he was enjoying an internal joke.

After a moment of absentmindedly tapping the table top, he continued, 'Perhaps a tour of the clinic will clarify the situation.'

Clemis gave commands to the droids in their strange language, and then stood up. Accompanied by his ruby companion, he strolled, with smoother movements, to the archway at the back of the hall. Nathan noticed a small metallic button at the base of Clemis' skull.

Nascent ideas of escape were dashed when the droids got them moving, with weaponry and garbled commands, now haltingly interpreted by their communications earbuds. Again, to lifts and down several levels, this time to emerge into a vast laboratory, where their attention was drawn to an array of glass tanks along one wall, in which, like insect specimens, the cast, film crew, and Martin lay immobile – except for their rapidly blinking eyes. Their heads were hooked up to a mass of wiring as though they had all acquired long, colour-coded dreadlocks.

Clemis, who, with his red, mechanical symbiont, was standing in front of the tanks admiring his comatose specimens, turned at their approach.

'I think your companions will be forever grateful for the new personas I shall install in them ...' His face lit up. '... the ones they are now being programmed with. The thing is, shall we also bless you with personalities from my long dormant trusted inner circle? What say you? Speak up, your reticence grows tiring.'

They remained mute.

Clemis's face clouded over, his eyes hardened, and a hand migrated to his forehead. After a moment, another internal debate appeared to have run its course, sufficient for him to continue his monologue.

'According to Theo, the show ends at sunrise when the couples exchange their vows with the dawn light giving them all a golden glow, creating new lives on a dead planet,' – he took on a saintly pose – '…all beautifully poetic, but as you can see, we are not quite dead, and the new lives will not be those in your script.'

A smirk enlivened his face, all too soon replaced by a venomous scowl, 'And then we shall track down Alerik and grind him into dust for abandoning us. But we fooled him, and his brood. Flesh can wither, but not the soul!' he said, tapping the side of his head, with manic eyes and a toothy, lupine grimace.

Once Clemis had settled, Nathan decided the time was right for some sort of counter offensive.

'You'll need us, as is, if you want to get off this worthless planet.'

Theo had been a footballer, and so Nathan hoped that Theo/Clemis would thus know little of spaceship protocols, time portals, or the physics of hyperspace. It was an ignorance he hoped to make use of.

'If you have access to Theo's memories, you'll know that after the dawn ceremonies we only have twenty-four standard hours to get back to our ship, and less than another forty-eight hours to get to the time portal.'

Clemis raised his hand, 'Yes, yes, all very inconvenient. Too much time, or not enough. It's always the same old problem.'

'You have less time than you think. If I don't report back,' he glanced at his wrist communicator, '… in one hour and twenty-two minutes, our ship has orders to abandon us and return home.'

'You think me a fool! You'll not abandon me, err, us. There are too many here in need of …' Clemis's voice wavered between two slightly differing intonations, as if the two personalities were momentarily fighting for control.

Speaking slowly, and with as much menace as he could muster, Nathan kept going, 'You're all the same, you self-serving sycophants. You think the universe can't do without you. Well, it can. So, get used to it. And only *I* have the power to rescind those orders, from up on the surface, and outside of the dome. I suggest …'

'Cease this insolent prattle,' Clemis screamed, before directing a group of workers to separate Galaxia. 'You two will await my pleasure elsewhere. Galaxia will come with me.'

Before they could react, both he and Stu were hit with electrical discharges that left them writhing on the floor. When it ended, Nathan, heart racing and struggling to breathe, caught a glimpse of Clemis, Galaxia, and the droids, disappearing through a door on his right.

The remaining mechanical guards then gave them orders, now more or less intelligible, to get up and move in the opposite direction. Like a pair of drunks, he and Stu struggled to their feet and were then cajoled down a corridor, and, not a great distance further on, goaded into a storage room and locked in.

A brief survey of their prison, revealed the only feature offering the hint of escape – a ventilation grill in the softly glowing ceiling, but it was out of reach and too narrow to be of any use.

After a while, Stu asked, 'You riled him on purpose?'

'Yeah. I figured that whilst Clemis's personality was still not fully in control of Theo's, I could stir him into doing something foolish. Something we could use.' He waved his hands, palms up, full of nothing, then sighed and resumed his thinking out loud.

'Clemis, and others like him, are vampires. To live they need to take over someone else's physical body. What we desperately need is some kind of silver bullet!'

Nathan, seeking inspiration, started stroking his chin. 'Clemis must know that digital immortality is fake. He probably can't make a physical copy of himself and so has to settle for inducing his personality and memories into the brain of a surrogate, which takes time. It's a slow process creating new neural patterns. He hasn't got that time here, on this planet. And did you notice how he goes nowhere without the red droid.'

Stu's confirming nods were enough for him to continue, 'I think Clemis is an avatar controlled by that droid. The droid is where Clemis resides, or rather, is stored.'

'That droid is the key. How it controls things I don't know. And I don't know what would happen if we destroyed it …' Nathan tapped his thigh pocket where the Peacemaker lay. 'We aren't without options. I just wish I knew what he has planned for Galaxia. He's dead meat if he messes with her mind.'

Nathan felt the bite of his fingernails from involuntarily clenching his hands.

'Before you put too much faith in Peacemaking,' Stu mimed, scanning the walls and ceilings for eavesdroppers, '… maybe Ignatius tried that and failed. We'd best have a plan B.' He motioned Nathan over, pulled out a metal gadget shaped like a flattened sausage from his back pocket and started whispering the many uses of his sonic multi-driver.

All to soon their plans were interrupted by the door opening.

Nathan gave his final whispered command, 'When the balloon goes up, Clemis is mine.'

The door opened. Outside in the corridor were a squad of worker droids, one of which walked inside and ordered them to follow it.

They were led back in the laboratory, which was now crowded with droids organising a cavalcade of trolleys, each carrying several glass-topped pods, sufficient to hold all the contestants, the film crew, and Martin. Beside a grinning Clemis was a trolley with only one pod, one containing a recumbent Galaxia.

Nathan demeanour grew murderous. His hand edged towards his thigh pocket.

'Go easy, nothing rash, we only get one chance, and it's not yet,' muttered Stu whilst placing a steadying hand on Nathan's shoulder.

Seeing them, Clemis announced: 'I have decided there is to be no delay. We move off once the pods have had their final checks.'

He then turned his attention to the red droid, which was rapidly moving amongst the pods performing silent ministrations to the control panels of each of them.

'In a few minutes, we shall proceed to the lander, then back to your orbiting spaceship and,' he paused to strike a heroic pose, 'go forward into a glorious immortality.'

Nathan replied with grim menace, 'It'll be a very brief immortality. You're going nowhere unless you release Galaxia.'

'My, my, you have become excitable. But I would advise against anything foolish. My droids' reactions are infinitely faster than yours, and anyway, what can you do? Join Ignatius! He was a regrettable mistake and a waste of a good specimen.'

Nathan quelled his fury, 'You still forget. I command the ship! Without my say so, we all starve in this mausoleum of yours. So, free Galaxia. Now!'

Clemis attempted to counter Nathan's fiery gaze but was first to blink. 'We waste time. First, we move to the surface, then we'll decide what happens.'

Clemis turned and, accompanied by his gold-collared droid, led the procession down a broad corridor.

Workers moved in to block any rebellious actions by their two prisoners, who found themselves taking their place at the end of the convoy of trollies. A short time later they were back in the dusty atrium, where they re-joined Clemis and his personal droid. On a bench, along the opposite wall, were their helmets and Stu's backpack.

With a face oozing smarmy contempt, Clemis addressed his recalcitrant guests, 'Stu, you are the technical man, put the Flight Co-ordinator's mind at ease and examine the delightful Galaxia. You will note that she is not wired up. She's just having some hypnotic preparation. A bit of history to prepare her mind for things to come.'

Stu took a breath, then obeyed and, after looking her over as much as he could, returned and reported back to Nathan. 'She doesn't seem to be wired up. She didn't respond to my presence, just lay there, eyes open, blinking occasionally, looking as if she is watching a particularly engrossing movie. So, maybe he's not completely lying.'

Nathan grunted but remained silent; he caught and held Clemis's gaze, determined to gain some psychological power over him, to psyche him out, to rattle his confidence. They fought a silent duel, in which the room disappeared whilst Nathan poured his soul and anger into Clemis's eyes. Again, Clemis gave way first. It was a victory of sorts that left Clemis briefly shaking his head, as if attempting to dismiss the incident.

After a pause, somewhat mechanically Clemis gave his orders. They were to don their helmets and then move off, with

Galaxia's trolley in the lead. The other trolleys would follow, then Nathan and Stu, and, finally, trailing at a safe distance, Clemis would, proudly "lead from the rear". Nathan presumed Clemis's closing remark was an attempt at humour/sarcasm? It was difficult to tell which.

Receiving no response to his witty rejoinder, Clemis ploughed on with his instructions to Nathan, 'Once outside the dome, you will contact the spaceship. You will inform them all is well and that you will be returning with all persons accounted for, after which you will proceed as per the schedule. There is to be no deviation from these directives or ...' He let a nod towards Galaxia's pod finish his sentence.

'We shall see what happens – outside,' Nathan replied, each word slowly and precisely spoken, partly to show his resolve, but more so to signal to Stu that on the other side of the exit doors was where they would make their move.

As directed, they went to the bench and clipped into their helmets. Clemis had his delivered to him by a droid, then struggled to put it on but eventually succeeded, after which he checked his intercom connection.

'Take up your positions at the rear. For your safety,' Clemis grinned, '... both of you will have droids to assist you,' this time a snorted chuckle escaped, '... and to ensure you fully comply with my orders. Go!' he said with a hand pointing at the rear of the column.

A red droid, but one with a silver collar, was in charge of Galaxia's pod, and led the procession into the airlock. The rest followed as arranged. Once the atrium's inner doors closed. Nathan endured a moment of rising unease. He swallowed hard to subdue it, regaining his composure just as the outer doors swung wide. His hand drifted towards his thigh pocket.

The leading pod was slowed by having to weave a path through the jumble of buggies. Those following then jammed up, allowing Nathan and Stu to catch up to the droid pushing the trolley in front of them.

Natham made his move. Praying the close proximity of the pods would hamper any responses from the droids.

Slamming into the droid on his left, he managed to tip it onto its face. Nathan fell with it, rolled over to wrench Ignatius's blaster from his thigh pocket, continued to roll until he faced Clemis, who stood slightly hunched, frozen with one hand on his droid seemingly unsure which way to run.

Nathan felt a surge of joyous vengeance explode in him as he pressed the trigger and saw its red beam slice across Clemis and his droid, searing a line of blisters on the droid and producing an ugly red slash across the white of Clemis's suit. Clemis gurgled once, then began to crumple.

Stu had performed a similar manoeuvre, knocking down his droid and blocking its weapon hand with his body. He had his multi driver aimed at Clemis's red droid, sending it a massive pulse of radio waves, more than enough to fry its circuitry.

Nathan's attention soon returned to his own fate when a deadly crimson beam from a nearby droid's blaster melted the pavement millimetres from his head. Pulling his blaster to bear on his attacker, he counted the milliseconds left to beat its next shot.

But none came. He didn't need to shoot. His opponent seemed to have blown a circuit: immobile, blaster in its metal hand, but apparently drained of any desire to use it.

Perplexed, Nathan returned his gaze towards Clemis, who lay twitching on the pavement, blood pumping from his slashed chest. His red droid, like its metal compatriots, had also seized up mid-motion, and, off-balance, had toppled over to join Clemis in the blood splattered dust. All the other droids were similarly frozen.

Suddenly, his laboured breathing, and Stu's, seemed overloud in the absolute silence that suddenly descended upon the scene.

Staggering to his feet, Nathan watched Stu do likewise, and together they studied the frozen tableau of droids, most standing like metallic stalagmites, with others collapsed on the ground in amongst the jumble of buggies and trollies. In the east, a pinkish grey was emerging, warning of the fearsome red sun's imminent return. Fear of frying forced reason back into his dazed mind.

'We can't hang around. Grab Clemis/Theo's head, I'll grab his legs. We'll chuck him in with Ignatius, then hook their trolleys up to our buggy, Galaxia's first, and then the rest of them. Next, we'll connect up all our buggies, which you can be in charge of. I'll lead the cavalcade of trolleys. We then hightail it back to the lander. The less evidence we leave behind of our presence here, the better. We don't want to muddy future history too much, do we!'

Stu was already moving. They carefully carried the corpse back, with Nathan hoping all the way that it wouldn't split in half. Thankfully, it survived intact and joined Ignatius in inert companionship. They then worked frantically to organise both convoys, a job made difficult by having to move unresponsive droids out of their way.

They were both sweating by the time they got going, Nathan leading the way, with their progress delayed briefly at the dome's middle door where he had to hook up Ignatius' abandoned buggy to the rest of them. An interminable time later they finally loaded everything and everybody into the lander.

Nathan contacted Mac. 'We're all back on board the lander, two dead, will explain later, get everything ready for our arrival and our rendezvous with the time portal. See you soon.'

The rising sun was starting to burn the topmost edge of the dome when they blasted off, Stu commanding the shuttle, Nathan the lander.

§

It took nineteen months before Nathan and, to a lesser extent, Stu, were exonerated for the various deaths, for the Navy to admit Ignatius as their spy, for the producers to drop the suit against Nathan for lost revenue caused by the cancellation of the final episode – they were mollified by increased interest in the following season's show caused by the publicity surrounding the court case – and for Nathan and Stu to receive their back pay, bonuses and damages, for the trauma induced by the reckless behaviour of the producers, and the Time Council for allowing the project to go ahead in the first place.

Nathan had arranged a celebratory lunch.

'How's little Jemma doing?' Stu remarked to a radiant Galaxia as he stepped inside their modest apartment.

Galaxia replied on the way to the balcony out the back, 'She's fine, having a nap. All that growing is a tiring business. She certainly loves her food. Just like her mum!'

'Doesn't show,' Stu responded after giving her a head-to-toe appraisal. 'Are you okay? The others are still having their brains unscrambled. Still in the Navy hospital I hear.'

'I'm fine, just fine.'

They joined Nathan, who presided over the barbecue, tongs in one hand and a glass of beer in the other. His face almost split in two with a welcoming grin. Abandoning the beer and tongs, he exchanged manly handshakes with Stu.

'Welcome. Wow! You're looking good. Spending too much time in a rejuvenator, or what?'

Stu, smiling, shook his head. 'No, nothing like that. But thanks anyway.'

Nathan again gave silent thanks to Galaxia for getting Stu to own up to the cancer, and then persuading him to have it treated.

'Rumour has it you've signed up for another production, Atlas Enterprises. I thought you would want to take things easy from now on.'

'Yeah – but it seems work is what I do. It appears I'm one of those types who doesn't do leisure. But it's an easy job. Should be fun, so …' He shrugged.

Kindnesses were exchanged, beers offered, and a convivial meal shared.

Later, when Galaxia had gone off to feed Jemma, Nathan and Stu were on the balcony kicking back in their recliners, sharing a minute's silence whilst watching the sun about to sink behind the apartment blocks on the other side of the park.

Nathan puzzled why, on all human planets, the star was always known as the sun, irrespective of its real name. He should be thinking Ceti is getting low in the sky not the sun, which could only rightly be attached to that angry red furnace they had narrowly escaped from. Escaping, brought his mind back to the ultimate reason for their celebration, a reason he pondered aloud: 'Now that you've lived through the bizarre world of reality shows, and the distant future, what have you learned from the experience?'

Nathan was secretly hoping Stu could provide some sort of ideological framework that *he* could build upon.

Stu gave a quizzical look before returning his gaze to the setting sun. A sigh followed, and then a reluctant reply.

'I reckon those contestants, fighting for their five minutes of fame, and Clemis and his lot, dreaming of immortality just to get revenge on their rivals, seem sadly ridiculous to me.'

'Do you want to expand on that?'

'Well, why do people want to become famous?' He paused, then answered, 'I'll tell you why. The same reasoning was driving both groups. Put simply: we all want to be remembered. The show's contestants, knowing deep down that they will die, hope their moment of fame will make them a little harder to forget.'

'Weren't Clemis and his crowd a little different?'

'No, not really. In their case, the development of "digital immortality" meant, in theory, they would never totally fade from their society's memory because they continued to physically exist, as stored digital data. This left open the possibility of finding ways to be reborn, and then regain the limelight. Which is what they wanted to do via our bodies. The moot point is: who exactly did they believe would survive into that future?'

He allowed Nathan time to offer a reply, but none came, and so continued, 'Is the Clemis in Theo's body going to have the same future as a Clemis in a Clemis clone? No, because our body's appearance and biochemistry affect our moods, and hence our actions, and then reactions of others to us. Thus, different bodies produce different histories, which in turn changes the evolving personas attached to each successive and unique body. It's like a game of Chinese whispers. A whispered message, fed through a series of minds produces a final message with no resemblance to the original. Capiche?'

Nathan needed time to think.

Stu, again filled in the silence: 'None of us really seriously consider, or answer, the question of who we are, and why we are here. My cancer forced me to confront my who and why. Perhaps, little Jemma will cause you too, to honesty ask, who you are, and why you are here.'

Stu took a sip of his beer, but maintained eye contact, with eyes displaying an unexpected mischief that Nathan found most disconcerting.

At least Stu appeared to have found satisfying answers to both questions, and had obviously decided to give life another chance. In contrast, he, Nathan Transon, had always lived day-to-day, never thought too much about the long-term. He'd always been convinced that life was too unpredictable for long-term plans. And he had certainly never given much time to his life's purpose, or purposes.

Nathan's silence appeared to encourage Stu to further elucidate.

'In the natural world nothing lasts forever. All living creatures are designed to die. I reckoned there must be reasons for that disturbing arrangement.'

Nathan wasn't about to offer any, so Stu continued, 'From what I've figured out, mortality forces us as individuals, as societies, and as a species, to come up with new ideas and new ways to adapt, so we can survive in an ever-changing universe. It appears death is needed to remove broken biologies and unhelpful ideologies.'

Seeing Nathan's grim, almost frightened look, Stu relented, 'Don't sweat. You don't have to get bogged down in philosophy, or religion, all you have to do is realise you don't have forever, so find out what you like doing, and why, and then arrange things to maximise the good bits. Simple!'

He smiled. 'I just hope you figure those things out a lot sooner than I did.'

The sun had set; the light was fading fast. It took Nathan a while to bring his scattered thoughts under control. All manner of themes had been set loose, too many, and he struggled to gather them in. A subtle change had occurred deep inside him. A vague shift for the better, though one he couldn't verbalise.

It was something he felt sure would become clearer as time progressed.

Stu seemed happy to let the silence linger. The man was definitely a whole lot happier, so perhaps talking about living and dying was a good thing after all.

Time passed. The light in the hall came on, followed shortly after by Galaxia.

'What are you two doing out here in the dark? Come inside and I'll brew up a pot of tea.'

Nathan let Galaxia escort Stu to the dining room, but lingered a while longer on the balcony. He noted the darkening sky still carried hints of orange along its crenulated horizon. Lights were winking on in the apartments across the park, then the street lights came on. He breathed deep the cooling air, and, filled with a strange, intoxicating contentment, he stood, then turned and walked into the lighted passage.

His joy expanded upon catching the muted sounds of Galaxia and Stu's cooing babytalk to little Jemma. In the next step it grew further. Hearing the gentle "clink" of a spoon on fine bone China, he suddenly understood the perfection its context represented.

Project Starfighter

The new CEO had been in place for less than a month and already rumours of a restructure were doing the rounds, spooking the staff, and none more so than Jimeon Boljar, Senior Analyst for East Asia Operations. He'd survived others but the recent poor performance of the Asian assets had put his division in the spotlight. As a mid-level manager, and pushing fifty, he was just the type for the chop.

Stepping out of the rotating maw of the concrete and glass monstrosity that was the bank's Perth Headquarters, the cool air and noisy normality of the CBD's Friday night exodus gave little relief from his rising unease.

Like a fox jumping into a lake to rid itself of fleas, Jimeon similarly required total immersion, of a different sort, to lose his biting anxieties. He turned, not towards the train station, but towards FunzHome and a session on the Starfighter Nemesis machine.

Only it could take him away from the depressing uncertainties of reality, to a universe where he was indestructible and fighting for a worthy cause, not the impossible task of placating the insatiable greed of bank executives but the achievable one of outgunning Klizav slavers.

It wasn't his day. A bunch of teenagers were crowding the Starfighter machine, watching their mate going for the record. The kid at the controls was good. His score was way above anything Jimeon had ever managed, which soured his mood more than it should have.

Averting his gaze, he debated how best to find an equivalent distraction. Escaping to his gaming chair in their spare room at home wasn't going to happen. Jasmin would expect, and deserve him to be the attentive husband, to be communicative, not selfishly hide himself away in another universe chasing childish fantasies.

Dragging his heels, and with no particular alternative in mind, he turned for the exit but had only managed a few steps when blocked by the grinning figure of the manager.

'Hello Mr Boljar. I couldn't help noticing your disappointment. I think I can offer you something much better. Come to my office. It will only take a few moments.'

Tony had a room out the back where he trialled new games and upgrades of existing ones, always in the latest gaming chairs. He had, on occasions, when Starfighter had been unavailable, let Jimeon spend time there trying out those new games and chairs.

His friendliness was a constant source of puzzlement because they had very different temperaments. Tony was the ebullient extraverted type and he? He didn't really know. Even after all these years he seemed different people in different situations.

At work, he managed to be reasonably outgoing; had to be to survive. Towards his wife, he was affectionate and doting, but in the Starfighter game he was a merciless hunter. Though even in that imagined world, and probably in the real one too, he was only ever Mr Okay, Mr Team Player, never Mr Inspirational or Mr Amazing.

Once inside Tony's office, Jimeon's nose battled an odd mixture of odours, the ebullience induced by the aroma of coffee, fighting noisome overtones of rotting garbage and stale cigarettes.

Tony was quick to pick up on his displeasure and moved to close the only window, which opened onto the alley behind the building.

'Sorry about the smell but it's the only "fresh" air available. There's a garbage hopper nearby and the smokers seem to find my window irresistible.'

Once he'd closed the window, he pulled a can of something from his desk and gave the room a quick spray. A rather pleasing mintiness took hold, after which Tony motioned him to take one of the two chairs on the other side of his cluttered desk. Once both were settled, he picked up one of several mobile phones scattered about his desk. He made a call, silencing Jimeon imminent protestations with an upraised finger and a friendly smile.

'Colonel Latimer, I've got the fellow you've been considering for your project. He's here in my office … Yes, that's right … you'll come down … five minutes … Okay. Bye.'

Though Tony's face radiated innocence and goodwill, it wasn't enough to quell a faint stirring of disquiet in Jimeon's digestion, setting him on the stupid path of wondering why his emotions always expressed themselves first in his stomach.

'Trust me, Mr Boljar, you're gonna love me for this. It'll be a better buzz than anything you've ever had from playing Starfighter. Colonel Latimer will explain everything. He'll be here in a few minutes. A nice guy. You're gonna like him.'

Tony filled the delay by shoving the latest issue of Gamer's Bible at him before fussing around making cappuccinos on his impressively new coffee machine. They were taking their first tentative forays into the froth when the office door resounded to two firm raps, startling Tony out of his chair.

The Colonel was tall, mature but trim, and disguised as a businessman in his dark suit, white shirt and red tie, and as such, would have blended into any boardroom but for his posture, which was too rigid, too military.

Once the Colonel was seated, introductions were made, with the Colonel's ID card flourished with practised ease. Tony then conjured up another cappuccino. Whilst waiting, Jimeon suffered that awkward uncertainty one gets when introduced to a stranger. Tony returned, handed the Colonel his coffee, then resumed his seat.

Nodding his thanks, the Colonel then turned towards him, 'Tony has recommended you highly, and I'm pleased to say that in the flesh, you are even more impressive,' – said with what puzzlingly appeared to be genuine affection.

To hide his confusion Jimeon had a sip of coffee, then replied in a neutral tone, 'I think you're drawing your conclusions on hearsay not fact, and I think that whatever plans you have in store for me …' He moved his head to catch Tony's eye, '… firstly needs explaining, and secondly, will probably result in my disappointing you both, so …'

Tony was about speak but the Colonel was quicker off the mark.

'Your words again confirm my confidence in you, but I think the best way to convince you of the terrific opportunity we have on offer, is for you to accompany me to a place where you can try out something much better than anything Tony can offer. I have a car waiting to take us to Pearce Airbase. I'll explain everything when we get there because it will be far easier for you to understand things once you see the set-up. Are you up to it?'

The Colonel's face softened into a mode that radiated sincerity. His shoulders eased and, in doing so, hinted at the human behind the military façade. In Jimeon, the odd thought emerged that maybe the Colonel was as fearful of his saying no as he was of taking up this bizarre and unexplained offer from a stranger who, logically, could be a shyster intent on doing him in.

For what seemed a long time the three of them stood frozen in place, immobilised by a fateful thought struggling to free itself from the depths of Jimeon's psyche. Suddenly aware he'd been holding his breath, he exhaled with determination, took a deep inhalation, straightened up, then looked into both pairs of eyes and heard himself saying: 'Okay. Let's go.'

The Colonel and his driver, occupied the front of the black, stretched Mercedes, whilst he was the sole occupant in the back. Tony had stayed behind. Not a word was said until they were checking in at the gates of the Air Force base.

The guard gave Jimeon an identity badge to sling around his neck. The Colonel had at some stage put his on; same too for the driver. Once inside they drove a while to eventually stop adjacent the entrance to a ten-storey office block, which hadn't been there the last time he'd been inside the airbase – all those years back. The building's drab design spoke more of Soviet Russia than the "free world" that the airmen here were pledged to defend.

The Colonel led the way briskly into the cold, fluoro lighting of the auditorium, empty except for a centrally located elongated bench that was flanked by two armed servicemen standing guard, either side of a seated, and attractive, female corporal, who seemed to be the gatekeeper. They were obviously expected as the Colonel only slowed marginally to exchange salutes before continuing on towards the lifts, behind the bench. Unexpectantly, he veered right and headed for the stairwell, only to stop at its base.

Turning, he smiled apologetically, 'The lab is on the ninth floor, we'll take the stairs, for several reasons. It's part of my fitness routine. I like to set a good example to the staff.'

He hesitated, measured Jimeon with some invisible rule, then, having made a decision, 'Look, the real reason is that I suffer from panic attacks in confined spaces, like lifts.'

Unabashed concern flooded his face as he waited to see the effects of his unmanly confession upon Jimeon.

The Colonel's admission induced a shuddering unease. How much did these people know about him? Was it possible that they knew that, long ago, he too had been traumatised in a lift? His mind shot back to his deep, dark past.

As a kid he'd always been averse to crowds, and tight enclosures, and had never been overly fond of heights either, all of which his classmates made use of during that Fourth Year History excursion to Sydney, when the class visited the Australia Square building to view the city from its observation deck on the forty-ninth floor.

The teachers herded them into the foyer then guided them into the lifts, where all his "mates" jostled him inside first, before overfilling the lift so that he was jammed in at the back.

They all squealed with delight when the lift rocketed into the stratosphere at a hundred miles an hour, whilst he was left terrified and ranting when his stomach fell through the floor only to shoot into his mouth just before they stopped. The rest of them found his reaction so much fun that, once out of the lift, they herded him, in his dazed state, to stand up against the balcony's glass panels, where he almost choked on the sight of the "ants" in their suits and dresses trudging up and down George Street, forty-nine storeys below.

It had taken a lot of counselling, and perseverance, to overcome the psychological scars of that horrid ride but he'd defeated his fears and even made a thing of taking lifts just to keep up his immunity. How could anyone else know this? Surely not his counsellors! He'd not told anyone else, not even his parents when he got home, knowing full well that they were big on children, especially boys, fighting their own battles as the best way to toughen them up for the adult world.

Maintaining a poker face, he captured the Colonel's gaze, determined to reveal nothing of his past battles with fear. The Colonel broke eye contact first, and, taking his silence as tacit agreement led the way up the stairs.

Even with stopping at every second floor, they were both puffing and "glowing" by the time they reached the ninth floor, where they spent a few minutes regaining their composure.

Jimeon had to give it to the old boy, he was breathing easier than he was – and he considered himself reasonably fit. This put him to wondering why he thought of the Colonel as being older, when his ID showed him to be a year or so younger than him! Perhaps, it was the association with military life, all that discipline and rigid structures leading to a more rigid world view – the sort of rigidity one associates with old age.

Jimeon had had a taste of Air Force life after leaving high school. It had paid for some tertiary education but he'd quickly discovered that the armed forces weren't for him. Despite that, the experience had been educational in many ways.

The Colonel walked them past the lifts to a door marked Class 1 Security Codes Only, and then ushered him into a huge room, undivided except for a series of widely spaced offices lining the southern wall. Though all the lights were blazing, the place seemed deserted, suggesting to Jimeon that Friday night would be the ideal time to launch an invasion of the country. The reminder that it was Friday night had him pulling on the Colonel's arm to call a halt.

'Time is ticking; my wife will be worrying why I'm late, so I …'

'Don't worry, your wife will be fine, you can call her from the landline in the office down there – mobiles won't work in this building.'

Pacified, he followed the Colonel to the designated office, which was equally well lit and also unexpectantly roomy. Along the left side was a series of desks separated by partitions. At the far end sat a row of gamers' chairs, whilst the right-hand wall held a large flat-screen monitor in front of which was a semi-circle of office chairs. The room had the faint perfume of peppermint, similar to that in Tony's office, producing the bizarre thought that maybe the Colonel was giving Tony cans of Air Force air freshener as a kickback. Further speculations upon the nature of the relationship between the two ended once they reached the desk with the phone.

'Before you make your call let me explain the situation. Our air defence needs not just state-of-the-art aircraft but also effective pilots. Our training is right up there with the best, but technology is continually pushing the boundaries of what is humanly possible, boundaries that we here are expanding.'

Glancing at his watch, Jimeon was alarmed at how late it was getting and struggled to contain his impatience.

Meanwhile, the Colonel kept going.

'If you can just delay your call by fifteen minutes, I want you to experience something that will explain more than any words I can use for you to join our project. Let's call it: Project Starfighter.'

Smiling like a kindly uncle, he led a reluctant Jimeon to one of the gaming chairs, which sported an upgraded version of the Starfighter Nemesis controls and display panel. Under the Colonel's guidance Jimeon settled into the seat and buckled up, knowing the seat would move violently on its gimbals in order to impart as realistic an experience as possible. The Colonel did likewise in an adjacent chair and gestured to Jimeon to don his Starfighter's helmet and to hit the "On" switch.

With all the screen's lights showing all gauges green, Jimeon's impatience over the delayed call was replaced by a wave of reassurance induced by being back in familiar territory, and in control.

Through the helmet's speakers, the Colonel explained, 'We'll have a five-minute warm up session, to get you familiar to this particular set-up. I'll be your wingman but don't let me inhibit you. I want you to go for a maximum number of kills. Okay?'

Jimeon was surprised to note a tremor of enthusiasm in the Colonel's voice.

But without comment he launched his fighter from the mothership and was immediately immersed in a swarm of Klizavs, flying souped-up X raiders. They immediately started blasting away at him with their photon torpedos.

It was a wild ride and he only lasted a minute or two before he copped an antimatter mine that turned the screen into fiery particles and ended with the flashing red letters of: "Game Over"!

His heart was pounding almost as much as when he'd conquered the stairs. Beside him, the Colonel's machine was still gyrating madly, emitting all sorts of violent sounds that continued for the full five minutes. When it came to rest it displayed a monstrously large score, glowing proudly on the top of the flight screen.

'Now we swap,' said the Colonel with calm features, but mischievous eyes.

Jimeon clambered awkwardly out, unsteady from adrenal overload, passed the strangely unaffected Colonel, and then strapped himself into the Colonel's vacated chair.

'Take a few seconds to get your second wind. When you press, "On", choose the option marked "New Pilot" and make sure your helmet is on tightly. Answer all the questions verbally, and truthfully. When the "All Clear" message appears, launch. Your machine will automatically fire my thrusters so we engage the enemy at the same time.'

The list of questions, was both long and peculiar, with most seemingly designed to prompt an emotional response. He must have answered correctly because the "All Clear" was given, and, after a quick nod towards an attentive Colonel, he jabbed the "Launch Mission" button.

As before, the star speckled void was buzzing with maniacal Klizav fighters who immediately swerved to the attack but this time he felt strangely detached and blissfully calm. The enemy spacecraft seemed to move as though flying in molasses, allowing him plenty of time to methodically pick them off with the ease of plucking grapes from a bowl. Each exploding enemy, gave the same pleasure as the sweet squish of flavour one receives when crunching on one of those grapes.

There was no fear, just a wonderful certainty in his ability, that was joyously reinforced with each Klizav destroyed. His delight was then compounded by the sight of his score reaching heroic proportions.

He was then stunned when he learnt his five minutes were up, and his machine automatically powered down. Temporarily, time had seemed to have lost its hold over him. During that game, he had never felt so self-assured. For the first time in his life, he had been totally devoid of anxiety. As if waking from a dream, he slowly unbuckled, removed his helmet, and climbed out.

The Colonel was sweating and his score showed why. It was far worse than his effort on that particular machine and it looked like the Colonel had fought hard to get even those miserable numbers.

'The machines are the same but the helmets are different. Your helmet is why you are here,' the Colonel announced as he guided him back to the desk with the phone.

'That helmet was originally the product of research into finding ways of curing post-traumatic stress in veterans. It dials down fear and anxieties. Research then moved into the prevention phase, towards conquering fear when it occurs. You felt the results just then. But so far, these helmets have only been used in simulators or during training flights with experienced pilots. What we and our allies, the Americans basically, want to do is trial it in real conditions, with an untrained pilot.'

Jimeon didn't try hiding his incredulity, 'You're not suggesting that I ...'

'Why not? You've never flown a plane of any sort, and finding any young person who hasn't played a fly and shoot game is no longer realistic. Being older also means you are right there in the maximum demographic, and with the added benefit of being ex-RAAF and thus still obliged to heed the Official Secrets Act. Remember, even after all this time, your pledge is still legally binding.'

By this time, they had reached the desk, where Jimeon stood for a moment dumbly studying the phone, all the while wondering what he would do, and what he would say to his wife.

After unknown heartbeats, he became aware of a surprising sentiment that resulted in him nonchalantly replying: 'Yeah. Why not.'

The Colonel let him settle, long enough to ready Jimeon for his next surprise: 'I was so confident you were the right man and so can add that there is no need to phone your wife, because she's already on her way here! She will be accompanying you on the flight to the Persian Gulf and will be living a life of luxury whilst you do your patriotic bit – and have the time of your life, testing this game changing technology – for real. And you know that, nothing beats reality!'

This amazing news stunned Jimeon to the point where his reality was becoming decidedly unreal. He seemed to have slipped into a parallel universe where this fellow, who looked like himself, was saying okay to all sorts of ridiculous ideas.

Less than an hour later, he found himself stepping into a US Air Force passenger jet, there to be seated next to his wife, already buckled up and sipping on a flute of champagne.

They seemed to have been given the First-class section, which they shared with the Colonel and Mrs Latimer. She appeared to be a charming woman in possession of an inexhaustible supply of chit chat that kept Jasmin amused for most of the first half of the flight. Eventually the conversation faltered and fatigue overcame all four of them and they retired to sleeping pods further down. They were awakened for the descent.

He and the Colonel bade adieu to their wives, ensconced in the limo destined for the luxury resort on the coast, whilst they rode in an air-conditioned Hummer through the blistering heat of the desert to the US airbase.

Two days later, having got his biological clock back in synch with local time, Jimeon found himself sitting in the Pilots' Briefing room, bracketed by the Colonel and an unnamed scientific gent in the mandatory white lab coat. At the lectern was senior fighter pilot, Toby Sasalwazk.

'Conditions are not ideal for a lengthy trial but we only need the morning, and should be back well before the weather closes in towards evening.'

Toby's announcement was delivered with his characteristic grim seriousness, but this time his demeanour somehow lacked conviction. Jimeon wondered if his report was the whole truth or an edited version.

After several sessions in the simulator, and an amazing actual flight, as pilot – though with a co-pilot as back up – today he'd be going solo in the one hundred-and-ten-million-dollar experimental F/40 Venom, on patrol over the Iraq/Iran border. They had awarded him a certificate that said he was qualified to fly, so perhaps they were right and he was ready to be let loose in the skies with the new plane and the new helmet.

By this stage of the adventure, he had abandoned reason's caution as well as any thoughts concerning the concept of "the future". He was now foolishly living solely in the moment and found the experience surprisingly liberating and enjoyable.

Was he their sacrificial lamb going joyously to the slaughterhouse? He should have been nervous as hell, but he wasn't. He was convinced that once he put that helmet on, he could do anything.

The Colonel was right, reality sure was way better than simulators. In the air, the plane inspired confidence with all its failsafe technology. It monitored his body to prevent manoeuvres that would have him blacking out, or stalling, or spinning out of control, it even had an array of defensive algorithms that took over if he was unsure how to save the craft.

The physicality of actual flight was so much more than he had imagined. The machine seemed alive; it shuddered and shook in extreme dives and turns, moved about in strong crosswinds and updraughts, and then there was the amazing experience of zooming around in three dimensions at G forces undreamed of. All this against the constant interplay of the blue sky and the khaki desert intermixed with strips of dark green around the rivers and far off mountains.

They took off with Toby in front and, he, and Big Albert as his wingmen. Albert was a tall, solidly built black guy who spoke to him with a minimum of words. The man was completely unsuccessful in concealing his disdain – presumably for devaluing his job by showing that any fool could pilot a high-tech fighter.

About an hour and a half in, they received a command to investigate a flare up in an unpronounceable village within spitting distance of the Iranian border.

Toby and Albert went down to show the flag, US of course, leaving him to do a big loop and guard the aerial high ground, and, presumably to keep out of their hair. They had only been gone a few minutes when a red light on the GPS warned him that he was about to stray into Iranian airspace.

About to, seemed provocation enough, because the next moment four Iranian fighters made a flashing debut on his screen. They were heading straight at him. He should have been panicking, but instead he quickly started planning his best escape route whilst radioing Toby, 'Coming under attack from Iranian fighters. They have given no warnings so far, but seem intent on combat. I will attempt to evade and head to…' An Iranian missile coming his way interrupted, and instigated his jerking back on the flight controls, initiating a steep climb, as per instructions for such situations, before he continued, '… towards Mosul.'

But he received no confirmation. The radio remained deadly silent during his wild ascent at an eye-watering pace that squished him into his chair and pulled back cheeks and lips exposing clenched teeth in his death's head grin.

His plane autonomously launched a counterattack of aerial mines, one of which did the trick and sent one of the Iranians to his reward of an eternity in paradise.

Somebody must have really upset the Iranians because the other three continued to pursue him well into Iraqi territory. They must also have been on maximum thrust, as he was, in his bid to maintain his narrow lead, but they obviously had the confidence that comes from full loads of fuel whilst his was rapidly approaching half, and if he couldn't arrange in-flight refuelling, which seemed likely, given the continuing silence from his "buddies" and Central Command. He would have to turn back, and turning is slower than going straight, leaving him open to the Iranians getting close enough to take another shot at him.

The flashing fuel light eventually decided things. He made a screaming left-hand dive to head south, back to base, and also get to a lower altitude for the added speed that the higher oxygen levels allowed. At some stage two of his pursuers had turned back and a while later his remaining combatant seemed to have exited the arena.

But he wasn't taking anything for granted and, once on a steady bearing, he maintained near maximum thrust, determined to gain a bigger margin of safety. But the Iranians must be smarter than the Americans would have you believe, because a few minutes later the two he'd "lost" resurfaced and appeared to be setting him up in a classic pincer movement, coming at him from opposing directions and creating a shallow triangle, with him at the head, they on the rapidly diminishing flanks.

In a worryingly short time, they simultaneously launched pairs of air-to-air missiles at him. This wasn't in the script, because even his amazing plane was going to have its work cut out dealing with four heatseeking missiles, from two directions. Under normal circumstances he would have frozen and awaited the inevitable gory ending, but indestructibility and omniscient still reigned. Calmly, he remembered that he was flying in Training Mode, which restricted certain suicidal strategies available in Combat Mode.

Now seemed the time to try them out. Switching off the Training mode, he waited the half second for Combat Mode to be confirmed, then pulled slowly back on the controls to gain a smidgen more height after which he cut the engines and dropped like a brick.

The altimeter became a mad blur of numbers as it tried to keep score. The charging missiles, losing his scent, picked up the only other nearby heat sources and fixed their deadly gaze upon their masters, the Iranians, who, delayed by human emotiveness, were too slow to respond and disappeared in fireballs of metal and flesh. All of which was but a passing thought because he was somewhat preoccupied with trying to reignite his engines to avoid a similarly violent and colourful end in the sandy wasteland now coming up at him at a maniacal rate.

The engines fired up, he fought back on the controls, felt the shuddering of the wings as he tried to flatten out, felt the bizarre bliss of conscious calm as he looked upon his imminent death, saw the sand dunes rushing up to take him in their deadly embrace, before the fierce glory accompanying the slowing of his trajectory, then its flattening out and finally returning skyward with the engines' fiery breath kicking up rooster tails of sand in the dunes metres beneath his wings. Surviving was a buzz, even if only an intellectual one, not visceral. But a buzz was a buzz.

When sufficient height had been regained, he dropped his speed to nurse his remaining fuel and then had another go to raise his "comrades", or Central Command. This time the airbase replied, with blandly stated bearings and a runway allocation, and not much else.

Once he parked up, back at the airbase, he found the ground crew were tight-lipped, and seemed a little displeased that he'd actually returned. At least Colonel Latimer greeted him with a happy face before whisking him away for the debriefing.

In the fullness of time, he and his dear wife were returned to Perth, their respective employers accepting the story concocted and adroitly delivered by the Colonel. He survived the restructure and life returned to normal.

A little over two years passed when an I.T. conference in Sydney offered up the opportunity for him to tidy up a few lingering items from his little adventure. He'd arranged to take a few extra days off, on the excuse of seeing friends, and duly found himself in George Street, looking up at the curved face of the Australia Square tower. It was Friday morning, ten thirty, and a tour bus was unloading a gaggle of primary school kids, all boys, in short pants. Everything was going to plan.

The Colonel would be waiting on the observation deck, the teachers were in on the act, so it was up to him to get a move on. Tugging his "baseball" cap a touch tighter on his head – to guarantee the best connections for the electrodes – he marched ahead of the children and made it to the lifts just before them. The two teachers, fellows in their early thirties, slyly nodded their recognition, then, when the lift opened, filled it with kids once he'd stepped inside to take his place at the back. One of the teachers squeezed in at the last, leaving the other, and the rest of the students, to catch the next lift.

The teacher explained to his excited charges that the lift would go up very quickly and so they should brace themselves for the downward pressure. None spoke a word, all their eager little eyes were trained upon their teacher, waiting for him to press the button.

A smaller, dark-haired boy jammed next to Jimeon seemed far less enthused than the rest. He looked up at him, perhaps in the hope of some adult reassurance. Jimeon looking down from the height of his adulthood, and possible wisdom, silently offered his hand, watched the kid hesitate, then felt him latch on when the lift jolted into action.

The other children let out a collective squeak of excitement, whilst Jimeon felt his stomach dropping and his hand being crushed by his silent companion, but most of all, he experienced a tidal wave of fear from his deliberate reversing of the emotional settings on the cap to exaggerate fear, not eliminate it. He was here to relive the terror of his boyhood ride, to again feel its crushing grip, again feel the shame of his cowardice, but hopefully this time, to truly conquer it.

In what seemed a moment, they reached their destination and collectively almost levitated from the floor, renewing the noisy delight of most. The ride ended and the doors slid open.

His breathing restarted. He swallowed, as if for the first time, and felt the grip ease on his hand. He gave his young companion a kindred smile, released the boy's hand and raised a finger to his lips to seal their bond of secrecy.

Though Jimeon's heart was pounding and his legs a little wobbly, he managed to feign dignity when he finally disembarked. Once outside he stood a moment to get his bearings, then walked, like a monk performing a motion meditation, over to where Colonel Latimer, dressed in expensive casual attire, stood, with his black attaché case at his feet, taking in the view north towards the harbour bridge.

The Colonel offered up his hand and asked gently, 'You, okay?' whilst limply holding a baseball cap, like Jimeon's, in his other hand.

Jimeon paused to take stock before answering, 'Yeah. I'm okay. Did you take the stairs, or the lift?'

The Colonel replied victoriously, 'The lift!'

They both chuckled, then turned and strolled to the glass balustrade. There, Jimeon was careful not to test his fragile victory over vertigo too quickly and so kept his head up, eyes focused in the distance and mind fixed upon an examination of the mansions and expensive apartment blocks of Sydney's North Shore. In due course, he lowered his gaze and eventually found himself studying, with dispassion, the tiny pedestrians scuttling along the footpaths at the base of the tower. There had been a momentary fluttering of the heart, that soon settled.

Turning towards the Colonel, he handed him his neurologically enhancing cap and asked: 'Are there any new developments in the *Starfighter Project*, ones that you can tell me about?'

'Nothing official of course, but it seems the project's combat applications are being downgraded. The top brass aren't enthused by the prospect of robotised, semi-cybernetic pilots. They reckon it's bad for morale.'

'Yes, I'd wondered about that. It seems defending one's country loses some of its appeal if soldiering involves giving up one's humanity, and sense of agency, through having one's decisions made by algorithms. You'd be just like an Uber driver, sweating for a computer app with little right of recourse against their bad or unjust decisions.'

'I won't speculate on the reasoning but we are no longer involved in the direct combat side but, as you can see, we are still continuing with the more humane applications of the technology.'

The Colonel bent down, retrieved his case and then placed their experimental caps inside.

'Had enough? Shall we go?'

'I might hang around for a bit.'

Jimeon was concerned about the scared kid. He'd wait and be there for him on the return journey, just in case the kid needed more moral support.

'Before you go, there is one other thing that still puzzles me. It's your seemingly amazing confidence in my saying "Yes" to your proposition, which, in the cold glare of hindsight, was very chancy of you.'

The Colonel suppressed a laugh, 'Not as chancy as you think. You were very carefully selected. Being ex-RAAF was the key. It made you one of us, at least subconsciously. And we had a few tricks which we were confident would renew that sense of belonging and commitment. Remember the mint air freshener?' The Colonel paused, eyes twinkling. 'It was heavy with oxytocin, which was just another aspect of Project Starfighter.'

Noting Jimeon's blank look, the Colonel continued, 'You really should keep up with developments in biology; it may help you in your career. You know, dealing with the hierarchy and customers and such.'

Jimeon remained unenlightened.

'Oxytocin is a hormone released by the body in a variety of situations, such as childbirth, when breast feeding, and in both sexes during lovemaking. Amongst its many effects are reducing pain, muscular relaxation and, an enhancement of inter-human bonding. People of the same tribe or peer group, exposed to oxytocin through nasal inhalation, are more co-operative and more generous to one another. They form stronger interpersonal bonds and hence are more willing to say "Yes" to suggestions from their trusted fellows. You were proof of that!'

Jimeon grinned. He'd been taken for a ride, well and truly suckered, but he wasn't complaining; his life had taken a turn for the better, at home, and at work.

They shook hands. The Colonel turned and strode confidently to the lifts.

Jimeon stood and watched, and eventually joined the kids in the lift for the return trip. He took up his previous position at the back, so too did the kid, who this time didn't offer up his hand, instead looked up at him briefly, and then seemed content to survive the plunge to the ground floor bolstered by the mere presence of a person who also, fully understood, fear.

Author's Note:

This story was homework for my writers' group meeting of July 2019. A new member had suggested the theme: *A high-tension elevator ride.*

Love and Luck

Prologue:

'Daddy, where did all their gods go?' demanded little Maisy, waving aloft the source of her concern: *The Pictorial History of the Romans* – her current favourite book. As a welcome home greeting, it was the last one Stefan Bostrom could have imagined.

Though rendered speechless by the force of her request, he still managed to squeeze past his six-year-old daughter, close the front door, then walk to the hall table, to dump his briefcase on the carpet, and the car keys in the drawer. Freed of encumbrances, he turned and picked up Maisy, and her book.

Countering the intensity of her gaze with his best serious face, he finally gave his reply. 'That's a difficult question to answer. So, you'll have to give Daddy time to think about it. In the meantime, we'll check on Mummy and see what's for dinner.'

Later that evening, the house quiet and him sitting in bed with his dear wife propped up next to him – engrossed in the latest tome from her book club – he abandoned the latest issue of *The Economist* in favour of examining the inadequacy of his reply to Maisy's question.

That innocent inquiry had forced him into a silent review of his life: from his humble working-class beginnings, winning the scholarship that opened the door to a better education, business studies, and then his rise within the cut-throat world of finance. Lucking upon a loving wife and then their wondrous Maisy, only to suffer bankruptcy and a social fall from grace, all thanks to the scheming's of Magnus Lucre. Then followed his slow, tottering journey towards depression, and divorce, that ended unexpectantly with Lady Luck's appearance, in the delightful form of Cognitive Therapist Lucia Denarius.

He'd never been religious, but the bankruptcy, and his ongoing recovery, had forced him to seriously consider the role of God, or gods, in his life.

Was his good, and bad luck, due to the one God's influence? Or did some of the old Roman gods that Maisy found so fascinating still hold sway over mortal affairs?

On either question he remained unsure.

§

In an unseen astral domain, Mars, the God of War, having crowed about his latest influx of believers, turned on his booted heel and quick marched back to his temple, kicking aside the perpetual ground mist just enough for Venus and Fortuna to glimpse the distant planet below them.

The goddess Fortuna was first to restart their shattered conversation. 'You won't be seeing much of your muscle-bound savage for a while, so now's the time for us to head on down and mix it amongst the mortals.'

'You really think your planned interventions will give us new insights, enough to convince more of them to believe in love,' replied Venus with a face clouded by doubts.

'Yes. And it's love and luck,' corrected Fortuna, 'People will always believe in war and thuggery. It's paying homage to us, and appreciating what we represent that needs rebalancing. So, gather your stuff: Miss Mia Ljubav!'

'Okay: Ms Lucia Denarius.'

§

At the lifts, Magnus Lucre flicked his eyes over the List of Tenants. Lucia Denarius and Associates (Psychological Services) Level 42, lay buried in a forest of brokers, financial advisers and accountancy firms – the only unexpected inclusion in a building overlooking the Stock Exchange.

A grin creased his clean-shaven face, handsome still at forty-six, and, seemingly untouched by three decades of remorseless dedication to avarice.

The smile was in recognition of his compulsion to doublecheck things he already knew, and, his sly glancing at his Rolex – to make sure he'd be a few minutes late. After which it lingered in smugness, because getting the facts straight, and starting negotiations late enough to niggle, were two of the foundations of his success.

On the way up, with the lift to himself, he diverted his thoughts back to the bizarre connection between miraculous escapes from financial oblivion for Alvis and Bostrom – his two greatest rivals – and their consultations with Lucia Denarius. Lucia's "part" in their resurrection was the hottest news on Saint George's Terrace, with some financial pundits now calling her "Lucky Lucia".

A snort erupted. There was no such thing as luck. More likely Ms Denarius had expertise in areas other than cognitive behaviour therapy. Or was it just another case of finance people – who should know better – being fooled by randomness? He'd soon find out, though, exactly how, remained uncertain, an uncertainty he knew he'd overcome.

After stepping into their tiny foyer, he marched up to the young African receptionist, and, from on high, announced: 'Magnus Lucre, ten-thirty appointment with…'

The girl cut him off.

'Lucia's office is the third door down the corridor. Just go in and take a seat.'

Treating him as a simpleton, she stared unashamedly back at him whilst pointing the way with a painted fingernail. Her unexpected rudeness, almost arrogance, dented his certitude enough to have him meekly complying.

With each step, his self-confidence reasserted itself, only to falter momentarily upon passing the second door. It was labelled: Mia Ljubav, Relationships Counsellor.

So, this is where she now worked. Even though it had only been a few months, he'd already forgotten about her and the tawdry end to their brief affair. He certainly had no intention of wasting time with her now.

Hurrying on, he ducked in through the third door, standing reassuringly open. Closing it, he took a breath, then strolled over to take possession of one of two well-padded recliners that guarded a large, polished Jarrah and Marri desk.

Ten-forty-two. Twelve minutes late. A lateness that was just right. Aglow with thoughts of Ms Denarius being nicely peeved, he stretched back and settled into his next task: seeking usable clues about her personality from the room's decor.

The first thing was an unobtrusive motion detector, and camera, up under the cornice to his right. It covered the entrance door, balcony entrance a few paces past the desk, and the narrow passage that led to two other rooms.

Did she use the camera to record her sessions? He would in her place, and added that snippet to the other information he'd already gathered about her, which, despite being extensive, revealed very little of her inner workings. An admirable trait. Many knew the details of his business dealings but he'd made sure none really knew what went on inside his skull. Perhaps "Lucky Lucia" might prove a worthy opponent.

The walls revealed an odd assortment of pictures: two paintings eulogising scenes from the days of Imperial Rome and, as contrast, over his left shoulder, near the entrance door, was an Art Deco poster showing a young woman, overflowing picnic basket at her feet, in a colourful thirties style sleeveless dress, one hand on the tiller of a small skiff, sailing towards a horizon split between sunny blue skies on the right and roiling thunder clouds sneaking up on the left. The odd thing was: the girl was wearing a blindfold. If it was supposed to be allegorical then he didn't see the allegory. But then, most of what others called great and profound "art" was just snobbish claptrap.

With a snort he dismissed the poster in favour of theorising about the doors in the passageway. Were they for a kitchenette and the toilet? Straining his ears, he could just make out muffled sounds in their direction, which took form a few minutes later with the appearance of a tall, stately brunette of indeterminate age. She looked late twenties but walked with the worldly assurance of a woman far older.

'Mr Lucre, you made it! Thinking you'd not show I scheduled my morning cappuccino earlier than usual,' she said, carefully raising the full cup in her hand before making her way to take up her seat behind the desk.

Placing the cup down, she ignored him to concentrate on making herself comfortable, after which she extracted an iPad from a top drawer, tapped, swiped, nodded to herself, and then put it away. Picking up her cup, she leant back, took an exploratory sip that coated her red lipstick with a kiss of chocolate froth, and finally, offered up a challenging smile, and then, an extended silence, for him to fill.

Her gaze was as bold and unwavering as the receptionist's. The silent impasse dragged on. But this time Magnus wasn't going be intimidated and so allowed his ire to show. It had no effect.

This battle of wills was wasting *his* time. Softening his stance, he tried a more conciliatory approach.

'Sorry about being late. Perhaps you can sip your coffee, and, start the session. I want to learn about this cognitive behaviour therapy stuff. Specifically, how it will help me in my business dealings. So, how does it work?'

Her response was to take another sip, before putting down the cup and, still with insolent eyes, made a show of seductively licking the accumulated froth from her lips. Just like Mia used to do! Were they in cahoots?

Further exploration of that disturbing thought was cut short by Lucia's abrupt and *un*seductive reply.

'How it works is: I ask questions. Your answers reveal the *words* you use to describe the world and your dealings with it. I then question the reasoning behind those words, which gives you the option of changing them. Once those changes become habitual, behaviours change, and so too your life's trajectory, usually for the better.'

'Hmm.' Magnus frowned. *All very unspecific and airy-fairy.* Before he could build a reply, Lucia interrupted.

'Your firm, *Cannae Investments*, is now Australia's leading non-bank lender, which wouldn't have happened if you didn't know your business. Therefore, you don't really need my help in matters of finance. So, what do you *ultimately* want, from me, from life?'

Behind his poker-face, Magnus was squirming, surprisingly unsure of how to respond to the force of her persona, and, her questions. Especially the one about his ultimate goal in life. Finding disclosable answers was made all the more difficult by her display of amusement, tainted with cruel pleasure.

Time became thick, heavy and arduous.

Obviously tiring of his silence, she produced further disquiet by extracting a deck of large playing cards from her top drawer, which she began to adroitly shuffle. Tarot cards. The charlatan was going to read his fortune!

Seeing his alarm, she laughed with such innocent joy that he should have felt relieved but instead was bewildered by her unpredictable changes in mood.

'Yes. Tarot cards, but don't panic, they're just a means of encouraging a conversation. After all, I can't examine your self-talk if you don't say anything. So, shuffle, split the deck, take the top card, place it face-up back on the deck and then tell me the first thing that comes up.'

After a hesitation, he obeyed, and, uncovered: The Lovers. What did it mean?

Her raised eyebrows and silence induced a surprisingly honest reply.

'If you must know, I was thinking maybe Mia has been bad-mouthing me and the two of you are secretly scheming to give me a hard time.'

Lucia's only reaction was to ask: 'Nothing about your messy divorce last year? The card is also supposed to represent marriage.'

'That! Ancient history. And anyway, Janine got the rough end of that stick.'

A gloating smirk emerged with remembrance of the scowl she had given him after leaving the courthouse. Nobody got the better of Magnus Lucre!

Lucia waited quietly, and then, once he'd calmed, gave him her summation.

Bad-mouthing, secretly scheming, hard time, and giving Janine, the rough end of the stick, are words that, to me, paint a picture of someone who doesn't like to lose. Who fears losing. Fears. And, fears losing what exactly? Money? Status? Your manliness? It appears you need to learn more about the role of fear, loss, and bad luck, but not just in business, more so in your relationships.'

'Rubbish! I'm not afraid of anything, or anyone. I also understand all about loss, that's why I hedge my bets. I always keep on top of the relevant facts and hence know when to cut my losses. Only sentimental fools stay in the game and suffer. And, I don't believe in luck, good or bad. Every event has aspects to take advantage of. I … make my own luck!'

Now breathing harder he felt the better for his emphatic reply. Lucia, on the other hand, radiated disappointment.

'Hmm. Anyway, I think we've made some sort of progress. Though you may disagree. You now have an idea of what I do, and I have greater understanding of your …' she paused, a wry smile enlivening her face.

'My what?'

'Nothing. Nothing important. Look, I think I've annoyed you enough for one day. Perhaps it's best to "cut our losses" and end early. Should you like another session, just arrange for an appointment. But before you go, there is one last thing. I want you to check all the cards, shuffle them, and then put the top five face-up on the desk.'

There was something in her serious tone that had Magnus obeying.

Six times he shuffled, and six times *The Lovers*, *The Fool*, *the Wheel of Fortune*, *Judgement*, and, *Death*, rose to the top, in that order. Boneless, he collapsed back into the recliner, confused, and filled with dread.

'I think you've seen enough. You may go now, but take the cards with you. Goodbye, Mr Lucre.'

Invisible forces held his mind and tongue. He found himself, standing, pocketing the cards, and felt unseen hands push him gently, but inexorably, towards the exit.

§

Later, back in their heavenly realm, and both comfortably seated in Fortuna's astral villa, a subdued Venus aired her disquiet.

'So, everything that happened during our excursion on Earth was all your doing?'

Fortuna replied with a blunt: "yes".

'But did Magnus *have to* die? Despite everything, I still liked him.'

'If he'd investigated the meanings in those cards, and been brave enough to answer my questions, truthfully, then he would have found spiritual rebirth, not an "apparently" untimely death. His business rivals heeded my words, honestly answered those questions and thus enjoyed good fortune, financially, and in their personal lives.'

Venus considered her companion for a long moment, then gave in to the inescapable truth: 'So, that's why all the other gods have faded except for Mars, you and I. Because lives are ruled over by only three forces: love, war, and uncertainty.'

'But, it's uncertainty – luck – that *ultimately* prevails!' smiled a triumphant Fortuna.

Author's Note:
This story was initiated by an anthology with gods and goddesses as its theme.

The Eternal Struggle

'Forget it. It has to be seven. It's a mystic number. The number of days it took to make the world – when you include the Sabbath. It's the number of the most influential heavenly bodies, the Sun, Moon and the five planets. It's the number of days in a week. No. Eight is one sin too many. That extra category is making the ramifications of sinning too hard to sell to our target audience.'

'Hmm. Okay. Seven it is.'

'You don't *sound* happy, and you must be happy or it won't work.'

'There's two things.'

'Yes?'

'Firstly: why me! A poor, old, and obscure scholar.'

'You may be the first two, but definitely not the last. We, above, are fully aware of your forthright views, and, it's because of them that you were voted the perfect candidate to initiate this campaign. You also have proximity.'

'Hmph. I still think your confidence is misplaced, but who am I to doubt an angel, God's emissary. As far as proximity goes, I'm hardly close. It is at least a week of hard walking, and will require plenty of luck if I'm to survive the gangs of brigands that infest the road to Rome. It'll be a miracle if I make it in one piece, and, once there, who's to say Pope Gregory will give me an audience!'

'Surviving such a *seven*-day ordeal is exactly the right touch. It will give your message added impact and credence. As for your reception, Head Office has it all arranged. So, there's nothing to worry about.'

Two silences then filled the small, frugally furnished room, one oozing implacable confidence, the other replete with nagging uncertainties.

Outside, the world began to stir. In through the tiny window above them slid the faint twittering of distant birds serenading the dawn.

That avian reminder of the birth of another working day prompted the visitor to push for a speedy end to the old monk's prevarications.

'So, what else is holding you back?'

'Well – dare I be so bold – there's the shock of your strange words and stranger concepts, things like: "selling to a target audience" and "Head Office".'

'Strange to you now, but it's the way of the future, and, since our plans involve securing a better future it was deemed prudent that I introduce some of the new terminology, and viewpoints, just to get you up to speed with the new processes we're implementing. Your greater familiarity with the language of our new paradigm will make you sound more authoritative, and hence more convincing.'

'Perhaps you're right. A bit of jargon does give the implication of understanding. My reluctance is just me being old, and the old disdain new ways. But, perhaps I'm not that old, because, of late, I have begun to doubt the effectiveness of the original, "Ten Directives", as you now call them.'

'Doubt?'

'Yes. They're all so negative, which seems to go counter to the church's "mission statement", to use your words. And now, to the Ten Commandments, sorry, "Ten Directives", you want to sanctify *seven* more prohibitions. I feel Christ's message of hope and love may become mired in negativity. One thing I've learnt in my years of monastic life is that goals are better achieved with a mix of praiseworthy rewards, reinforced by reminders of the punishments awaiting sinful and unthoughtful actions.'

'At last, you've hit the nail on the head! We are now of one mind. We too agree with your summation – just wanted you to get to it in your own time. I knew we had the right man! But to allay any remaining doubts, we propose to add seven *cures* to counterbalance the seven mortal sins. Here, have a read.'

From beneath the folds of his perfectly white robes – spoilt only by a speck of soot on the hem – God's celestial messenger extracted a vellum parchment.

'It would be best if you cease kneeling on the cold floor, and study it sitting on your bed or you'll ruin your knees, and then never manage the trip to Rome.'

The monk obeyed, took the scroll, creakingly transferred himself to his straw mattress, and then unfurled the document:

<u>Proposed Amendments to the Conceptualisations Required to Promote Greater Brand Awareness and Customer Loyalty.</u>

Sin	Virtue
Pride/Hubris	Humility
Greed	Charity
Lust/Fornication	Chastity
Envy	Gratitude
Gluttony	Temperance
Wrath	Patience
Sloth	Diligence

'Ahh, yes. Perfect balance. Good,' replied the monk after a thought-filled pause.

'We in Head Office also recognise the benefits of balancing the bodily needs of our flesh and blood representatives – like yourself – with their spiritual ones, and hence will continue to support the church's established remunerative policies of tithing their followers, as well as the selling of indulgences. The church must have effective funding *and* programs, if it is to maintain – and hopefully expand – its share of the growing pool of mortal souls on offer. It's the only way to outcompete our opposition, who, unfortunately, remains eternally, and fanatically, against us.'

'But surely feeding the church's burgeoning coffers will continue to encourage the sins of greed and pride?'

'True. But there is no sanctity without trials, no wisdom without effort, no piety without temptation. Don't worry, it's under control. Head Office always considers things from a much bigger and longer perspective than is possible for mortal minds. If you ever need questions answered, we're just a prayer away.'

'Y-e-s, hmm ...'

Contemplation of the enormity of his forthcoming mission had the old monk suddenly feeling immensely older. Whilst he brooded, a thin ray of light probed tentatively in through the window, a ray that grew emboldened, then, with a burst of enthusiasm, entered fully, bathing both occupants in its flaxen light.

'I am being called. I must leave you to your task. Have no fear, you *will* succeed. Farewell.'

With a gracious bow, the angel folded its wings and began to condense from a being that dominated the room all the way down to a tiny glowing sphere of white light, which then floated out through the open window and ascended briskly into the coming day.

But the sphere was not totally pure, within the white was an infinitesimally small mote of deepest black.

Halfway to Heaven the sphere slowed, then stopped. It's perfectly smooth and gleaming surface began to contort in response to an internal rebellion until, with a thunderous crack, it split into two smaller spheres, one white, the other black. For a moment they hung touching, before a flash of repulsion cast one upwards, to the stifling everlasting calm and regimented order of Heaven, the other down to Hell, to the realm of eternal and uncontrollable assaults upon the damned via a relentless, random alternation of unbearable ecstasies and unimaginable agonies.

In between lay the no-man's-land where the superpowers of order, and of chaos, waged their eternal struggle for possession of that marvellously finite, semi-ordered, sometimes comprehensible, and always messy world of mortal men and women.

The struggle continues still.

Author's Note:

In September 2022 my writing group tasked us to produce a short piece on the *Seven Deadly Sins*. My research on the topic revealed that in AD 590, Pope Gregory the First, revised the list down from eight to the current seven. This story is my explanation of how it might have happened. It is what happens when an overactive imagination meets an ignorance of religion.

One Fear in the Darkness Binds Them

In a dimension unimaginable to human minds, a meeting had concluded.

'We are agreed. We have no choice. The direct intervention must go ahead as discussed.'

As one, the three attendees voiced their approval.

§

With the closing of the door, Dr Dominic Oporto had to shake his head to remind himself it was still Saturday and a mere handful of hours since that breakfast phone call – from the Vatican of all places!

No sooner had he hung up than the doorbell rang, announcing the arrival of the limousine that rushed him to Zurich airport, then a chartered jet to Rome, all so he could have a private luncheon with the Pope – purportedly to discuss matters of great relevance to his work as Director of the CERN Particle Accelerator.

In truth, little had been said of nuclear physics; instead, the Pontiff had concentrated on trying to persuade him to take up a senior role in the social media platform the church was setting up. To be called *Faith and Reason*, its remit was to find ways to use the seemingly opposing forces of religion and science to counter the spread of conspiracy theories, lies, and online thuggery that sidelined both civil religiosity and balanced, rational debate. After the meal, Dominic was scheduled for a tête-a-tête with the platform's Content Director to discuss the details.

He'd only agreed to attend once he'd learnt it would be held in the Sistine Chapel, which, the Pope had assured him, would be devoid of gawking tourists and chattering tour guides. As such, it provided a once-in-a-lifetime opportunity for Dominic to study, unhindered, the chapel's famous murals.

Their lunch had proved surprisingly convivial, with excellent food and a pontiff who surprised him with carefully crafted questions that had him agreeing with the goals of the Pope's new online endeavours. Dominic was less convinced by his arguments suggesting that *he* had the special talents that could help bring about the desired rebalancing of public discourse. When Dominic had asked his, sometimes confrontational, questions, the Pope had fended them off with surprising adroitness. If it had been a football match, they left the field, amicable and happy with a well-played nil-all-draw.

The Pontiff had now departed, leaving Dominic in sole command of the chapel for the ten or so minutes before his appointment with the unnamed Content Director. Putting aside his misgivings attached to the upcoming meeting, he set off on his much-anticipated task of studying the wonders of his surroundings.

Sadly, after his initial walk around the room, he found less joy than expected.

His muted appreciation was the child of a mind unable to tear itself away from the pointlessness of the coming interview. There were just too many exciting developments unfolding at the collider for him to divert precious time onto new commitments, especially towards those as futile as the one on offer.

The lunch *had* been interesting, but he should have been more forceful and made it clear that his seeing their Content Director was time-wasting for both sides. And should have also voiced his belief that no individual, or church sponsored website, could do much to change the algorithms and financial incentives that produced the internet and social media's misdeeds.

That last implacable truth soured his mood further to the point of inducing an energy-sapping dejection that left him standing, gazing up with unseeing eyes, swallowing saliva imbued with a ghostly bitterness.

Time slipped.

A deep inhalation, a forced blink, and a furrowing of the brows wrenched his thoughts back onto the chapel's architecture and embellishments. A cursory glance with his more enervated mind had him conceding that the chapel *did* have a pleasing airiness, and the lighting definitely imbued Michelangelo's depictions of God's work with a soothing, golden hue.

Emboldened, he set out on a second circumnavigation, this time one of deeper consideration, that ended, again, with disappointment!

Back at his starting point, Dominic felt like a visitor to a country whose favourable first impressions are diminished by the shortcomings revealed in subsequent visits. The chapel now reminded him of the trophy homes of the nouveau riche, stuffed to the gills with items designed to show off their wealth and superiority, and hopefully to induce envy in lesser beings.

Were the chapel's paintings and statuary there to proclaim the unassailable and unmeasurable power of religious faith in order to humble those who only have puny science and its flawed rationality to sustain them?

It was a thought he'd never considered possible within the confines of the Sistine Chapel. Was he being too harsh? To check, Dominic decided to use the last moments left to him to re-evaluate the chapel's most famous depiction.

Walking a short distance, he gazed up and again saw God! Leastwise, Michelangelo's concept of the divinity: a man of Mediterranean extraction, white-haired and bearded, with a muscular body and a strong face. God's arm was outstretched, finger extended, caught in the act of putting the *spark of life* into the similarly extended finger of his greatest creation – a supine and somewhat dazed-looking Adam.

Dominic smiled. If only life, the universe, and everything, were so simple!

His nuanced amusement ended abruptly upon the sound of a door closing. From the incomprehensible heavens, his mind was "cast down" to grubbing around in the more understandable experiences of earthbound mortals.

Approaching footsteps coalesced into a tall, well-built, mature gent, in an expensive grey suit over a crisp white business shirt, open at the collar. The man gestured him over.

'Doctor Oporto. We meet at last. I am Angelo Literelli.'

Accepting the proffered hand, Dominic noted the dry grip, with just the right amount of pressure to express friendship and yet suggestive of vast reserves that could be weaponised – if required.

By mutual consent, they disengaged, then stepped back to study the other. A brief analytic silence followed, which dissolved into synchronous amusement.

'Do I meet the grade, Doctor Oporto?'

After making a show of looking him up and down one last time, Dominic replied: 'Yes. You seem normal enough.'

'Good. Let's get down to business. As His Holiness has undoubtedly informed you, the Vatican feels that the tenets of Christianity are failing to gain traction amidst the noise and nonsense that overwhelms the minds of today's populace, especially since the advent of the internet and social media empires run purely for profit, regardless of the long-term negative consequences.'

After hearing the man's rushed explanation and noting the passion in his concluding remark, Dominic couldn't quite stop a certain measure of pity from entering his smile. He, too, was painfully aware of the consequences of the growing anti-science "zeitgeist" infecting cyberspace. It had made getting funding for ordinary science, let alone theoretical physics, so much more difficult than in times past.

'You find the situation amusing!' accused Mr Literelli, his face suddenly thunderous. Beneath the suit, the man almost trembled from barely contained wrath.

Taken aback, Dominic raised a placating hand, 'You misunderstand me. I laugh not at you, but with you, because I, too, am personally acquainted with the evils you rail against. It's not just religious faith that is being undermined. Balanced scientific reasoning is no longer able to make headway in the minds of the public, or their erstwhile leaders.'

The tension dissipated as quickly as it had arisen. His bonhomie restored, Mr Literelli stepped forward, placed a welcoming hand on Dominic's shoulder, and then gently guided him over to an alcove he'd not yet encountered.

'Let's sit and chat. It's now clear to me that you are a man well chosen for the task at hand. One capable of reasoning and yet, hopefully ...'

'Yes?'

'... not completely estranged from faith, shall we say?'

Immediately after, two armchairs, positioned either side of an ornate coffee table, came into view, and Mr Literelli motioned Dominic to a seat, but continued on to a side table that hosted a tray containing a coffee pot, cups, and a collection of small cakes and treats.

'We took the trouble to learn your favourite postprandial

desserts and beverages. I hope they meet your approval?' announced Mr Literelli upon returning with the tray.

Accepting the cup of espresso, Dominic was immediately rewarded by its robust aroma, but placed it down untouched – it being too hot for tasting. From the selection on the tray, he chose a Bacci and took his time to carefully unwrap the foil. Once he'd extracted the chocolate, he placed it in his mouth and proceeded to enjoy its crunchiness, from the hazelnut, countered by the soothing sweetness of the dark chocolate. It was a classic treat that never failed to please him.

Mr Literelli had also concluded the coffee was too hot and followed Dominic's lead by also picking up a Bacci. He appeared happy with his choice and then continued to mirror Dominic by extracting the slip of paper from the wrapping to likewise discover its message.

This had Dominic declaring: 'Mine says, "Love conquers all", and yours …'

A triumphant smile preceded Mr Literelli's reply: '"The *heart* knows, what the *mind* does not!"'

Dominic chuckled, 'Is it a *sign* that faith knows what reason does not?'

'Perhaps, but let's not get ahead of ourselves,' replied an amused Mr Literelli as he leant forward to pick up his cup.

Dominic followed suit, and, for five or so minutes, both concentrated on paying homage to their coffees.

Eventually, the cups were drained, with both glancing at the dregs, perhaps both unconsciously hoping for premonitions of the future, before returning their cups to their saucers.

Dominic waited.

Mr Literelli took the hint and asked: 'Doctor Oporto, have you considered why, of the world's thousands of scientists, it is you in particular that we have chosen to take charge of our new online portal?'

'No, not really. It remains a puzzle, despite the Pope's best attempts to inflate my attributes and achievements.'

'Hmm. Let's put *you* to one side and instead consider the scope of what we wish to achieve.'

Dominic raised a hand. 'Before you continue, I must insist that I simply don't have the time, or the inclination, to participate in your website, or whatever it is, no matter how commendable its objectives – objectives that I feel are beyond any one institution's power to control.'

Mr Literelli brought his hands together, forming an archway over which he gazed at Dominic, much like a teacher unsure of how best to emplace a morsel of wisdom into the mind of a recalcitrant adolescent. A few breaths later, a strategy appeared to have been decided upon.

'Dominic … may I be so bold as to call you Dominic?'

'Certainly. But being friendly won't make much difference. I just don't have the time.'

'I hear you, Dominic, but I still feel compelled to try and change your mind. Will you permit me that?'

'Yeah. Okay, but please remember I'm a realist. It will take *real* reasons to move me.'

'Real. Realist. Reasons. Your *belief* in the real may have its logic, but it seems to have clouded your understanding of that which is insubstantial.'

Dominic saw the hopes in the upraised eyebrows and tilting of the head, but was impervious to their silent entreaties for him to soften his stance.

Mr Literelli sighed, then continued in patient tones, 'Dominic, as a physicist, surely you, of all people, must know that the "real",'; he made the quotation marks with his hands, '…is described by words and numbers, which are *imagined* constructs, and that machinery, buildings and other manufactured items start as *unreal* ideas, theories and attitudes, which are then applied to the real, to create what wasn't previously part of reality. Apparently, like many others, you grossly underestimate the power of the unreal, of beliefs and ideas, especially those that current thinking deems *un*reasonable.'

Dominic frowned. 'Hmm. Look, we're drifting into the murky waters of philosophy. Let's just say that I have some appreciation of the power of "an idea whose time has come", and am also much aware of the difficulties that new ideas face before they are widely accepted and acted upon.'

'Good. So, you also understand that science goes through periods of normality, in which existing ideas are used and extended, interspersed by periods of "revolutionary science", when bold new ideas arise that radically change how we understand the world. Darwin's concept of biological evolution via natural selection, and the discovery of DNA, revolutionised biology. In your field, atomic theory, the link between magnetism and electricity, and later that between mass and energy has gifted humanity with the many marvels of modern technologies, as well as their negative impacts upon the environment, and societal attitudes. Surely, ideas count as much as things. Yes? No?'

'Okay. Yes. I agree. But this doesn't affect my position regarding ...'

Mr Literelli interrupted, 'It *will* once I have revealed some vital information you seem unaware of.'

Pushing back into his seat, with arms tightly folded across his chest, Dominic awaited illumination with unenthused silence.

'Consider the effects of online campaigns against nuclear research, all that ranting about atom smashers threatening to create black holes that would engulf the Earth ...'

Incensed, Dominic interjected, 'P-l-e-a-s-e, nobody of consequence takes any of that ridiculous nonsense seriously, no matter how vociferously they preach it.'

'Not so. You underestimate the power of social media and the interests of the "cyber-feudalists" who control the algorithms that mould the course of online chatter. That chatter is behind the mothballing of America's mega-collider. Even the Chinese have succumbed. They have scaled back on theoretical physics and diverted the funding towards new AI-augmented weaponry and cyberwarfare. Your paymasters at the EU, constrained by current economic and political dramas and facing growing anti-science sentiment in their electorates, are planning to drastically reduce the funding for your establishment. You will be lucky to be kept on as a part-time consultant.'

'Okay, I know about the situation in America, but the rest is mere hearsay. *I* would have heard something. And anyway, our research is vital to developing the new technologies needed to …'

Dominic faltered, distracted by the loud buzzing coming from the inside pocket of his jacket. Fumbling from embarrassment, he extracted the offending device whilst silently cursing the person who'd dared disobey his strict instructions not to be contacted for *any* reason – except for the most dire of emergencies.

Once he'd unlocked the phone, he stabbed the text message and was confronted by an emergency that *was* unreservedly dire. An earthquake had caused significant damage to the main collider. Worse, the higher-ups had immediately announced a suspension of all activities until a thorough investigation could be completed, which, knowing those currently in the ascendant, would take years, if ever.

'Bad news?' remarked Mr Literelli, with an air Dominic would have sworn hinted of foreknowledge.

Annoyed, he responded with an acidic: 'Yes.'

'The earthquake?'

'Yes! But how did *you* know?' Dominic replied with growing unease.

'You forget that the church, whilst not what it once was, still has many ears it can call upon – including ears in high places.'

What could Dominic say to that? Nothing!

After brooding for a minute or so, he abruptly stood up and announced, 'I'm needed back in Zurich. I'll have to knock on quite a few doors if I'm to get the collider repaired and back on schedule. I trust the Pope will be true to his word and expedite my return journey.'

Not waiting for a reply, Dominic began marching towards the exit. He had almost reached halfway when hammered into immobility by a bellowed command.

'Stop right there or the next step will be your last!'

The hairs on the back of his neck stood to attention. The rest of him seized up. A breath later, he cautiously turned and was shocked anew, this time by the horrifying sight of Mr Literelli, standing, rigid, grim-faced, holding an automatic pointed unerringly at Dominic's solar plexus. Dominic felt death's chill presence enter the room.

For an indeterminate length of time, they stood studying the other. Mr Literelli maintained an ominous silence, standing as unmoving as a statue, with the only signs of life being the delayed blinking of eyes filled with deadly earnestness.

Dominic tried to bluff it out by attempting to outstare him, but the windows to Mr Literelli's soul were like two black holes. The harder he peered into them, the closer he came to being sucked in and consumed by them. A vertiginous desperation took hold. His pride at controlling others, built up from defeating hecklers when scraping a living as a standup comic during his university days, and later on in conquering the inflexibility and ignorance of colleagues, bureaucrats and politicians, now seemed ill-founded.

Suddenly, he realised he'd lost the battle and felt he was slowly being turned inside out, until all his innermost workings were exposed to the mercy of an implacable opponent – a mercy that seemed extremely unlikely.

Slamming his eyes shut, pride fled, and his knees turned to water. He collapsed to become an unseeing and unmoving jumble of limbs despoiling the intricate mosaics of the floor. But his numb respite ended too soon. A new command from Mr Literelli restarted directed thought, and his desire to act.

'Get up. Return to your seat. We are not finished here.'

Forcing his eyes to open, Dominic looked up, slowly got things into focus, and once more saw God and Adam above him, as self-absorbed as before, and hence thwarting foolish hopes of their divine intervention to dispel the madness that held him.

To conserve the vestigial control left to him, Dominic concentrated upon the tangible task of moving from the horizontal to the vertical. Once standing, he took a moment to grow steady, then, with eyes concentrating on the patterned floor, shuffled back to his seat.

Keeping a watchful eye, Mr Literelli waited for him to settle, then sat down, all the while keeping the gun levelled at Dominic's midriff.

'It pains me to be forced into acting in this rather brutal fashion, but I believe it will help you better understand who I am, what I am capable of, and what we need to accomplish. I will start with an instructive demonstration.'

Dominic puzzled over the man's mercurial return to civility, at least in his voice if not his actions – the eye of the automatic still glared at him with evil intent.

Though fully conscious, Dominic came to realise that he couldn't move any part of his body, except his mouth. That he'd become a ventriloquist's dummy waiting for its master to bring it to life – or was it death? – because, as he sat, he watched, in stunned horror, Mr Literelli's trigger finger contracting, and then discovered that his time, and Mr Literelli's, were not flowing at the same speed.

In ultra-slow-motion, Dominic saw the shock wave exit the gun's muzzle, then the puff of smoke, and finally the bullet's achingly slow progress towards him. The slow flight of the dull-grey lead projectile became his mind's total preoccupation.

But not for long. Mr Literelli interrupted by resuming his one-sided conversation: 'Before the bullet meets your chest, we have a number of things to sort out.'

Releasing his grip on the gun, which remained floating in midair, its owner carefully leant around it to pick up another Bacci, which was unwrapped and unhurriedly consumed, after which Mr Literelli returned his attention to Dominic.

'Please be aware that this current demonstration does have a rational explanation – if one possesses sufficient knowledge and comprehension – both of which are unfortunately well beyond the abilities of humans, as they currently exist.'

He paused to allow Dominic to respond and seemed pleased with his silence.

'Good. You are prepared to listen. Let us begin. Firstly, the purpose of your current predicament is to convince you of the omnipotence of your "interlocutor". We can manipulate time, mass and energy, amongst other aspects of reality. You may be pleased to know that we are also not restricted by the speed of light, that bugbear of physicists, but not science-fiction writers. Humans, individually and collectively, are nowhere near ready to wield a millionth of these powers. They will be barred from you until your social and mental evolution develops the attributes needed, either via natural selection, or perhaps, by other means.'

Dominic gave up on disbelief and decided to temporarily accept the science-fiction nature of the world he now inhabited. In doing so, he found the power to ask, with a measure of hope: 'Other means?'

The fish had taken the bait! An indulgent smile smoothed Mr Literelli's face and then flowed into his reply.

'The full potential of your species could be realised with a bit of genetic tinkering, and considerably more social engineering, after which significant exchanges of truly transformative technologies could be considered.'

Emboldened, both by the bullet's barely measurable advancement and the lure of unimaginable knowledge, Dominic forgot his impending doom and sought answers to the barrage of questions that had arisen in him.

'Before you continue, perhaps now is the time for you to tell me, who are you, what are you, what you're doing here, and what, specifically, do you want of me?'

Mr Literelli chuckled, rubbed his clean-shaven chin, then found words. 'Many a being has asked those first three questions of themselves, and found their answers inadequate. I think you will find mine similarly unsatisfactory.'

His smile widened, then returned to neutrality. 'As far as names go, Angelo Literelli is as good as any I've had over the years, so it will have to suffice. What I am ...' He paused to assess his audience's capabilities, then decided to be bold. '... is whatever you *believe* me to be! After this is over, you may see me as being ...'

In open-mouthed amazement, Dominic gulped, then stared as Mr Literelli morphed into a replica of Michelangelo's God.

Only for his mind to be assaulted as *God* melted, to be replaced by a red-eyed, black-faced, horned man whose breath was flames. A blink later, Dominic beheld a being that was squat and scaly, with an ugly toad-like head, a huge fanged mouth and eyes on turrets, like those possessed by chameleons. The next blink brought thankful relief when the human Mr Literelli returned.

'... any of these three, or whatever else your imagination can come up with, and *believe.*'

He paused, let Dominic's breathing return to normal, then continued, 'Perhaps, as a working hypothesis, we consider that I am, largely, what I appear to be: a mature man of good education *and* means – though of considerably more means than most! What I am *doing* is what I want you to do: influence others. We are here to resolve the direction of that influencing, its rationale, its worthiness, and then the mechanics of achieving the desired behavioural changes in those key individuals whose words, and deeds, craft societal norms and their enforcement.'

Despite serious concerns over the frighteningly indeterminate nature of *what* Mr Literelli was, Dominic muzzled his incredulity, and fears, and reminded himself that he was a scientist and that bravely seeking the truth is what scientists do. With that in mind, he decided to ask the many questions that had been brewing up in him since the morning's fateful phone call, but firstly, those pertaining to his immediate predicament.

A considerable time later, with Mr Literelli's humanness tentatively accepted, and all of his questions answered rationally and devoid of emotive adornments, Dominic found himself possessing a very much expanded picture of how the world actually works. Though mentally and physically fatigued, he was surprised to find himself seriously considering giving up nuclear physics in favour of joining Mr Literelli's "coalition of the willing" to fight the unwise use of new technologies and so prevent the disastrous consequences they would generate.

After Mr Literelli had outlined the nature of the other people and resources being mobilised, Dominic was further astounded to realise he actually believed that Mr Literelli's grandiose utopian ambition might be both real and achievable! As a scientist and a man devoted to the long-term and the public good, it was an outcome he would have previously deemed an impossibility.

But his wonder and relief that a way forward had finally been found now meant he could no longer divert his attention from the "creeping" bullet, now less than a handspan from his chest.

Trying not to let panic enter his voice, he asked: 'Now that we seem to be in agreement with what needs doing, and how best to achieve it, I think it's high time to do something about that bullet. I won't be of much use to anyone if I'm dead.'

'Oh, you'd be surprised at how often dying can be a great career move!' Mr Literelli cheerily quipped, whilst blithely watching the bullet suddenly increase its rate of progress.

Dominic's control shattered. 'Stop. Stop it! Now! Now!' he yelled, all the way up to the moment of impact, the sting of which shocked him into a silent acceptance of his death.

The bullet then had a miraculous change of heart! It reversed and flew back to its roost in the gun's barrel. A gun, now back in Mr Literelli's grip. A gun that didn't explode but merely resumed its inert state of unblinking readiness. Mr Literelli then calmly slipped it back into his shoulder holster, buttoned up his jacket, leaving the weapon safely hidden from the eyes of the innocent.

'Sorry for the lateness of the rescue, but we wanted you to have a scar, a stigmata, to remind you of the reality of this afternoon's events *and* commitments.'

Glancing down at his chest, Dominic saw the charred circle in his shirt, felt the discomfort, then probed the hole with a finger, which came back daubed with a speck of blood. It was only then that he realised that he had been given back control over his limbs. A deep inhalation and a jiggling of toes and flexing of fingers had him feeling the uncommon joy of a Lazarus resurrected.

After silently celebrating being back in control of his body, Dominic next performed a quick, cold re-assessment of his new attitudes and goals and discovered they remained surprisingly resolute.

'Are you still with us?' asked an observant and relaxed Mr Literelli.

After a pause and a deep inhalation, Dominic replied with a definitive, "Yes".

'Good. Over the remnants of the weekend, give yourself time to digest all that has happened here. On Monday morning, around ten, someone will contact you to arrange for you to meet some of the key personnel at the European office, which, conveniently for you, is located in Zurich.'

'When will you and I meet again?'

Straightening up in his chair, Mr Literelli crossed his arms, then seemed to silently consult the ceiling for the right words, before eventually answering: 'I'm afraid this will be our one and only meeting. I am merely an influencer. My small part in our worthy cause is to persuade people to willingly join our struggle. Once they are on board, my role is at an end. It has been a pleasure making your acquaintance. You exceeded my expectations. Our interactions, I found both rewarding and educational, and hope it was the same for you too.'

'But, what about – "other means"? You hinted that your kind of human, or whatever you are, understand and control all manner of powers beyond our imagining. Powers that you so effectively demonstrated today ...' Dominic jabbed a finger into the hole in his shirt for emphasis, '... and which you said might one day be shared with us.'

'Yes, I did let that slip. It is understandable that you'd like a shortcut to the marvellous knowledge, challenges and rewards that our possible involvement in your future might offer.'

'And?'

'Sadly, any such actions would depend upon the nature of the progress made in our corrective endeavours and how long it takes for those corrections to "solidify". Unfortunately, we are a long way from that juncture. But don't give up on that hope. Who knows … humanity may progress faster than expected, in which case …'

Disappointment clambered across Dominic's face to the point where he was on the verge of speech, until halted by Mr Literelli's amused smile and calming movements of his open palms.

'All I am saying is that the powers I demonstrated today *may* one day be fully understood. Only then will they be given into humanity's care. That won't happen until your current project has won, not just the day, but the future. I'm sure you are wise enough to realise that too often technology gets ahead of wisdom, with disastrous results. Humanity is at a tipping point, not just regarding planetary environmental parameters, but also in its societal ability to wisely use technological innovations. Your road ahead diverges; one leads to disaster and extinction, the other is a longer, happier one that requires a wisdom not yet developed and, certainly not yet *innate*. Your new career is your contribution towards building the foundations of that inborn greater wisdom.'

For a minute or so, Dominic's face underwent a series of contortions reflecting the unsettled waters of his mind, before eventually returning to placidity. A sigh signalled a begrudging capitulation to the truth of Mr Literelli's words.

'You are right. The influence of the plague of half-truths, lies, and corrosive ideologies, as well as the active silencing of facts, if left unchecked, will inevitably lead to terrible consequences. It is such a pity I feel compelled to join your fight, because I now must sacrifice my exploring of the many intriguing puzzles still unresolved in physics, especially those concerning the fundamental forces underpinning reality. I fear I will never get the chance to solve them in my lifetime. But such is life,' sighed Dominic.

'Yes indeed,' replied Mr Literelli before standing.

Dominic followed suit, and together, they strolled to the exit.

§

Later, the three entities reconvened to discuss progress made in their worldly interventions.

The second spoke first. 'I think my actions were well received. The balance between order and disorder has improved, but will require ongoing monitoring for a while yet before a more sustainable harmony is achieved.'

Number One then opined, with a hint of understated appreciation, 'As Mr Literelli, you were more than correct to have remarked upon how *educational* your time with Dr Oporto had been.'

Number Three felt it "educational" for them all to be reminded of what had been done and what had been narrowly averted.

'We immortals may have mastery over all the fundamental forces, but surprises still happen. Dr Oporto, and the trajectory of his research was one such. If his nuclear experiments were allowed to continue, he would prematurely have come to understand, and perhaps use, ideas too dangerous for an immature mind beholden to a barbaric species.'

'I think you are being too harsh. From my time in their company, they, with a nudge or two from us, may well prove your words to be ill-chosen,' countered number Two.

'Perhaps,' conceded number Three, 'But one thing is certain. Dr

Oporto highlighted the truth of that bland statement in that holy book of theirs, the one they used to export from Byblos, Bible, or whatever they call it these days. Specifically, the line in it about man being created in God's likeness.'

A ripple of contrition spread amongst them before Number One retook the baton.

'Yes indeed. Unbeknownst to Dr Oporto, he reminded us that *we*, like humans, share the same basal fear. The same fear that stalks them in their darkest moments. The fear of death! They either try to deny its reality, or annul it by convincing themselves that, after their body dies, their spirit lives on. *We*, on the other hand, are immortal, all-powerful and *incorporeal*, hence impervious to outside influence, or destruction, and yet ...'

Number Two stepped in. 'Dr Oporto's experiments would have led to a small rip in the space-time continuum, which would have hastened the reversal of the universe's expansion, hastened its contraction and its next rebirth. We had temporarily forgotten, or chose to forget, that that reborn universe may not have us, *as we are now*, in it. Their fear of death now haunts *our* darknesses too!'

A synchrony of nodded agreement stirred the countenances of the three, resulting in a humbled, but amusingly so, Number Three speaking their thoughts.

'We, at least, have the time, and capacities, to fully appreciate our "lives", and, to find meaning in our possible non-existence after the next, "big bang".'

With that expressed truth as their guide, the three then disbursed to contemplate their expanded reality.

Author's Note:

This story was my response to a writers' group exercise with fear as its theme. It induced me to ask: What do we humans fear the most, and why? And then: What do *gods* fear?

The Jovian Dirk

Thian's dark features grew darker. Taking up this role as Chief Security Officer on the *Ragusa* was supposed to be the start of his slow, cruisy path towards retirement, but the semi-naked body sprawled face down on the floor of the Presidential Suite suggested the Earth-Jupiter run had unsavoury aspects not mentioned during the job interview. It also meant the higher-ups would soon be on his back, pushing him to find the culprit and to keep the whole thing under wraps.

Stifling a groan, Thian turned his attention to the steward.

'So, his friends asked you to investigate why the deceased was late for their card game. You came up, saw him dead, then called me, immediately. Is that correct?'

Without looking up, the steward answered in the affirmative. His expression seemed to alternate between fear, revulsion, and a morbid fascination with the elaborately carved knife handle protruding rudely from the passenger's back. Understandable really; this sort of thing, hopefully, wasn't a common occurrence on these outer planets resupply trips.

Though it wasn't the handle that piqued Thian's curiosity; it was the lack of obvious signs of a struggle.

'So, who was he?'

'Jonas Boag. An asteroid miner returning from Earth.'

Thian noted the condescension in the steward's voice. Again, understandable, but not the sort of sentiment encouraged in staff aboard a Solar Federation spaceship. The harsh physical and erratic financial realities of an asteroid miner's existence had often been used to explain their violent and unruly ways, but they were as human as everyone else and deserved the same dignity, even in death.

But quietly killing each other out amongst the asteroids was one thing; doing it on this spaceship, on his first voyage, was another. Thian leaned forward, and, with a gloved hand, slowly extracted the knife and bagged it. It was the first he had seen in the flesh, and it couldn't have been any more in the flesh. The crossbar at the base of the wooden handle had been half buried in the victim's aged skin!

It was a weapon peculiar to the colonies on the Jovian moons, especially of Adamstown, the capital of Europa, but what did they call it? He knew the official description: a *Jovian, oak-handled dirk*, but there were several colloquial terms used that temporarily eluded him.

'What do the locals call these things?' he asked of the steward, under the assumption his years in space meant he knew more on the topic than he did.

'Around Europa and the other moons, they're usually called *Jovian Pig Prickers*, but the asteroid miners prefer *Jokers*, from Jovian oak-handled ...'

'Yeah, yeah, I get it. *Pig prickers* and *Jokers*, oh dear!'

Thian rolled the body over, making sure his chest camera got a good view, for the investigation to come. The first signs of rigor mortis were appearing, the eyelids were half open, the limbs were on the verge of seizing up, and, on the tanned, bony face, as wrinkled as a walnut, were the beginnings of the *smile of death*.

All of which suggested the time of death was about three hours ago, around 06:30 to 07:00 ship's time. A post-mortem would be more precise, but if his estimate was right, then the man had possibly gotten out of bed to let in an early visitor, who, from the lack of a struggle, he presumably knew, but obviously not well enough, because the fellow had skewered him as soon as the victim's back was turned.

It was interesting that the killer hadn't removed the knife. Was that a mistake? Had he been interrupted? Or was it deliberately left behind as a warning for others to take note of? The murderer had certainly killed with passion, which hinted of more dramas to come. Thian hoped not.

But why was Jonas Boag killed? And how did the killer smuggle the knife on board? Too many questions, and no answers.

Turning back to the steward – Theobaud, according to his name tag – Thian asked, 'If you have no objection, for the course of the murder investigation, I'll have you seconded to Security, which will give you a temporary pay hike. You okay with that?'

'Yes, sir. Fine, sir.'

'Good. In which case, the first thing you can do is go back and explain to Mr Boag's buddies that he won't be making it to today's session, or any others – inform them of his demise, but just say it was from a fatal heart attack, which in a way is true, since his heart most certainly was attacked!'

Thian noted Theobaud's lack of response to his attempted levity and sighed. The younger generation appeared poorly endowed with a sense of humour.

'Continue your normal duties, but keep an extra ear out for any whispers concerning his friends, and also go out of your way to check up on the other asteroid miners on board. We don't have much time to solve this murder, as we will be at Asteroid Junction in just over twenty-four hours, at which point the miners will trans-ship and with them Boag's probable killer. At the end of your shift, please report to my office, unless you have some important or unimportant news, in which case phone me or send a text message if I'm unavailable.

Understood?'

'All quite clear, sir.'

After the steward departed, Thian contacted Jenkins, his Deputy, explained the situation and asked him to start trawling through the CCTV footage of the corridor outside Boag's room, and outside the rooms of the other miners. Afterwards, Jenkins was to go through the records of the victim and those of the miners on board. Hopefully, a picture would emerge of the personalities involved, their finances, and their recent comings and goings to and from Earth.

Next was Doctor Flintock. Thian got lucky – he picked up almost immediately. 'It's Thain Logos of Security. We have a situation that requires your expertise. An asteroid miner has been murdered, and I need you to organise the removal of the body and to get a post-mortem underway.'

'Humph. I don't suppose you have any idea of who the culprit is?'

'None, but the finger points to it being another miner.'

'They're a pretty closed-mouthed lot. So, they'll not be much help. Got any clues?'

'None, apart from the murder weapon … a knife, a Jovian dirk. But I'm open to your input.'

'Good. I have your location on the screen, and if you're at the crime scene, I suggest you leave it immediately and wait for me outside. I *may* be able to help.'

Feeling a little more confident, Thian left the cabin, locked the door, and awaited the doctor's arrival. Whilst waiting, he phoned the captain with the bad news.

The captain's warnings to be thorough and discreet were still reverberating around his skull when Doctor Flintock and two assistants arrived, with a stretcher and a metal suitcase.

'I'll take some air samples first, then swab the area for DNA, film it all, and send you a report once I get him back to our operating room, which doubles as our morgue.'

'Not a very reassuring setup for your live patients!'

The doctor chuckled. 'We only tell them of its dual nature if they are particularly obnoxious!'

Thian left their ghoulish humour behind, then wandered off to the closest dining room for a pot of tea and a chance to mull over the situation.

Sitting back in one of the paired recliners in the alcoves along the walls of deck C's main dining and recreational lounge, Thian wondered why the old miner was returning to the asteroid belt. If he could afford their most expensive suite, then he must be loaded. If so, why leave behind the comforts that abounded on Earth to return to the privations of the asteroid belt?

From his cursory glance around the suite, it seemed the man had lived like a monk in a palace. Scrolling through the room's terminal had revealed that Jonas Boag had consumed hardly any booze, had ordered the most frugal and basic of meals, and had slept in the smallest room. Its wardrobe contained only the barest minimum of clothing – and not of any great quality – and had watched only the news, the planetary weather summaries, and stock market reports.

Not for the first time, Thian puzzled over why some, if not most, of those who accumulate wealth from their own sweat don't seem to know how to enjoy it. It was as if the game of accumulation consumes them until the day arrives when they have a mountain of cash to use, but then can't remember why they wanted it in the first place.

The humbling notion then popped into his head that, once *he* retired, how would *he* spend his remaining days, and his modest "pot of gold"?

It was a question for another day, though it highlighted the key to solving the case: finding out who would inherit the old guy's cash.

Hopefully, Jenkins' digging would shed some light on that. One thing was certain, once his death became official, some mistress, ex-wife, loving niece or cousin would emerge from obscurity to "feast on the corpse"!

Later, in Security's small domain, the public part of which lay outside the long wooden bench, whilst inside, he and Jenkins had three desks, and, down the corridor, the holding cells, storeroom, kitchenette and a bathroom to lord over, though on this occasion, they sat either side of Thian's big desk, munching sandwiches and summarising their discoveries.

Jenkins started. 'We have seven miners on board, Boag is the oldest, his three card-playing colleagues are in their fifties. Boag and the others all work for the same syndicate, on various asteroids, all not too distant from each other. They usually keep together and have had Boag join them on at least the last three resupply trips, which seem to occur about every two to three years. Nothing suspicious there, to my mind.'

Thian grunted and kept eating.

Jenkins continued, 'The CCTV footage clearly shows Boag's early morning visitor entering and leaving shortly around 06:35. Dressed in the usual miners' trench coat, broad-brimmed hat and wearing those miners' goggles they use for seeing in an expanded spectrum, to help pick out the seams of rare earth minerals they are chasing. The goggles also help them read the physiological "tells" that signal the emotional state of us humans, which is why they aren't allowed when playing cards...'

'Yes, yes, no lectures. So, can we recognise him?' Thian butted in.

'No. Wrong build, too broad and has a shambling gait that fits none of the miners or any other passenger for that matter. The big beard is also a hindrance. All the miners are either clean-shaven or have very trim beards. I reckon it's a falsie. The whole get-up is a disguise.'

'Heard anything from Theobaud, our roving spy? I haven't.'

'No. I can chase him down if you like?'

Thian shook his head, scattering crumbs, 'No. We don't want it to be too obvious that he's in our pay. Anything else?'

'I followed the killer's movements, he seems to have originated from near storage hangar 5C, the cameras thin out down there, so I lost him. He must have a secret hangout out of reach of the cameras, which suggests great familiarity with the ship and its monitoring systems.'

Thian leaned back, chased a morsel inside his mouth and then surmised, 'This puts the killer as a regular passenger, or one of the staff.'

Unfazed by the last remark, Jenkins continued, 'There's one other thing. We have another missing miner. He hasn't been seen since dinner last night, a poorer and younger one, a Mr Placer, Atlan Placer, it's only his third trip and ...'

'And what?' Thian glared, suddenly ill at ease.

Jenkins, unperturbed, continued, 'And he works, sorry, worked, for Mr Boag.'

Thian thought it was strange that Theobaud hadn't reported such an event, so he picked up his desk phone and made the call. It took a few moments before the steward picked up. In the background was the sound of clinking glasses and a low-key dance band.

'Theobaud, I hope I'm not creating a scene for you, but we have another missing miner ... Mr Placer. How come I haven't been informed?'

'Placer! He's always last one up. Usually surfaces before the last lunch sitting. So thought nothing of it. As far as collecting gossip goes, I've heard nothing useful apart from snatches of conversations between Boag's card-playing buddies, mostly complaining that they'd lost their chance to win back the money Boag had creamed off them in their last session. Accusations of card tampering were mentioned. I don't think Boag was overly liked by any of them. Do you want me to check on Placer?'

'Yes. If it can be done without comments being made.'

After he hung up, he asked Jenkins to run a computer search for all relevant information on Theobaud. Jenkins cleared away the scraps of their combined lunches, then went to his desk and started tapping away.

A few minutes later, Theobaud called in. Thian put it on speaker.

'Placer is dead. The same M.O. as Boag. Knife in the back, with a handle of the same sort of wood as the other one, but carved differently. He's stiff as a board, so I guess he's been dead longer than Boag.'

'Stay there. I'll get Dr Flintock to come over with his boys to collect the body. Whilst you're waiting, have a quick look around without disturbing anything; film it on your communicator. Once the doctor arrives, come report to me at security. Okay?'

The steward said yes, and Thian hung up.

'Jenkins, forget what you're doing and come over to my desk; together we'll watch the CCTV footage outside Placer's door from midnight onwards. Two pairs of eyes may be better and faster than one.'

There had been very little foot traffic, until just after seven in the morning, a male cleaner in a cap, sporting heavy rimmed glasses with thick lenses, clean-shaven but with a pasty white complexion and puffed out cheeks. He was of average height, and was pushing his trolley down the corridor. He knocked at the door. There he waited briefly before letting himself in with his key. He re-emerged less than five minutes later, then trundled off in the direction of the storage hangar 5C, where he disappeared from view.

Thian snorted in disgust, 'This guy is taking us for a ride. Is he a miner dressed as a cleaner, or a cleaner dressed as a miner, and where is he getting these knives?'

'Probably from his victims,' Jenkins replied, before elaborating. 'It's a sort of tradition, a miners' ritual. When they set up a mining operation, the first thing they do is carve a unique handle for their dirk, which they then carry with them everywhere – supposedly as a good luck charm – including, it seems, on this ship. I reckon they've devised a way of smuggling them on board, probably in with their mining equipment. I think you will find that at some early stage they each made a trip to the storage hangars, "to check on their equipment", but really to retrieve their dirks. Legend has it that they sleep with them under their pillows.'

'You seem well informed; pity you didn't share this earlier.'

'Sorry, sir, but the situation seemed so unreal. All that stuff was just fairy tales that my father told me of his brief stint as an asteroid miner upon leaving school. I always thought he was making most of it up, just to scare an impressionable kid, me.'

'Humph. Anyway, when Theobaud arrives, I'll get both of you to search the cabins of the miners with a combination scanner and confiscate any knives. They can have them back when they trans-ship tomorrow. Hopefully, this may put our killer off from striking again. With any luck, he will depart with the rest of them. Two unsolved murders, but what's the alternative? If we find those disguises and get some DNA samples, maybe then we'd have a chance but …' Thian shrugged his shoulders and looked glum.

Shortly after, Theobaud reported in, with nothing much to add. Thian dispatched him and Jenkins off to round up as many dirks as they could, leaving him with the unpleasant task of informing the captain of the latest developments.

Once he had the office to himself, he began trolling through the personal histories of Theobaud and Jenkins. The thought that either one or both of them could be murderers had him getting itchy between the shoulder blades. How straight were they? The energy-dampening fog of distrust tainted his thoughts and slowed his actions.

Even at his plodding pace, he eventually ran out of questions and the resources to answer them, all of which revealed biographies not suggestive of grand passions or latent criminality.

Jenkins was thirty-seven with both parents still alive and back in London, admittedly in a working-class area. After high school, he did ten years in the army and ended up assigned to their intelligence unit. Once his contract was up, he moved to other areas of employment, mostly in construction, until applying for his current security job eight years back. He'd been on the Jupiter run ever since. He had a "partner" back in London and one kid, just starting high school.

Theobaud was younger at thirty-four, of mixed Asian and European descent and also a British resident. He'd had a more checkered life. Born in Glasgow, with no mention of a father, the family, as such, moved to Manchester early on, where his mother had struggled to find work, and even had a few minor scrapes with the law. But, despite circumstances, she still managed to get him a good education, enough to start a degree, but presumably not enough to complete it. Theobaud dropped out to join the Manchester constabulary. He did well, getting to Detective Sergeant, but, when undercover, got wounded and presumably decided another line of work would be healthier. This resulted in him joining the Earth-Jupiter run as a steward. Divorced, no kids and no apparent love interests.

Though Thian didn't have the time, or means, for an exhaustive investigation of their finances, the company's records showed both with healthy retirement fund balances, both with AAA credit ratings. Thus, both had no obvious money motives.

Bizarrely disappointed at finding no greedy murderers amongst his helpers, Thian turned the screen off and eased back in his seat. The lack of red flags left him little to go on. He put his mind into neutral and sat quietly, listening to the silence, gazing unfocused at the empty desks and allowing his mind to dawdle where it would.

He must have dozed off because he woke with a start at the noisy return of his lieutenants, who made a spectacle of dumping a collection of dirks onto his desk, to then stand back as if expecting rapturous applause for their handiwork.

An unenthused: 'Any trouble?' was all he could offer.

'Plenty,' replied Jenkins, 'but we settled them down by threatening to charge them with possession of offensive weapons, even conspiracy to take over the ship, and said if they didn't co-operate, they'd find themselves languishing inside the Adamstown goal, awaiting a trial who knows when. That quieted them down, especially when we said we would return their property when they trans-shipped tomorrow.'

'Good work. Lock those knives up in the secure section of the storeroom, and don't forget to log them into the records.'

Thian waited for them to return. When they reappeared, he doublechecked the evidence log – all the dirks were there – and then gave his orders.

'Now that the dirks are nicely squared away, you, Theobaud can return to your snooping duties.' He flicked his hands until Theobaud took the hint and left, then turned his attention to Jenkins. '… you can do a bit of backtracking down the corridors used by our killer. Don't rush, try and think of where, and how, he could have stashed his disguises. If he'd dumped them in a recycling chute, they'd be ground down and shredded beyond retrieval by now, but give it a try anyway, we may get lucky.'

They didn't. Neither turned up anything of use. The evening, night, and following morning produced no new bodies, which had Thian breathing easier, especially once all the miners took the shuttle to Asteroid Junction, along with *all* their equipment.

It was after lunch; Jenkins and Theobaud were away doing their usual tasks, which involved strolling the decks and keeping a watchful eye on the punters to ensure they had a smooth, safe journey.

Back at his desk, feet up, near horizontal, Thian was pondering what more he could have done when Theobaud stepped into the office.

'Excuse me, sir, but do you still want me gathering intelligence now the miners have gone, it's just …'

'Ah yes …' Thian had forgotten about the steward's extra duties and cleared his throat. 'Ahh, maybe not, I think the crisis has passed. Thank you for your efforts. I'll just have to get you to sign the Higher Duties form to make sure you get that extra cash in your next pay.'

No matter how high-tech the world became, some paper always crept in. Thian got up, went to the office's sole filing cabinet and started hunting for the correct form. The phone on his desk rang. They both stared at it. It kept ringing.

'Could you take that, and tell them to wait.'

Theobaud picked up, listened without comment, then said, 'You'd better hear this, sir; there's been another knifing, another death.'

'What?' Thian turned in disbelief, 'Not another one of those damned pig prickers! Who was it, and how long ago?'

'According to Jenkins, the dead man is a Mr Glemace, a solicitor, on his first trip to Europa.'

'And? The weapon – and when …?' Thian pleaded, arms wide and shaking his head in disbelief.

Theobaud asked the question, as put, held the phone closer to his ear, frowned, then replied, 'Jenkins says: "It wasn't a joke, and he wasn't smiling".'

Slamming shut the drawer, Thian let out a muttered curse, then moved back to his desk, 'Looks like you'd better continue sleuthing for us for a while longer! Again, join Jenkins at the scene. Where did it happen, by the way?'

'I forgot to ask and Jenkins didn't say …'

Thian dropped into his chair, picked up the phone, and made the call. He found out, after admonishing Jenkins for not providing the location, and then told Theobaud to get on with his usual work, but again to keep his eyes and ears open and report back any suspicious behaviour or useful gossip.

After informing Doc Flintock of the new body awaiting his tender mercies, Thian was on the verge of terminating the call when, out of desperation, he asked, 'We've found no physical evidence so far. Do you have anything to suggest? Some new techniques I've overlooked?'

'Well, yes and no.'

'Arghh! I don't need …'

'Hey! Calm yourself. It's only that what I suggest we do may give clues, but nothing that could be used in court.'

'Doesn't matter; I'll try anything.'

'Good. Then meet me in my surgery around four-thirty. By then the boys will have gone, and the computer will have had time to come up with something.'

A few minutes past their agreed time, Thian entered the white aseptic world of Doc Flintock's realm, after passing his two assistants in the corridor outside.

'Come into my office, I've done some preliminary analysing and might have some insights to offer.'

Taking the proffered chair, Thian sidled next to the doctor, who sat tapping away on a keyboard with the attached screen obediently responding by flashing up pages of text and graphics, the last of which was some sort of summary sheet.

'Right. It's half what I expected. But before we get to that, you should know that, for safety reasons, the air in the ship is constantly monitored for its chemical composition to detect poisonous gases or poor air quality. The other lesser-known aspect of this procedure is that it can be used to detect who was where, when and for how long. Sort of.'

He held up a hand to ward off Thian's impatience, then continued, 'When we humans enter a space, we leave behind traces of our scent *and* some of our microbial assemblages floating about in the air. If one can obtain a sample of a person's body odour …' He turned to Thian, noted with amusement the slight wince induced by the all-too-common embarrassment associated with human odours and couldn't repress his smile. Then steadying again, he kept going, '… I can use the log of air quality like a bloodhound to sniff out who went where and when.'

'So, what have you "sniffed out"?'

After a nervous cough, Flintock gave his explanation: 'Well, what I've done is programme the computer to analyse the scent tracks of the following people: the three victims, all the miners, you …' He paused for a reaction, saw none, then went on with greater confidence, '… your two helpers, *myself*, and my two assistants. I also gathered scent readings from the relevant cabins and of the places these people most frequent, such as workstations and other regular haunts, like favourite seats in dining areas.'

'And?'

'As I said before, these findings wouldn't stand up to legal scrutiny, but if you had to bet on the favourites to be involved in all three murders, then …'

'Come on!'

'I'd suggest that Jenkins and Theobaud are the best bets, then yourself, with myself and my assistants tied for a distant fourth place.'

Thian's facial contortions reflected disappointment. 'This still doesn't get us any further. Both Jenkins and Theobaud, by the nature of their jobs, must travel the ship; same for me and you to a lesser extent, and so we all had opportunity. To get further, I need evidence of means and motive. And having opportunity makes the means relatively easy since nothing hi-tech was involved.'

'Assuming the murderer isn't you, or myself, have you checked the backgrounds of the other four for possible motives. I can't say I know the lives of my boys intimately, but from what I know of them, no motivations spring to mind, but …'

Thian's disappointment had him butting in, 'I've checked my two and also found nothing suggestive of a motivation. All I can do now is to dig deeper into the lives of …'

'…of me, and my assistants!' said a smiling Doc Flintock.

'Well, yes. Who knows what evil lurks behind the most innocent façade? Hmm? To be fair, I suggest you check out me and my two as best you can, and we'll report back tomorrow evening, in a quiet spot in the main dining room. There we shall partake of good food and, perhaps, indulge in some unexpected character assassinations. Yes?'

After the doctor had agreed, Thian left him communing with his screen, and returned to his office to do the same.

The next evening, at the allotted time, again it was a disappointed Thian who dined with a less disappointed Doc Flintock, the less so because he'd had lower expectations.

'Don't look so glum. It was always going to be a long shot, and on the bright side, no more punctured bodies have surfaced,' remarked the doctor during the wait for their meals to arrive.

'*You* can make light of the situation, but I've got to come up with something that will placate the captain, the investigation sure to be raised by the Solar Federation's hierarchy, and satisfy any grieving relations and beneficiaries.'

'Rather you than me,' was the doctor's unhelpful response.

Moments later, their meals arrived. They tacitly agreed to enjoy the food and talk of things more uplifting than murder, things such as music and books.

The rest of the trip to Jupiter flew by without incident, and the same was true for the return to Earth. Then, for a week or so, Thian was kept busy by the official inquiry at the Federation's London head offices, before the inevitable conclusion that the murders were committed by persons unknown, despite all due process having been done to find them. Thian received no communications from irate relatives and only cursory interest from the media, for which he was most grateful.

After a few weeks at home enjoying his wife's company, he received notification of his next resupply trip. Hidden in the documentation was the crew listing. Absent from it were both Jenkins and Theobaud. Why?

Checking with Personnel, both had reported that they'd had enough of being separated from friends and family, and that the trauma of the murders had added to their motivations for resigning – all very plausible, but also open to other interpretations, interpretations that needed more information. This ended in him contacting an old colleague, George Jacobi, now quite senior in the ranks of the police, and arranging a get-together to discuss old times, but more so to examine his unease regarding Jenkins and Theobaud.

They met in their favoured lunchtime café not far from London Police headquarters.

'George, it's great to see you again. You're looking a bit trimmer than last time. Wife got you on a diet?'

'No, doctor's orders. But I have to admit this healthier lifestyle is paying dividends, which I'm glad to see you noticed.'

Thian gave thanks that the menu hadn't changed and so ordered his usual lunchtime fare, a ploughman's lunch with a half-pint of bitter. George ordered skinless chicken and salad, but allowed himself to be guided by Thian's choice of beverage. Not until the food was eaten and the beer was kissing the bottom of their glasses did their business get its airing.

'So, George, did you manage to come up with anything on my two suspects?'

'I had to dredge back quite a ways; forty years for one, and almost as much for the other, to find any connections between your two and the three dead guys, all of whom were crooks and often in cahoots.'

'My enquiries were limited to the Solar Federation's database, which, though extensive, probably aren't as comprehensive as yours.'

'Yeah, probably. But, Thian, as you know, not everything is available digitally. I called the few remaining colleagues and lawyers, still alive, who had some direct dealings with the legal cases involved. They could only hint and give unsubstantiated opinions, but …'

'What cases? I think you'd better tell me the whole story, as you see it. Even if I can't do anything with it, I'd like some clues as to what actually went down on my ship.'

'For Jenkins, you have to ask: why he joined the army after high school, why he wriggled himself into their intelligence section, and then why he quit, when he was up for promotion and higher pay, to go work in the shark-infested waters of the London construction game?'

'And?'

'Well, it all starts with his father, who, as a young man, was apparently suckered into joining the rush to mine the asteroids. It was there that he encountered the likes of Boag and Co. There was a lot of claim-jumping and scams going on, and I suspect Jenkin's dad got badly burnt by one of your two dead miners. When he returned home, he married, but his economic circumstances were never great, which is why Jenkins, a bright lad by all measures, had to join the army as the only way up via the decent education the army provided. He probably switched to the London construction scene upon learning that Boag and his mates had moved into the building game after the asteroid belt became too hot for them. Here, they were involved in a few building scandals, dodgy workmanship, collapsed finances, all of which always seemed not to hurt them, probably due to the financial and legal wiles of a young Mr Glemace.'

'Sadly, yours is a story as old as time. Are you implying Jenkins took up a security job on the Jupiter run in the hope of getting an opportunity to revenge his dad's grievances and his own tough childhood?'

'Possibly. Because Boag and buddies went back to the Asteroid belt when the London authorities started getting too hard to put off, that was around eight years back, which coincides with Jenkins' new career in space.'

'Interesting. If so, Jenkins knows how to hold a grudge. But it's the sort of thing that eats a man up inside, such that it eventually shows on the outside. And yet I never saw any evidence of it. Perhaps he considers his actions more than revenge. I'll have to think about it. Anyway, how about Theobaud? How does he come into this story of yours?'

'With him, it's probably even more personal, because Jonas Boag was his father! Tracing his mother's location and those of Boag before and after the date of Theobaud's birth, put them in the same places. I dug around for DNA evidence and hit the jackpot. Boag had to give a sample when arrested for one of his building scams, one Glemace managed to extricate him from. His mother was involved romantically and financially with Boag, it seems. Though from a relatively well-off family, she lost her money and reputation almost undoubtedly because of Boag. Got so poor at one stage that she got nicked for shoplifting, which resulted in a DNA sample. I got Theobaud's from Space Federation records, then had them compared and found out the genetic relationships. Abandoning and fleecing your mother is something few would let go of.'

Thian's eyebrows took a while to descend after that last bombshell; it then took a breath or two before a response could be offered. 'And again, Theobaud showed no signs of becoming twisted up inside by dreams of revenge. I wonder if the two of them discussed their mutual histories, which resulted in both adopting a new ethical disposition? Perhaps more will be revealed when we see what happens to Boag's estate. How long do reckon that would take?'

'Years, if not decades, according to my mate in corporate crime. The complexity scammers use to keep the taxman and creditors at bay also makes inheritance a nightmare, but with millions at stake, I'm sure they'll eventually get to the bottom of it and find a way to allocate any funds left after the lawyers have had their fill!'

'Y-e-s. But none of this gives me much joy. It appears one, or both, were involved in one, or all of the murders, and it looks like they'll get away with it.'

'Well, Thian, you can't win them all. Perhaps new evidence will come to light that will lead to a conviction. But I wouldn't hold my breath, or lose too much sleep over it. The three "victims" were despicable predators few would mourn. Myself included.'

'I suppose so. Anyway, it's been great catching up and finding out what probably happened. I just hope I'll never run into those two, as I'll not know how to react.'

'Yeah, life's like that sometimes. Things get fuzzy and uncertain, and right and wrong get hard to tease apart.'

They parted, and that was that, until Thian's farewell-do four years later.

The crowd at Federation HQ was starting to thin. Most of his colleagues had early starts, encouraging him to make his final exit. He'd gotten to the side table holding the various mementos of his years in space, when he realised that there was one parcel still unopened, which was strange.

Ever cautious, Thian put the others in the carry bag – thoughtfully provided by one of the ladies – then took the bag and the mystery package into the kitchenette, to find a knife to cut the strings with which it was expertly secured.

Inside was a polished wooden box, containing … a dagger. A Jovian, oak-handled dirk and a typed note proclaiming:

"Evil triumphs when good men, the law, and the state, do nothing. Doing nothing is easy. Doing something incurs risks, sometimes revulsion, and always unflinching resolve. The easy way makes you dirty, the difficult, purifies."

There was no signature. Thian needed none.

Author's Note:

This story began in April 2019, as a writing exercise. We had to create a short story that would have the last line: "It wasn't a joke, and he wasn't smiling" – from *Yellowcake Spring* by Guy Salvide. But that line left my readers, and myself, hanging. This extended version is, hopefully, better.

The Joker

Captain Niob watched the door of the bridge guillotine, with silent finality, the retreating figure of his second-in-command. Velon's departure had been surprisingly good-natured, no smirk, no poorly disguised scowl, no hunched shoulders or truculent final words.

Maybe Velon had finally made peace with Starfleet's decision and was going to respect their wishes, was going to make the best of the privilege of being second-in-command of a battlecruiser. If he behaved himself, further demonstrated his undoubted competency – he was a genius at untangling software glitches – and learned to be gracious in taking orders from those higher up, then his chances at the next round of promotions were looking up.

Niob pushed back in the commander's chair, swivelled to glance over the readouts on the control panel, noted all was well, and then contemplated how to fill in this rare moment of solitude.

Their minor repairs had been completed. Velon was piloting the shuttle down to Macron, the *pleasure planet*, to rescue the crew from a week of sampling the planet's extravagant delights. Niob should have been thinking of what to do in the next few hours, or the voyage ahead, but somehow couldn't drag his mind from the peculiarities of his 2iC.

A frown briefly played across Niob's unlined face. Velon was nine years his senior, though still young at forty-one. He was clearly upset that, again, he'd missed out on the captaincy and was irked at having to take orders from a younger man. Or, was it not their age difference, but because he was from Oberine, and Velon was a Gamlen.

Of course, it shouldn't have made a difference; both planets had been in the Federation for over a century and a half, and at least six or seven generations and countless intermarriages — clinging to the hostilities of the distant past seemed an unthinkable absurdity.

But, as he had learnt at the Academy, humans are good at believing all sorts of absurd ideas and are masters of rationalising their opinions, no matter how ridiculous they appear in the cold light of reason.

As Captain, Niob had to guard against that weakness in his own thinking, and that of his crew — a much harder task — because he had to allow for a diversity of views, to give flexibility. As a consequence, he had to accept a certain amount of interpersonal friction, so long as it didn't hinder the smooth operation of the ship.

It was an art, not a science, and Velon's apparent change for the better was a hoped-for vindication of his tolerance of his niggling ways and occasional acerbic remarks.

The latest phase of Velon's discontent had been engaging in practical jokes — thankfully, mostly harmless. When he was found to be the perpetrator, he justified his actions as a way of bringing a bit of comic relief to their otherwise humdrum life. Boredom, he claimed, was their greatest enemy in this exceedingly peaceful section of the galaxy. His jokes were there to liven us up, to keep us on our toes. But those jokes were wearing thin. Hopefully, Velon's new attitude would herald an end to them.

Tiring of his musings, Niob gave Lashish, his Chief Engineer, and only other occupant of the ship, a brief call to make sure the new software upgrades had bedded in.

All apparently was in order. So, he then checked the chronometer and estimated that he had just under three hours before the shuttle returned, which left plenty of time to blast the flight deck with some real music, not the manufactured muzak that quietly anaesthetised the air in the corridors and lifts. Niob selected his play list, pushed back to a near horizontal position, tensed his ears for that first dramatic chord, and then, hit the go button.

An indeterminate time later he was surprised to find that he had apparently nodded off, the music was still going on and he struggled to lessen the volume to allow his befuddled mind to assess the situation. Something was wrong. The air seemed stale, he was hot, his forehead beaded with sweat. Breathing was hard work.

His clumsy adjustment to a more vertical position almost catapulted out of his chair. Holding the chair's armrests in a death grip, he then concentrated on getting his eyes to focus on the control screen, which, surprisingly, indicated all was normal. Unsatisfied, he tried for a second opinion from Engineering but the comm didn't respond. Confused and annoyed, he abandoned his chair and shuffled off to the exit door. It refused to acknowledge his presence and repelled his attempts at a manual override.

On the way back to the comm, he saw the low oxygen alarm winking on the main screen, but *without* an accompanying alarm bell. Something had gone drastically wrong with life support *and* communications. It was as if the ship had locked down the bridge and was incapable of registering his presence.

The screen refused all attempts to stir it into life. Niob glanced at the chronometer, still another hour at best before the shuttle returned, but the oxygen readout blandly estimated fifteen minutes left before he would lose consciousness. But how did it know that, if it did not recognise his being there?

All the other screens acknowledged no malfunctions and no human presence on the flight deck, and yet the air quality sub-screen continued its countdown to oblivion, when it should have realised that the increasing CO_2 and decreasing O_2 levels meant the room was occupied and hence air quality needed to be maintained. The software was clearly malfunctioning.

But he would soon be dead. What to do? The sweat now dripping into his eyes and down his neck wasn't just from the heat and stuffiness. Sliding from his chair, he stumbled to the panel that concealed the emergency spacesuits. Naturally, the damned thing refused to open. On the cusp of panic, he remembered the blaster he'd strapped under his chair – in case of mutiny, or other such emergencies.

Like a drunk, he staggered back, fumbled, but eventually dislodged the blaster, returned to the spacesuit storage and cut the panel off with the blaster on needle beam. The smell of molten metal choked him, but it was a fair price to pay as he scrambled into the suit and felt the heady glory of fresh air.

Swaying slightly from his exertions, he turned carefully and then returned to the captain's chair. Staring at the screen, his mind boiled with murderous thoughts as he watched its malevolent countdown of the air's deteriorating quality.

Numbers started flashing at the level any occupants would have become unconscious, the next moment a picture of a Joker, the playing card, appeared on screen. Underneath was a flashing subtitle: "*Sweet dreams, Captain!*"

It wasn't a joke and he wasn't smiling.

At least, not until he began planning his retribution. It was then that the carnivorous smile of the ravening wolf took hold!

Author's Note:

In April 2019, my writing group tasked us with creating a story with the last line: "It wasn't a *joke, and he wasn't smiling*" – from *Yellowcake Spring* by Guy Salvide. This story, and *The Jovian Dirk* resulted.

Beethoven's Galactic Legacy

With the meeting's ending came the familiar sounds of desultory banter, shuffling feet and the swish of departing capes until only the Secretary General, Syntras, and his personal assistant, Gemina, remained to give life to the pillared, domed vastness of the Galactic Alliance's Decision Hall.

At a nod from her boss, Gemina gathered up their tablets and stowed them in her latest shoulder bag, before boldly enquiring: 'So, you've decided not to mention the report on our "bit of space junk", whose messages our experts now claim to have finally decoded?'

'Yes. And, you'll probably not know why.'

Gemina's smooth, leathery face luminesced briefly, from embarrassment, because it was all too true. Having no real idea why he had decided to shelve it, she tried guessing.

'Is it just your poor opinion of experts in general, or something else?'

'Both. I'll explain once we get outside,' he said, with a lift of the head that gave the suggestion that the open air would somehow make his reasoning easier to understand.

In a few minutes they had slipped in amongst the tourists strolling around the lake's shore, and like many of them, they also picked up hot drinks from one of the vendors along the promenade, and likewise sought out a vacant bench, to sip, and enjoy Toshan's sun painting the torn clouds with oranges and reds as it descended towards the forested horizon.

'Well?' asked Gemina once both had made some inroads into their coffees.

Syntras dutifully responded, 'Experts have their place, but to become one, they must specialise, which makes it hard for them to appreciate the wider picture, and longer timeframes. They thus have trouble seeing the dangerous side of the simple and primitive, especially when it is mixed with complexity and imagination. Which is exactly what that alien probe exhibits. Even its name, *Voyager*, appears simple, but is it? Is *Voyager* merely a travelling advertisement, or is it part of a spying mission?'

'Surely you can't be suggesting that it is in some way dangerous! It's a primitive, almost childish piece of equipment, hardly the product of an alien race of much sophistication, or, with any potential to harm us. The Alliance represent billions of high-tech, educated and civilised people from eleven species, who have been co-operating and overcoming all manner of social and physical challenges for millennia. This first evidence of intelligence from the periphery should be a cause for celebration, not fear.'

The Secretary General was slow to respond, his mind mired in grim remembrances of the history of misunderstandings and wars that characterised the Alliance's earliest days.

Gemina responded to his silence by adding: 'You do realise that if we were to backtrack the probe, we'd likely find nothing left of the probe's makers.'

Syntras replied with reluctance, 'Yes. Yes. I am all too aware of how self-defeating and destructive intelligence can be, of what happens when too much technology meets too little wisdom.'

An awkward silence then developed, with both choosing to concentrate on their drinks, unfocused gazing at the lake, and the thinking of separate thoughts.

Gemina, being younger, was first to grow impatient.

'We *do* have other things to do. So, not to waste time, perhaps you could list what the probe has, and lacks, and record your mood to each item. Doing so may clarify the situation enough to convince me, and others, of the reasoning behind your reluctance to further investigate the probe and its makers.'

The sensory whiskers on Syntras's broad face quivered from unexpected surprise at all that good sense coming from one so young.

'You really are a most perceptive assistant. That is a brilliant idea!'

He extended a hand.

Gemina delved into her shoulder bag and, with smiling deference, passed him his tablet.

After a brief pause, he started typing. Two lists arose that kept growing until …

'You have found the problem?' inquired Gemina.

'Perhaps, yes.'

After signing out, Syntras returned the tablet, waited until it was back in the bag, then turned slightly to better engage with his assistant.

'Scientists and experts so often see only objects and interactions and miss or downplay the *invisible*.'

He could almost smell Gemina's incomprehension and allowed his amusement to show, then waited for her to relax sufficiently for him to elaborate.

'To make that spacecraft required a civilisation with the command of metals and an understanding of physics, to the point of using nuclear energy, in its case nuclear fission, all of which means they are intelligent. Just like us. Yes?'

'Yes, of course, but …'

Syntras held up a hand. 'But what do the messages it carries tell us about what we *can't* see? Things such as their motivations and their mental disposition towards themselves, and towards those not like them. Taming the destructive forces of tribalism has been the Alliance's greatest achievement. But it's something scientists and experts can't *objectively* measure, and yet, it exists. It is the *invisible* glue that holds *our* civilisation together. If we were to no longer understand that invisible force and so fail to continually encourage it, then doom awaits. You *do* understand?'

A reluctant nod from Gemina encouraged Syntras to continue.

'The primitive technology of the probe, and the rather childish pictographic attempts to explain what they look like — dimorphic bipedal beings that provide more proof of convergent evolution, if one needs any more — and where they come from, to my mind, is not reflected in the contents of its golden disk of sounds.'

Gemina joined in, 'It certainly gave the music experts a hard time, especially when trying to reverse engineer the instruments and then use them to reproduce the melodies. All the instruments were made of wood, brass, animal skins and such, which is about as primitive as one could imagine. Not many of them thought any of the contents particularly sophisticated, or inspiring, and definitely not disturbing in any way. So why does it bother you?'

'You are right. Most of its contents were forgettable, *except* for the piece titled: *First Movement, Beethoven's Fifth Symphony.*'

'I remember that one. It *was* different, though it still didn't make much sense to me, but it certainly wasn't anything to get upset over.'

'Maybe for you and everyone else. But *I* find its simple theme, da da, da, dum, and the composer's seemingly infinite and coherent imagination both magnificent and disconcerting. Disturbing because of the piece's unexpected, and sometimes violent, changes in pace, volume, and instrumentation.'

'But why is that so important?'

Struggling to find the words, Syntras's broad shoulders slumped; his gaze fell upon the multicoloured, randomly arranged pebbles of the path at his feet. After a moment of silent contemplation, he returned to the upright with enlivened eyes.

'To my mind, we should avoid contact with the makers of that craft because they are *too* primitive, *too* primordial. We don't want to be contaminated by their dangerous mix of barely controlled passions combining intelligence and soaring imagination, passions and imagination that can produce musical masterpieces such as that *Fifth Symphony*. Such a mix is equally likely to produce imaginative horrors too. All eleven species of the Alliance had to survive the bloodletting and destruction of such past primitiveness, and then miraculously survive each of their nuclear and biological comings of age. They survived only when they separately learned to reliably master their primitive motivations. Are we prepared to risk going through that traumatic and uncertain task again?'

'So, you believe it best to not seek them out, to not engage with them?'

'Yes.'

'All because of one piece of music!'

'No. All for what that piece of music *represents*.'

It was Gemina's turn to be silenced by disquiet and a mind dealing with unfamiliar ideas, ideas that eventually induced her to speak.

Turning her gaze, she saw an amused Syntras waiting patiently for her reply. She nodded, luminesced, and finally obliged him with her conclusions.

'Technologically, the society that sent that *Voyager* probe was no match for any one of the Alliance's member species, let alone the combined efforts of all eleven. There has been no other evidence of intelligent life in that sector in the millennia it took to reach us, all of which suggests their civilisation hasn't survived. But what if they had?' She paused, perhaps expecting a response, got none, and so continued, 'Surely to survive to the present, the algorithms of convergent evolution imply that they would have found similar solutions as the Alliance species, and so would be as civilised and approachable as us? At the very least, we should send a probe to investigate them.'

'No. If they still survive and encounter our probe, it may induce in them the same disquiet that I feel. What their reactions would be is anyone's guess. I firmly believe our best option is to quarantine that arm of the galaxy until more evidence of their disposition is received.'

'If you vote for that, as far as disposition goes …' She paused to gather her words. 'Well, you'll never know, will you?'

'You and *I* will probably never live long enough to know much about them, but not knowing everything, or solving every puzzle, are just some of life's many challenges,' he replied with smug finality.

The Glorious Enlightenment

Chapter 1

Out past Pluto, in the emptiness where comets are born, a starship materialised, and, for the briefest of moments the unblinking stars beheld a gleaming burgundy rocket. Its sleek lines were embellished by a golden stripe that snaked its way up from the shark-finned base to the spaceship's bold name that formed a golden collar below the nose-cone of the command module.

The ship's impudent presence lasted but a moment. Cloaking technologies were activated, leaving it invisible to prying eyes and scanning devices. Soon after, the ship began its historic journey towards the third planet.

Inside, evening meals were underway in opulent dining rooms. But in the First Speaker's suite, food was the last thing on the minds of its three occupants.

Astride his saddle-like bench at the head of the expansive, semicircular, polished wooden table, First Speaker, Unarad, adjusted his bulk to a more relaxed position, and, being in the company of trusted confederates, let slip his greater comfort with a splash of iridescent colours to dance briefly across his thick rubbery hide, before fading and returning it to its usual uniform and uncommunicative midnight blue.

Unarad swivelled his gaze right, towards his second-in-command, who sat stiffly on the edge of a conventional biped's chair.

Requiring no further prompting, Glarg summarised their conclusions: 'Our preparations are sufficiently advanced to be able to cope with the new schedule. We are ready to begin sowing dissent amongst the Altlani's inner worlds.'

His announcement was uttered in a heavily accented English replete with starchy pride.

The human female, pushing back in the recliner on Unarad's left, suppressed a smile. Despite the Korg's inbuilt bias against females, alien or otherwise, he'd still made the conciliatory effort to speak in English, in spite of the difficulties imposed by his body's vocal architecture, and the Korg mind's abhorrence of the disorderliness inherent in spoken English. She was flattered by his efforts.

When the First Speaker glanced her way, she in turn gave her opinion upon the wisdom of their proposed actions, as slowly and as concisely as she could, out of respect, and to prevent misunderstandings.

A considered silence followed. Unarad closed his enormous eyes. Glarg sat staring at the desktop, whilst the human rolled further back in her chair to study the kaleidoscope of pictures covering every millimetre of the curved ceiling. After a time, the opening of the First Speaker's eyes, and the long wheezing inhalation peculiar to the Mulani, alerted both that a decision had arrived.

'It is inconveniently early, but circumstances ...' colours rippled across the broad muscular torso in tune with unreadable emotions, '... require us to implement Phase Two, now, and not as previously planned.'

The words, deep and gravelly, received two confirmational nods and the meeting broke up.

Leaving the First Speaker's suite, human and Korg strolled together towards the T junction with the circular perimeter corridor where they would part company.

For a while they walked in silence, until, as if talking to the air, Glarg reiterated his concerns, 'The Altlani are unpredictable. So far, they have been cautious in their explorations of this arm of the galaxy, but who knows when they will discover your little planet.'

'Which is why we are ramping up our preparations. Hopefully, we will be ready in the event of an Altlani incursion.'

She felt the exaggerated beating of her heart and a slight flush of heat, both emanating from knowledge of the responsibility she had undertaken, mixed in with the annoying presence of wounded pride. The Mulani had for millennia allowed humanity to progress at their own faltering pace but now the empire building Altlani were getting uncomfortably closer. Humanity had to lift its game and grow up fast. She was embarrassed and fearful that she, and they, would be found wanting.

But there was nothing to be gained by advertising her doubts; instead, she boldly added, 'I am confident our program of *influencing* …' She paused to allow Glarg time to remind himself of the complexity of that innocent-sounding task, then continued, '… of remoulding the *motivations* driving our elites, will soon be achieved. Once possessed of more constructive "reasons for being", they will spread them to the bulk of our population. After that, rapid progress will be made in our ability to repel the Altlani.'

By the time she'd finished her confidence-building statement, they had reached the T junction.

'Mistress Sorensen, let us hope both our efforts bear fruit. Until next time, fare thee well.' He bowed stiffly and then marched off to the right.

Ana Sorensen hoped she'd not oversold her and humanity's abilities, then dismissed her worries. Gathering her pride, she walked briskly to the departure docks, where her high-speed shuttle awaited to take her back to Earth.

§

Five months earlier, Raif Hautman was, like most, completely unaware of interstellar aliens involving themselves in human affairs. He had other issues on his mind, one of which was his looming thirtieth birthday.

His dear wife, Leese, who was only a year younger, should also be thinking about the ticking of time, and the unresolved issue of babies and the next phase of their shared lives.

Of more *immediate* importance, though, was finding an alternative to his life as a globetrotting salesman for S.E.T.I.L., *Sorensen Environmental and Technological Innovations Limited*. Being one of Ana Sorenson's minions increasingly wearied and disgusted him. The trouble was, equally well-paid jobs were hard to imagine in the current economic climate.

He'd gotten off the autobus at the Rockingham Beach Marina to stretch his legs after the tedious flight and to contemplate his next moves. About halfway to his favourite café near the old jetty, he baulked at the sight of the queue outside it, and gave up the idea of a quiet coffee in favour of grabbing the first vacant bench under the huge Norfolk pines that stood guard over the adjacent beach.

Propping his feet on his suitcase, he let his body relax and left his mind to drift where it pleased. It started easily, with a study of his all too familiar surroundings.

The sky was a cloudless and desiccated blue. It was given some life by a flight of pelicans in a shaky V formation, making an unenthused traverse with a minimum of wing beats.

The pelicans' laboured progress pushed Raif's eyes onto the enormous white cube that dominated the Garden Island Naval Base across the bay, a building *purportedly* home to Earth's first interstellar spaceship, but whose featureless walls had hidden all evidence of progress on such for over twenty years. Despite the occasional press release, most, including Raif, had concluded the project was a con, one of those public/private white elephants. At least they'd gotten the colour right!

The negative sentiment induced had his glaze sagging to the subdued, steely-blue undulations of the sea and then onto the beach, a sweep of sand that raced north in long and short leaps, impatient to lose itself in the hustle and bustle of Fremantle.

The beach held a scattering of mostly younger folk of two apparent varieties: those who intended to eventually swim, and those who chose the easier task of strolling along the water's edge. He abandoned both to concentrate on the young mother, an attractive blonde in a black one-piece, who had pitched her beach umbrella on a patch of sand directly in front of him. Once the towels had been spread, she directed her efforts towards supervising her two toddlers – girls as blonde as she – who appeared to be having their first encounter with sand and waves.

After a few minutes of their entertaining antics, Raif was on the verge of departing when stalled by a particularly loud burst of delighted squeals from the toddlers, who were chasing the tiny breakers, but spent most of their time falling down and clumsily getting up – with long delays in between brought on by the distracting pleasure of squeezing wet sand between fingers and toes. Their unburdened joy unleashed a sigh of deep melancholia, born of his comparing their child-world of marvel with his world of battered expectations, foregone ideals, and discarded dreams.

It took a passing jogger to clear the depressing mind fog that had seized him. The distraction allowed him to drag his thoughts back to the present, then towards the future he wished to create.

He realised then that the now clearing gloom was undoubtedly a side-effect of removing his *Sorensen Emotional and Cognitive Enhancer.* Unbidden, his left hand rubbed the base of his skull feeling for the scar, and naturally felt nothing. The surgery was far too sophisticated for anything as crude as scar tissue.

A slow, deep inhalation later, having given up on coffee, he stood, increased his grip on his suitcase, and, with eyes set on the autobus stand just beyond the cafes, began marching, with home his destination.

Chapter 2

Back in their apartment, Raif dumped his bag, brewed himself a coffee, then, mug in hand, headed to the balcony to sip his espresso and drink in the restorative view over Safety Bay.

The bay was an unruffled deep blue, its waters undisturbed except by the occasional passage of a handful of pleasure craft. The sight should have calmed him, but, out past the confines of the far-off seawall, slowly becoming redundant as the climate inched back towards normality, was the unexpected and disquieting silhouette of Ana Sorensen's floating palace, and S.E.T.I.L. corporate headquarters: the mega-yacht *Excelsior*. That boat's presence added to the unease generated by Leese's unexpected absence.

Seeking reassurance, he returned inside, flopped onto the lounge, and rechecked his phone. It was Friday and her rostered day off, so where was she? He pressed the contact marked *Lisle* and again wondered why he'd been so pedantic inputting his wife's true name, when he always thought of her as *Leese*. Whether *Lisle*, or *Leese*, the response remained: "Please leave a message …"

Damn!

It looked like he'd have to phone the receptionist at the lab. Leese often got so immersed in her work that all else ceased to exist. Convincing her to schedule time away from work to have babies wasn't going to be easy, even if he opted to become the househusband, though, financially, and probably emotionally, a dual effort was probably their best long-term option.

'*Sorensen Environmental and Technological Innovations Limited*, how may I assist you?'

The girl's oft-spoken words were offered up with such amazing freshness that Raif was taken aback.

'Err, I'd like to know if Lisle is at work this morning, it's …'

'Oh, it's you! Sorry, Mr Hautman, it's been a while since I've manned reception. I was a bit slow in noting the caller ID. Let me check the roster.'

The silence that followed was punctuated by the sound of keys being tapped, which ended in a surprised intake of breath: 'Humph! Now I know why I haven't seen her for a while. Your wife is part of the contingent staying on board the *Excelsior*. Some sort of in-house training is being run by Ms Sorenson. Lisle won't be back on shore until noon tomorrow.'

A day and a bit. Raif fought two competing forces, a surge of unreasonable anger at the delay, and the brain numbing incredulity that Leese, a lowly lab manager, was aboard the mothership, the holy of holies, and, being instructed – groomed? – by the mysterious and almighty Ana Sorensen.

'Was there anything else, Mr Hautman?'

'Ahh, y-e-s. Could you, umm, give me a number I can contact her on?'

'I'm sorry, Mr Hautman; I can't even do that. It's a silent conference, no phones or contact with the outside world. I guess you'll just have to wait until she's back on dry land. Sorry.'

Annoyance surged. His reply was unnecessarily brusque, 'That's okay. I understand. Thanks. Bye.'

Mercilessly, he jabbed the disconnect button and immediately felt a wave of contrition douse the flames of his petulance.

A deep breath later, Raif belatedly admitted that readjusting to unaugmented emotional reactions was going to take a lot more practice than first envisioned.

The other thing the call had unveiled was that Leese, and by attachment, himself, were now somehow enmeshed in unknown corporate machinations, scheming he urgently needed to learn more about.

Leese had only recently been promoted to laboratory manager, and the stuff she *said* she'd been working on had sounded fairly routine. Both of which were at odds with her being one of the *chosen few* to receive the personal attention of Ms Sorensen.

With no direct options readily at hand for gathering information, Raif conceded he'd have to try indirect approaches. Sampling the gossip in the work canteen was a good first step.

Revived by a quick shower, and resplendent in his most stylish suit, an emboldened Raif Hautman rode the lift down to the ground floor lobby of the employee's accommodation tower, then strode across the marble tiles to pass beneath the arched gateway into the staff's cavernous and tastefully decorated canteen. Once inside, he stopped at the buffet counter to pick up a menu.

Whilst pretending to study its cornucopia of options, he intermittently glanced up, as if weighing up the choices, but actually to scan the tables for familiar faces.

A bit late for breakfast and too early for morning tea, there was only a handful of employees to choose from, all of whom were busy with their phones. Casting his eyes further afield, he spied the distinctive profile of Dave Watkins, helicopter pilot, scuba diving buddy, and sole occupant of a table on the terrace outside.

An absurd plan sprang to mind. It required a few props, and so Raif dumped the menu and made a hasty exit.

In less than half an hour, he was again on the march, this time in the opposite direction, along the treelined path that crossed Sorensen Park's manicured lawns to the business twin of the company's accommodation tower. Its first two floors held Sales and Administration, buffering the floors above, where the real work was done in a labyrinth of research laboratories, attendant storerooms, innumerable offices, and a dozen or so seminar halls.

Once the hidden electronic surveillance systems had allowed him through the front doors, he drastically slowed his pace to an amiable stroll so as not to unsettle the sole occupant of the overlong, polished stone and timber bench that dominated the beautifully crafted but minimalist lobby. The lovely young lady tapping away at a screen was the kindly human face of the far less forgiving organisation they both worked for.

But he had armed himself for the coming encounter. Across his shoulder was his leather satchel containing his tablet; in his right hand, he gripped the straps of an oversized insulated cloth bag, bulging with gourmet vegetarian pizzas. This was countered by an enormous bouquet in his left hand – the buying of which had allowed his memory to drag up the receptionist's name.

'Good morning, Camellia, it's me again. This time bearing gifts. A delivery man in a hurry entrusted me to deliver these pizzas after he'd seen my ID and I signed for them. The flowers are my way of apologising for my snappy behaviour on the phone earlier.'

He handed over the bouquet, dripping water onto the uncluttered surface of the bench in the process. Camellia held the flowers at arm's length, looking somewhat confused as to what to do with them. It was sadly apparent that she didn't receive too many such shows of gratitude.

Raif stepped in with a suggestion. 'Perhaps it would be best to get them into a vase before that puddle gets much bigger. I can man your desk for the few seconds it will take. There's unlikely to be too much happening at this time of day, and I'll stall any who do turn up.'

He smiled his most deprecating smile.

A brief internal battle between protocol and embarrassment took place before she replied, 'Okay. Thanks, Mr Hautman. I won't be long.'

Abandoning her chair, she carefully gathered the flowers and, holding them at arm's length, headed off around the corner to a nearby staff room and its attached kitchenette. As soon as she'd disappeared from view, Raif sprang into her chair, still warm from her shapely derriere, and started swiping through menus to locate Dave's number. Extracting the headphones from his bag, he inserted the lead into the screen's auxiliary jack – to cut Camellia from the conversation – took a deep breath, and, pressed *Enter.*

'Yes?'

Dave had always been a minimalist with words.

Raif sweetly replied, 'Good morning, Mr Watkins, this is Camellia from Admin, sorry to disturb you this early, but there is a small but urgent job for you. Could you please pick up Mr Raif Hautman at the helipad; he has an urgent delivery for Ms Sorensen.'

Raif held his breath. He'd always been good with voices; but how good?

'Right … okay … be there in five, ten, max.'

Dave then hung up. Raif's paralysed breath escaped in a rush. Dave didn't sound overly convinced. But it didn't matter much, so long as he got him over to the *Excelsior.*

Raif was beginning to sweat but kept going, swiped until he had the number for the *Excelsior,* then made the call.

'Hi, this is Camellia from Admin. Mr Hautman is flying over to give his presentation and also to deliver Ms Sorensen's special breakfast order.' The other side hesitated. Raif pushed. 'I know. It's always the same. They can't stick to the schedule, but …'

His hands were shaking by the time they gave their okay. Somehow, he disconnected his headphones, secreted them in his shoulder bag, and then raced back to stand on the correct side of the bench. A quick wipe of his brow and hands with a handkerchief helped restore a semblance of normality – or so he hoped.

Was he mad! These theatrics of his would be recorded somewhere, but what the heck, he was going to quit, so he might as well have a little fun beforehand.

Besides, there was something going on with Leese that he didn't like. They'd never had secrets before, but now he wasn't so sure.

It was a disturbing thought.

Chapter 3

When the receptionist returned, he exchanged a few pleasantries that he hoped would quieten any suspicions she might have before departing ostensibly towards the Sales Department, but once out of sight changed course for the loading docks and service exits, one of which led to the helipad and its hangars.

The morning air was still cool, helping to dispel the heat of his subterfuge. The walk then calmed his nerves to the point where he was almost jovial when he spied the rotund outline of Dave Watkins fussing over his precious machine.

'G'day Dave, long time no see. Catching any off Point Peron?' he said whilst instinctively ducking his head under the rotors, despite them being stationary.

'Not recently; too much going on with *Madam* in town,' Dave said with his usual gruff expression and a nod in the general direction of Ms Sorensen's ship.

Raif survived the brief flight by plying Dave with questions about his dogs, his boat, the helicopter, anything to distract him from their current circumstances. It was with much relief that he waved him farewell, after promising to get in touch to organise a fishing expedition.

Slightly stooped over from the blast and noise of the departing helicopter, Raif met his reception committee, a committee of one, in the form of a tall, thin fellow in a fluoro orange and green shirt, tucked into dark green trousers.

'Raif Hautman,' said with a well-practised flash of his ID tag.

The man had a glance, nodded, then returned to his little hut, coming back with a plastic bag containing a pair of headphones and a small device like a miniature phone.

'The headphones will guide you down to the kitchen and from there back up to the dining room and the main conference room. Just scroll through the menus like this ...' the man demonstrated on the tiny screen of the navigational aid.

Most of the destinations were greyed out, but Raif was happy to have at least three to choose from. He nodded his thanks, put on the headphones, pocketed the "finder", and then, aided by a pointed finger, walked as confidently as he could through the gate on the left and then on towards a doorway on the landward side of the ship.

Doors slid silently open.

'In forty-six metres, at the lifts, select level Three, and ...' intoned the headsets with carefully enunciated feminine charm.

The pale pink corridors with their slightly curved walls gave the fleeting impression of strolling through the blood vessels of a monstrous metal whale. Thankfully, all was deserted. His footsteps hardly registered on the dimpled floor, the only sound being the muted movement of air in the ventilation ducts and ceiling vents, accompanied by the murmur from a far-off engine room. The air was cool but had the artificial freshness of sterility and disinfectants.

Raif wondered what would happen if he decided to go exploring. At the first intersection, he had a four-way choice; of the four corridors, his lifts were to the right according to the whisperings in his ear. Ignoring them, he studied the schematic on a wall-mounted screen. Pleasingly, it allowed him to swipe through the various screens to give him a general sense of the ship's layout. He located the kitchen, the two dining halls (the lower one presumably for the crew), the sleeping quarters, the conference hall, the gyms, the pools, and the laboratories.

The last piqued his interest. The laboratories on level Five took up the front half of that deck and were probably where the answers to his questions lay. But first, he would try the enquiries section of the screen. He tapped in: "Lisle Hautman". The reply, in the small answer bar was minimal: "Room 723, presently at Laboratory 547."

A shadowy reflection grew larger on the display, alerting him that his solitude was about to end. Hastily, he punched in "kitchen" and pressed "Enter" just as a crewman in a white short-sleeved shirt and dark blue shorts stopped behind him.

'Can I be of assistance?' the man asked with calm assurance.

'Err … just making sure I won't get lost if the batteries die on me,' replied Raif, tapping his headphones for emphasis.

'Where are you headed?'

The man eyed the bag containing the pizzas with a mixture of suspicion and digestive desire.

'Not sure if I gave the guy at the helipad the right destination. I've a special delivery for Ms Sorensen which needs to go to the kitchen, but you seem to have two.

'Only one kitchen but two dining areas.'

The man's eyes hardened, marginally.

'Ahh … Yes. Yes. I was getting a little confused. Never been on board before.' Raif tried a weak smile.

The fellow, Adrian Foulks, according to his name tag, pointed towards the lifts. 'Level Three. Turn right when you leave the lift, you'll hear the sound of banging plates so you can't get lost.'

'Thanks.'

He turned and walked to the lifts, feeling the eyes of crewman Foulks digging into his back.

Luck was still running with him. There were two older gents in white lab coats in the lift, and they'd selected level Five. To hide his nerves, he announced: 'Special anniversary gift for Lisle Hautman,' then smiled and raised the bag containing the pizzas.

The two scientists nodded politely and then continued their silent wait for the doors to open at Level Five. When they arrived, Raif dawdled and then followed the two at a safe distance, still unsure as to what he was going to do next. The corridor curved slightly to the right, and the two scientists were soon out of sight. He maintained an air of confidence that appeared to fool the few crewmen and scientists strolling towards him. The laboratory numbers ticked away until 547 came into view, on the left.

Most of the other labs he'd passed had windows that gave a view of the activities within. He'd glimpsed the occasional person in white moving about, or perched over microscopes, or some other piece of equipment, but 547 had no windows. *Fortune favours the bold*, so he tried the door. A small blue light glowed in the doorframe overhead, resulting in the door opening with silent mechanical obedience.

Raif found he'd stepped into a small holding room, or airlock. It was devoid of all items except a touch screen next to the door opposite, which presumably gave access to the lab. It too had a flashing blue light on the lintel.

Stepping forward, he managed two paces before a subdued hissing was followed by the caress of moist fog on his face. His eyesight blurred, his legs gave way, and the antechamber's pink turned into deepest night.

Chapter 4

Leaving the lectern, Ana Sorensen maintained her air of dignified confidence that had become her public persona – after much deliberate cultivation. She nodded benevolently to her gathered scientists and technicians now standing, clapping their appreciation after her rousing update of their grand plan. She had convinced them all that progress was going better than expected, which it possibly was. She wouldn't know for sure until Unarad and the Mulani fleet had been assembled and were in orbit, ready for the "big parade", as they jokingly called it.

But that long-awaited day still seemed years away. Right now, she had an internal security breach to sort out. Sadly, it involved two of her more promising staff members, Lisle and Raif Hautman. She would tackle Lisle first, simply because she was less likely to be compromised.

Once back in her private suite, in the deck below the *Excelsior's* bridge, she made herself comfortable behind her unencumbered desk. She contacted her Head of Security.

'Max, any developments?'

'No ma'am.'

'Raif is still …'

'Sleeping like a baby, in the operating room.'

'And Lisle?'

'In there with him, fretting.'

She paused, unsure whether to laugh or be alarmed at Raif's weapon! 'And the *package* he was carrying?'

'As innocent as it appears, pizzas of a superior quality, in fact, just the sort to impress you, ma'am,' Max replied, definitely with more amusement than concern, before adding, 'There is one strange thing.'

'Yes?'

'His S.E.C.E. has been removed, which may partly explain his odd behaviours since returning from Uzbekistan.'

'Now *that* is interesting. I'll be down shortly to chat with the girl. In the meantime, keep Raif sedated and … umm. That will do for now. I'll see you shortly.'

Before leaving, she went to her secure room, closed the door, checked the sensor readings, and then made a very long-distance call. Unarad needed to know about this development. She saw distinct possibilities in it that, with his great mind's input, could be turned to their advantage.

Their chat lasted longer than expected, but greatly expanded the scope of the opportunity that Raif represented. But first, she had to get more details of his mental disposition. Perhaps he could become a secret weapon to deploy against the Altlani, if only they could prepare him properly and …

By the time she was approaching the guard outside Lab 547, she felt an optimism she hadn't dared to entertain since learning of the Altlani threat. Stopping before the guard, her beaming smile puzzled him, but he did the right thing and insisted she place her palm on his analyser. To his obvious relief, it flashed green, allowing him to stand aside for her to proceed into the laboratory. She commended him for his diligence, then strode inside.

Once through the second airlock door, she was greeted by Max, who guided her to the office where Lisle was sitting rigidly in one of the visitors' chairs that bracketed a coffee table. The girl jumped up the instant they made their appearance.

'Bring us some chamomile tea and a pot of honey, some of the local varieties, then leave us be for a while. I need to spend a bit of time with Lisle.'

Max departed without comment.

A deeply concerned Lisle willingly sought the reassurance on offer in Ana Sorensen's outstretched hand, before rapidly and ardently asking: 'Ms Sorensen, could you *please* tell me what's going on? Why is Raif here? Why is he being held sedated in the operating theatre prep room? Why am I ...'

'Please, be patient. We don't have all the details yet, but with your help, I am sure we will be able to answer all your questions and allay your concerns. I have great confidence that the situation is much less troublesome than it appears. Come, sit down and we'll sort things out over a cup of tea.'

Once seated, Ms Sorensen opened the conversation with intelligent questions about Lisle's work, then, after the tea had arrived and Max had departed, moved on to asking about recent events in Lisle and Raif's domestic life.

This brought a pause, Lisle hesitant to admit that things lately had become strained and that she, to her shame, hadn't made much of an effort to investigate the causes of Raif's unease, at home, and with his work. Perhaps it was out of the fear that doing so would somehow upset her career and further damage their domestic harmony.

As if reading her mind, Ms Sorensen asked, 'We need to understand what's going on, because work and home interact, often with one supporting the other or ...'

Averting her gaze, Lisle took a moment to gather her thoughts and her courage before looking up and answering.

'It's probably two things: Raif is thirty this year, and I think it has made him extra conscious of the passing of time, of wanting to do things differently. Though he hasn't raised it specifically, I think he wants us to start a family, before ...'

'Before it's too late!' suggested Ms Sorensen.

'Yes. I'll be thirty next year, so I'm also increasingly aware of the ticking of my biological clock, but ...' She replaced further explanation with a frown.

'Lisle, you must realise that with us, family commitments are no barrier to advancement, just talk to any of the women higher up than you. They will all say that having children and still working can be happily done. In fact, doing both enhances one's wisdom, makes for a more balanced person and a more effective employee. You are lucky to have a man like Raif in your life. I missed out in that department. You don't have to.'

Lisle nodded slowly, then shook her head as the other problem came to mind. A sigh escaped, leaving space for resolve to enter her face.

'I think the bigger problem is that he has become very disillusioned with his work. He objects to his having to sell the exorbitantly profitable "Deluxe" enhancers to the world's privileged and selfish elites, to turn a blind eye to the negative consequences that doing so has had on their countrymen ...' She ran out of courage, and understanding, because of the growing amusement entering Ms Sorensen's face, when it was anger at the criticism that was the logical, and feared, reaction.

'I am sorry if I seem odd, but ... I shouldn't be saying this ... but Raif is one of the few sales reps to realise the apparent foolishness and unethical nature of our marketing strategy, and, to squeak! It now seems he is also one of the few to do something more about it.'

Puzzled anew, Lisle asked, 'What do you mean?'

'Before we proceed further, I want to assure you that I am most impressed by your progress *and* Raif's. But you need to learn the full scope of what our business really is, and what it really hopes to achieve. Both of which will involve you meeting an amazing character by the name of Unarad, which will require you, Raif, and I to go on a space flight. Are you up to it?'

Lisle was confused; hopes mingled with fears, fears borne of not knowing the details of what she was being asked to become involved in, and the uncertainty over how much she trusted Ms

Sorensen. Lisle looked into her eyes and saw nothing but concern and respect. Her fears subsided.

'I still don't understand.'

'No need to say any more. As I said, all will become clear shortly, especially once you meet the dedicated team behind me, and meet my friend, Unarad.'

She smiled at Lisle's hesitancy. 'Don't fret; life for you and Raif, and a whole lot of other people, is looking decidedly rosier.'

With that, Ms Sorensen motioned Lisle up.

'Our first stop is Raif, and then an impromptu meeting in my suite with our senior staff, which you have now joined. Congratulations, Lisle Hautman, *Special Operative - Level Five*!'

Dressed in his business suit, face up, and asleep on the white operating table, Lisle found Raif's presence vaguely absurd and disturbingly out of place in amongst the plethora of overhead mechanisms, screens, hoses and robotic armatures, whilst being fussed over by a white-clad doctor. Her unease quietened with a reassuring pat on her arm from Ms Sorensen.

Upon sight of Ms Sorensen, the doctor, Dr Moors, joined them, and immediately gave his report: 'He's still sleeping like a baby … a baby who is in top physical and mental condition.'

'Good. Let's keep it that way. This man has a mission ahead of him that may prove critical …' Then, seeing Lisle's apprehension, added, '… assuming he will see its benefits and agrees to carry out the tasks required of him. By the way, this …' pointing to Lisle, '… is Raif's concerned wife, Lisle, who, until today, was one of our laboratory managers but is now a Special Operative, Level Five, whose next duty is to join me in a meeting on Deck Two. We'll be back once it's concluded. Until then …' She left the rest unsaid, then guided Lisle towards the exit.

Max joined them in the lift.

'Lisle, this is Max Weber, Head of Security. Max, I've made Laboratory Manager Lisle Hautman a Special Operative, Level Five, for the foreseeable future. She knows nothing of our, err, "broader operational imperatives", shall we say. After the meeting, I would like you to give her a brief history of myself, Sorenson Enterprises, and tell her the gist of the galactic situation we are facing.'

Max's sharp intake of air and stiffening posture had Ms Sorensen smiling and placing a hand on his shoulder. 'Do the best you can. I have promised Lisle that she and I will be meeting up with Unarad as soon as he comes within range. I have assured her that that meeting will make the stories you and I will tell her, real, rather than science-fiction.'

Returning to Lisle, Ms Sorensen added, 'Hold onto your trust a while longer, and try not to disbelieve too much of what is said, or what is decided upon in the coming hours. It would be best to listen first and be generous towards what is said, as well as the reasoning behind the opinions expressed. I will make sure your input is both heard and taken seriously. They are all good people, so I'm confident a way can be found to satisfy your concerns and those of this organisation.'

Further talk was terminated by the lift's arrival. Flanked by Max and Ms Sorensen, Lisle walked in through the double doors opening into the executive suite's circular meeting room.

There she was surprised by the four people arranged around the large oval table, on either side of the three empty chairs at its head. As far as she could see, Max Weber and Ms Sorensen were the only members of the company's Board of Directors. Of the other four, she only recognised one: Bill Harris, Senior Implants Technician. The other three belonged to the faces of overall-wearing workers, occasionally glimpsed in the canteen at headquarters in Safety Bay.

Ms Sorensen guided Lisle to the seat on her left. Max took command of the chair on her right. As soon as they were settled, Ms Sorensen addressed the surprisingly incurious company.

'I am sorry for the lack of warning but a fortuitous situation may have arisen involving Raif Hautman, and his wife, Lisle Hautman ...' She nodded in her direction, then continued, '... who was running Laboratory 547 until today, but now is a Special Operative. She, thus, has become one of us, though one who knows little of what we do and why we do it. So, I ask you to remember how it felt when you were first introduced to our real mission, and later met our patron, the unforgettable Unarad!'

Nods and knowing smiles were exchanged. The air in the room then seemed to emit a subliminal sigh of acceptance, which did much to allow Lisle to relax – a little.

Turning to Lisle, Ms Sorensen put a finger to her lips to encourage her to listen first, before turning to give the meeting a brief account of Raif's history and recent changes in his perspectives and actions, with emphasis on his having his S.E.C.E. surgically removed and today's unauthorised entry aboard the *Excelsior*. After a brief pause to give them time to gather their thoughts, she asked them to introduce themselves to Lisle, stating their names, their official position, as well as their roles connected to the organisation's true purpose. Max was given the task of being first.

After the last biography, Ms Sorensen asked Lisle if she had any questions or concerns.

'Well, I'm a bit stunned by all these revelations about …' She waved her hands at the gathering, and the room itself, in an attempt to encompass the ship, Ms Sorensen's organisation, and the impossible stories she'd just heard, before meekly conceding that she'd leave her questions for later.

Ms Sorensen accepted Lisle's decision with a nod, then continued, 'We shall now move on to Raif, and what he possibly represents. But firstly, I confirm that operation *Change of Heart* will begin, immediately! The sooner we get world leaders and influencers questioning the status quo and enacting *our* policies, the better. But we mustn't rush. Their change of heart must not be associated with our emotional/cognitive enhancers; it must be perceived as being their own brilliant idea, and proof to themselves and others that they are strong enough to change tack, as *they* feel fit. All going well, it will generate the mindset that will make the next phase easier for them to own and implement, all of which will be necessary if the planet is to successfully redirect the Altlani's love of conquest away from us.'

'How, exactly, does Raif fit into this?' asked Bill Harris, receiving approving nods from the others.

Ms Sorensen's face lit up with a mischievousness few had ever witnessed. 'He is to become our most effective weapon! But before I elaborate, we should ask ourselves to consider our foe. Specifically, what do they *get* from conquest, and what is it that they *fear* the most? Any takers?

'No? Well, just let me say that what I, and Unarad, have in mind is turning Raif into a Trojan horse. Not one hiding and then projecting "hard power", but one that delivers a *terrifying existential fear* into the mind of the Altani commander currently leading their efforts against us. The plan will require Raif to undergo some specific mental conditioning, and then to be captured by that Altani commander. All going to plan, the commander will be "infected" by Raif's enhanced, but subliminal, fears. He will then scurry back to their home planet to unwittingly spread those exaggerated fears and confusions amongst their elites.'

She ended her speech by miming the release of an invisible gift. The mythic dove of peace and salvation, perhaps?

Turning to Lisle, Ms Sorensen's face returned to full seriousness. 'The thing is, to get it to work, Raif must be mostly ignorant of his role, and definitely ignorant of what his subconscious will hold. Otherwise, the Altlani commander won't "swallow the bait", and it is critical that he does so. We want him "infected" with Raif's fears and uncertainties that we will have exaggerated a hundred-fold.'

She paused to allow the gravity of their plan to sink in, then added, 'But the specifics must be explained to Lisle first, because it is her permission that is needed before Raif can become: the *Saviour of Mankind!*'

All eyes turned towards Lisle. Eyes filled with a breathless expectancy that had Lisle suddenly growing hot and sweaty.

She blinked hard, then began a slow, stumbling reply, 'Well, I'm not ...'

Chapter 6

Raif Hautman stared slack-jawed at the main screen of his Recon Dart. His eyes smarted with each flashed "EMERGENCY OVERRIDE", whilst his brain battled two stupefying distractions: the screen's tracking of the missile coming at him from the blue and white planet below, and, the morbid, unhelpful distraction of his mind dredging up that ancient joke foisted on him over a decade ago, when about to board his first flight to Mars Central. Then, it had been another forgettable example of Granddad's odd sense of humour.

"… a screen jock at NASA Mission Control yells to his supervisor: "Hey! We've just discovered intelligent life on Mars."

"How do you know?"

"They just shot down our Mars Lander!"

But now, the joke's poorly timed recollection was either his subconscious mind's attempt to laugh at death, or death's way of laughing at him!

The debate, over which it was, barely started before it was shut down by the unflappable female voice of the command console announcing: "Impact in twenty-one seconds. Prepare for emergency ejection."

§

He survived the landing, and, for a day and a night, had avoided becoming a meal for the planet's frightening array of predators, or slowly and painfully dissolved in the camouflaged traps of the larger of its carnivorous plants.

That freedom ended abruptly whilst exploring a forest pathway and subsequently being ambushed by a troop of sentient bipeds. They were humanoid in form, though thinner, taller, and with smooth, transparent skins that showed the pulsing of their blood, and, if defrocked of their unimaginative, knee-length leather tunics, would have made the task of diagnosing digestive ailments extremely easy.

By shooting him down, they had also proved themselves intelligent, leastways by Granddad's criteria. And, if curiosity was another sign of intelligence, they had repeatedly demonstrated it during the days since his capture.

Like a prized exhibit, they had set him up in a well-appointed, covered cage placed pridefully in the centre of their massively walled city, walled, presumably, to discourage the local carnivores and incursions by rival cities. His accommodation thus allowed the natives a maximum of opportunity to study his every move, and utterance, both of which they found extremely amusing, if the animations and jabbering he elicited in them was any measure. Embarrassingly, they were particularly entertained by his excremental activities.

Though they had removed his blaster, they'd left him his wrist communicator, as well as the Medi-kit and emergency ration packs in the pockets of his flight-suit. The communicator was automatically beaming his position, in code, to the mothership to expedite his rescue. The shooting down of his reconnaissance Dart should have initiated an immediate response, but, so far, no rescue had apparently been instigated.

Stroking his stubble, Raif tried not to contemplate the disturbing notion that he was being deliberately abandoned. The Mulani, whose amazing technology included the starship that had got him into his present predicament, and whose knowledge of galactic affairs had convinced the Sol Confederation to mount this joint "fact-finding mission", were perhaps waiting for the right moment to act.

The rudimentary machinery, architecture, dress, and foods, which were at least edible, were at odds with the natives' technology to first negate the cloaking technology of his Recon Dart and then shoot it down – all of which suggested the *Oddles* – the name he'd given them on account of their odd appearance and behaviours – were either good at hiding their superiority, or, were low-tech minions to high-tech alien overlords, whose technology extended to being invisible to the Mulani robot probes that had preceded the expedition.

Maybe his capture was proof that the Mulani's fears were real. That their evolutionary cousins, the rapacious Altlani, were indeed sniffing around the spiral arm home to unsuspecting humanity and other ripe plums ready for their picking.

Perhaps Mission Control's reluctance to rescue him was based on the hope that his extended presence would allow for maximum information gathering before circumstances required his "emergency extraction" – an extraction that increasingly brought fearful associations to dental crises of the same name. Adding to his gloom was the thought that, at his present rate of intelligence accumulation, he'd be a grey beard before any rescue eventuated.

What to do?

No sooner asked than answered! His sparse crowd of onlookers, in a Mexican wave, suddenly looked skyward, then downwards, before bolting for doorways and alleys. Following their gaze, Raif saw, in the blue above, a point of light rapidly transformed into a shimmering, opaque sphere descending at supersonic speed. He threw himself on the floor, hands cradling his head, and, with a blank mind, awaited his doom.

But instead of blissful atomisation, he merely heard a hiss, endured a brief swirling of dust, noted a sound like steam escaping then beheld a deafening silence broken only by his laboured breathing. Turning over, he propped himself up on his elbows and was confronted by the sight of three beings exiting an enormous metallic sphere through a lens-like portal.

The leading figure looked like a younger version of Unarad, the Mulani's commander-in-chief, who he'd briefly met just prior to his leaving Earth's orbit. The other two were natives, adorned with bandoliers and holstered weapons, marching obediently on either side of their alien master.

The sight induced the sour reminder that every conquest is made possible with the collusion of a significant number of the conquered. It also had Raif questioning whether Unarad and the other Mulani were *truly* humanity's allies? Was the alien commander striding towards him on his four lower tentacles whilst gleefully rubbing together the handlettes on his torso's extrusions an Altlani, a Mulani disguised as an Altlani, or some other combination?

Stopping in front of him, the tentacled alien asked of his left-hand escort: 'So … what have we …?' *In English!*

Receiving no response from his goons, he gave orders in their guttural gibberish, which caused one of them to wave a device at the lock of the cage's only doorway. They entered, grabbed his arms and hustled him outside.

More unintelligible orders were given, and together they marched to the gigantic brushed metal sphere, entered through the oversized "camera lens", ending up in a spacious airlock. The Altlani commander departed, whilst Raif was herded right, towards a lift that deposited them on the third of the four upper levels. A bit more walking ended with him being tossed into a barred holding cell, which held a minimum of accoutrements: a basin and tap, a metallic privy, and a padded bench upon which to sit or sleep.

Both ceiling and floor consisted of small, opaque glass tiles, with the ones making up the floor less shiny from having their surface slightly roughened. Deciding not to waste energy in fruitless speculation, Raif stretched out face up on the bench, hands cushioning the base of his skull, wondering what they would do next. More importantly, he wondered if Unarad had planned for an eventuality such as this? He hoped so.

This brought him to admit to being surprised at his quiet acceptance of his fate resting in the hands of others, one friendly and one not. His philosophic musings were interrupted by the tiles, above and below, lighting up and moving in tandem across his cell. When they passed over him, he felt a nervous tingling and visceral strangeness, both of which dissipated when the lights went out.

No X-ray or ultrasound had ever produced such an odd response, one of which was an immense lassitude. Yawning, he moved his hands from his head to rest, clasped across his abdomen. Soon after, he drifted off into carefree slumber.

The waking was far less civilised. He was shaken unceremoniously back to consciousness, and then manhandled by his two guards to the vertical before being forced into another excursion within the spherical ship that ended on the second lowest deck, in what looked like a First Aid room. There he was strapped to a mechanised chair and left to contemplate this new development – a situation that appeared decidedly ominous!

Unfortunately, his only real option was to wait and work on staying calm. Panicking was definitely a counter-productive strategy, even if it offered the false happiness of seeming to be doing *something*.

The patter of tentacled feet brought the Altlani commander into view. He was alone, but his skin, that had so far been a dull, dark grey, now rippled with colours, which, in the Mulani, could have represented unease. It was then that Raif regretted not learning more about Mulani and Altlani communicative skin displays.

Stopping within grasping distance, the Altlani looked him up and down, inducing new colourings – suspiciously suggestive of disdain – before announcing in well-enunciated English, 'I see you once had one of those pathetic emotional/cognitive enhancers implanted. Damning proof that you are a Mulani spy. Doubtlessly one of old Unarad's hapless slaves. Well, we know much about his attempts to get you apes to do his fighting. Your presence here is proof he has some new scheme of interference under way … a scheme I shall soon know *all* about.'

He rubbed his torso-handlettes together, setting off a flush of red and yellow dots coursing downwards from his rounded head to fade into the grey of his lower extrusions.

'I *could* instal one of *our* enhancers, but it would take too much time to calibrate. A tedious task that ultimately is not accurate enough for my needs. We Altlani have a better way!'

The red and yellow dots did an encore, followed by the Altlani moving closer until Raif's nose was jammed up against the alien's iron-hard, grey chest. Two handlettes glued themselves to the back of his neck, a stabbing pain followed, blood then briefly trickled down onto his shoulders. The pain subsided to be replaced by the immensely greater horror of feeling something flowing into his neck, that began pushing its way up into the base of his skull.

All sensation stopped. Darkness came. Time faltered.

Raif woke with arms flailing, screaming to flee a parasite-filled nightmare. Eventually, he escaped the clutches of horrid dreams to find himself lathered in sweat and happy that the crawling sensations inside his head had gone. Gone too was the smothering wall of grey skin that he distantly remembered as having, at some stage, exploded into starbursts of green, yellow, violet and a million unnameable colours.

His back registered the cool, unforgiving hardness of the floor on which he lay. Uncertain eyes registered the domed roof, then the bars of the cage, the city square beyond and the drab buildings enclosing it. With dulled comprehension, he observed the unhurried movements of thin, sallow humanoids strolling past his cage, humanoids who seemed indifferent to his existence, when, he vaguely recalled, they hadn't always been so disinterested in him.

Moving to a more comfortable position, he became aware that the cage's door was wide open, and just inside, was a bowl of strange fruit and, what looked like bread, next to which lay a gourd, presumably of drink. Getting groggily to his feet, he touched his neck and came away with specks of dried blood. It was then that he remembered the monstrous, metallic sphere, and realised it had gone.

Was he free to go? Go where and for what?

His brain fog suddenly cleared, revealing the humbling truth that he had no solid ideas of what had happened to him, where he was, or what he was doing here.

And, were these faintly familiar aliens friends, or foes?

Chapter 7

Why, exactly, had he called the natives Oddles? After a month or so in their company, he was beginning to think they needed a more noble badge. After all, they had allocated him to the care of a childless widow, who had assiduously taken on the task of feeding him, and teaching him the local customs and language, which was beginning to sound less discordant to his ears.

It was a morning the same as any that had become his new existence, when assisting his aged alien benefactor, Ergal, with preparing the "porridge" and "yoghurt" – their descriptions were still too unappetising to be used in association with food fit for eating – that a commotion could be heard rapidly approaching their ground floor apartment.

"Aliens are coming! Hide! Hide!" was the gist of the approaching crowd's babble.

Upon opening their door, Ergal eventually calmed down the leader of the mob, which completely clogged up the alleyway, and, after much banter and gesticulating on both sides, a semblance of order was restored. The leader then waved his followers back towards the town square. They followed with distinct reluctance.

A downcast Ergal reported back to him: 'You must go centre. You friends come. You go?'

Was his almost forgotten rescue about to materialise? Or had the nightmare monsters come back?

Either way, Raif had to find out.

'I go. You stay. I come back. I come back, hear?'

After giving her a very human hug – which she still found disconcerting – he donned one of their unisex leather tunics to help disguise his flight suit, then slipped out and made his cautious way towards the town square.

It lay empty of locals, though the surrounding windows sported many a prying eye. The cage had been dismantled soon after his release; in its stead now stood a shiny Recon Dart! Outside the spacecraft's open hatchway, two figures sat chatting on folding chairs.

One had the distinct profile of Dave Watkins. His female companion induced a heart palpitation! Hers, too, by the way she violently shook Dave's arm just before jumping up and dashing over to him.

Raif may have forgotten much, but that lithe female sprinting towards him suddenly brought into mind a tidal wave of remembrances and emotions that drowned all recent forgettings. He stumbled out into the square – or was it love's arena? He didn't care; he wasn't thinking. He was restricted to being and feeling.

Lisle almost knocked the breath out of him with her exuberant embrace, then recoiled at the sight and tickling of his lengthy beard.

'I leave you for a few weeks and you turn feral on me! Looks like I'll have to keep a closer eye on you from now on.'

She gave him a quick, but dangerous kiss, then goaded him towards the Dart. Dave and the chairs had already disappeared inside.

Leese was about to pull him bodily in through the door, but was surprised and concerned by Raif's sudden reluctance to enter.

He had just glimpsed Ergal creeping out of the shadows of an alleyway.

'Leese. Stop! Before we go, you *must* meet my adoptive grandmother.'

Without further explanation, he dragged her away from the Dart, across the paving, to meet up with Ergal, who had inched further into the open.

Awkward and unintelligible introductions were attempted that ended with Raif giving Ergal another hug, followed by a reluctant Leese doing likewise. The two women then eyed each other, and, after a moment of silent assessment, seemed happy with what they both saw.

Soon after, Raif and Leese boarded the Dart, and, within minutes, with Dave Watkins at the helm, they were cloaked and roaring upwards to a rendezvous with the Mulani spaceship in orbit around the planet.

Despite the Mulani having mastered faster-than-light travel, the journey back to Earth still took a number of on-board "days" to complete. The first of these was taken up with medical procedures, debriefings and celebrations.

The next two were spent talking to Leese, Dave, and assorted crew members, mixed in with plenty of doing … not much. Reaching the Oort Cloud on the edge of the Solar system late on the fourth day of the return, Raif and Leese were transferred to the waiting Mulani flagship, the *Bwal Narjim*.

Not long after they'd settled into their new cabin, Raif received a summons to attend a private breakfast with First Speaker, Unarad, at seven the next morning, by which time they would be in high orbit above dear old planet Earth.

What worrying new intrigues were in store for him? It made for a restless night.

Chapter 8

The Mulani flagship was not only considerably more luxurious but also much larger than their previous conveyance, and hence it took Raif the better part of ten minutes to navigate his way to Unarad's private suite.

Along the way, he reflected upon the whirlwind of the last six or so months. He'd met aliens, both good and bad, flown in starships and become involved in galactic shenanigans. But the development that eclipsed them all was Leese now enthusiastically agreeing to start a family.

His employment was still up in the air, but, for reasons unknown, he felt there must be something better to do than flogging enhancers to demagogues and their cronies, to improve their abilities to enrich themselves at the expense of those they effectively enslave.

These musings ended upon spying a modest sign on a nondescript door that declared, in three languages – one thankfully English – the title: "First Speaker". The door had sensed his approach, decided he was a friend, and opened with sufficient notice as to allow Raif to enter without breaking step.

Once a few paces into the huge circular space, he stopped to check his wrist communicator – he was two minutes late. But so too was Unarad. The room was vacant, giving him a few moments to take in his surroundings.

It was dominated by a large semicircular table, arrayed with normal chairs except for an oversized saddle-like structure at its focal point. Further afield, near a closed door, was a glass-fronted display, followed by a cluster of large and small recliner chairs and a saddle seat, which provided comfort to a coffee table. By then, his attention became captivated by the walls and ceiling, both completely covered in tile-screens, sporting images of aliens, exotic creatures, occasional humans, cityscapes, and landscapes, all slowly refreshing to reveal new images of a similarly diverse nature. It was like journeying slowly through a person's memories. Unarad's, presumably.

But where was his host?

The question returned his gaze to the table, there to be shocked, and a little embarrassed by the image of the Mulani commander slowly emerging from what had initially seemed thin air above the strange seat.

'Please excuse the party trick, but sometimes I can't help having a bit of fun at my guest's expense. You are obviously unaware that we Mulani evolved from creatures similar to your octopi. Like them, our skin can "see" and then arrange its chromatophores to mimic its background. Our ability to "disappear" was very useful in the distant past and remains so even now.'

'Well, it certainly works. I had no clue that you were "lying in wait", so to speak.'

'Your words are well chosen. Camouflage works for both prey and predator!'

The last words induced a shower of coloured specks to flicker across Unarad's torso, to be absorbed in the darkness of the thick upper regions of his grasping tentacles. This was followed by him giving a loud, short command in a strange language that resulted in a smaller, presumably younger, and possibly female Mulani emerging from the closed door, carrying two trays of food and drink. The servant's appearance had Raif embarrassed to realise that he knew very little of Mulani biology, or history for that matter. Once he, she, or it had departed, he joined Unarad at the table.

'We'll make a start. Enjoy the food, and if you have questions that need answering, just ask, no matter how foolish or seemingly impertinent. In private, the truth, civilly uttered, is a treat that should be given and received with appreciation.'

With that, Unarad selected a morsel and suggested Raif do the same before the food got cold. Needing no further encouragement, Raif happily complied.

The food was good, but around halfway, Raif found he wasn't doing it justice, or being an attentive guest, because he couldn't suppress disturbing speculations centred around aspects of his host's physicality and disposition. What did he *really* know about Unarad, the Mulani, the Altlani, or even the Oddles for that matter? Not just embarrassingly little, but dangerously little!

He, and humanity, were putting their lives and futures too much in the hands and tentacles of strangers, beings possibly more incomprehensible and wilful than the most obstreperous or devious of humans. Unarad's talk of camouflage, predators and prey had suddenly taken on menacing new connotations.

A sudden flickering of colours beside him made Raif realise that his anxious thoughts had frozen him in the act of lifting fork to mouth – for who knows how long – and that Unarad had noticed.

'The food grows wearying? Or is it the company?'

'Err …'

When wired into an enhancer, he would never have gotten himself into this situation, and never been at a loss to find flattering words or a disarming aphorism to get him out. Now he was struggling mightily to find a safe way between the competing forces of truth or lies, and being forced to decide on the basis of either scant facts or unlimited speculations. In the end, it was Unarad's talk of appreciating truth, civilly uttered, that decided him.

'Perhaps, if you permit me to be rude, it is the company! Or rather, my ignorance of your true nature and true disposition towards myself and humanity.'

An exuberant colourful lightshow followed. It raced across Unarad's exterior before fading into dark uniformity and finding new expression in the spoken word.

'You surprise me again. Few have the audacity to seek the truth, especially to a more powerful entity such as I.'

To emphasise the point, Unarad suddenly rose up on his thick lower tentacles to tower over Raif, before swiftly grasping him under his arms and lifting him effortlessly aloft, there to wave him around, as if showing him off to an invisible audience. After this, he gently returned a stupefied Raif to his seat before resuming his own. He let silence have its way, a silence Raif was presumably meant to fill.

A breath, and furrowed brows preceded his reply.

'If your demonstration was somehow meant to reassure me, it failed miserably. In fact, it did the opposite. I now think …'

Unarad interrupted, 'You are wise to fear the powerful. But, as your Marie Curie once remarked, *Nothing is to be feared, only understood.*' His dome-shaped head briefly turned a speckled, glacial-blue that made his huge eyes appear even larger. 'I think it is time for me to fill in some of the blanks in your knowledge of the Mulani.'

Part of Raif listened to the tale of the Mulani transition from small ocean dweller to large terrestrial and social animal. His attention spiked when learning that each Mulani limb possessed an auxiliary brain, which worked in tandem with the central brain – behind the eyes – but could also work independently. A limb cut from the body, or voluntarily ejected, as a lizard discards a tail to avoid capture, could either transform into a smaller version of the adult, or reattach and reintegrate with it.

These backup brains were more often used as a means of direct neurological communication between adults. Two Mulani could agree to allow one to inject an auxiliary brain into them, via the blood, with brain cells migrating individually into the other's brain, to diffuse within it, there to read and/or write information. Once the process reached a critical juncture, the immigrant cells left the host, travelled back, and returned to their usual location to inform the central brain of what they had shared.

A stunned and horrified Raif managed to exclaim: 'So that's what happened to me on …'

'Yes, and, *no*,' cut in Unarad, before pausing to find the best analogy. 'Crudely put, that *is* what happened to you. But, like human sexual congress, our *meeting of minds*, done *our* way, is equivalent to your lovemaking at its most heavenly. The Altlani version is rape of the most vicious kind. Theirs is a ransacking of the other's mind, leaving the victims memories battered whilst filling theirs with stolen information.'

Raif was silent for a long while, aware of a buried disquiet that was struggling for air and light. Thankfully, the Altlani's assault on his mind had faded but the related theme of mental manipulation produced a question.

'When I got back from Uzbekistan and found Leese/Lisle, mysteriously aboard the *Excelsior*, I remember scheming to get aboard to see her. I remembered the pizzas, finding her lab, but after that, it gets blurry. The next memory is meeting Ana Sorensen, and being told that it was fortuitous that I had arrived on board because my show of initiative was just what they needed for their new project. After that, the interstellar espionage mission blotted out all thoughts of the improbability of my involvement in these events. Was it luck that they were so understanding, Leese included, or was there more to it?'

A slow passage of greyish-blue blotches drifted from the top of Unarad's head, down his chest and tentacle-arms, before fading away. Only then did he offer up a long explanation of how Raif's disillusionment and distrust was artificially exaggerated and locked into his subconscious, feelings and attitudes that his mind was conditioned to remember, but only if it suffered an invasion by foreign neurones. Those exaggerated fears and paranoia towards authorities would then infiltrate the invader's mind. It worked. The Altlani commander scurried back to their home world and dutifully spread Raif's enhanced panic to his Altlani peers.

Time slowed as Raif silently chewed over what had been forced upon him, by whom, and to what ends. Grudgingly, he concluded that those involved could be forgiven and that he should, perhaps, even be proud to have proved so useful, even if unwittingly so.

With that resolution, other lesser items came to mind. The walls were one.

'What's with the walls and the pictures?'

Unarad lit up.

'Few figure it out that we, I include myself, are what we remember. Sadly, negative events carry twice as much power as the positive. Knowing this, I have arranged for these repeated happy images to act as a corrective to that bias. They help encourage a more accurate picture of who, and what I am. Their corrective context helps generate better and more nuanced decisions. You should try it yourself.'

'Hmm. I think I see your logic. Interesting. But what about this tracksuit you insisted I wear?'

'Consider it your graduation gown! The graduation ceremony requires us to step outside and go for a stroll along the exterior of the *Bwal Narjim*. Comfortable clothes are an essential inside a spacesuit.'

Raif protested, but eventually capitulated. Forty or so minutes later he clumsily followed the ridiculous sight of the suited-up Mulani out through the lowest airlock and into the dizzying, star-spangled void, there to try and stand upon the sharply curved surface of the ship, just above the tail fins.

'Take your time to get used to the odd feelings. The pills should reduce any space vertigo, and the ship's gravity field, though less on the hull, will still keep you from falling off into orbit. All we are going to do is slowly walk along the golden thread to the upper airlock near the ship's name. You lead. Say nothing, just observe. Okay?'

Raif disobeyed immediately by saying, "Okay", which inspired a wry smile and a shedding of anxieties.

The band of gold writing that had always seemed so thin from a distance was actually a metre or so wide. It made a splendid road to travel, but one that involved the sacrilege of trampling upon the written wisdom of the Mulani. The only consolation was that, not being able to read the writing, he was blissfully ignorant of what he was being sacrilegious to.

Raif clomped his way up the burgundy cylinder, trying not to look "up" at the blue and white, and green and brown, planet Earth, dangling "below" his head – the impossibility of "above" actually being "below" added to the difficulty of moving his legs in heavy boots and lower gravity, both of which produced images of his slipping off into the blackness to end his days burning up on re-entry into Earth's atmosphere.

He was within three or four metres of the T junction formed by the enormous fonts of the ship's name when Unarad called a halt. Then, he had him reverse back to the beginning of the last inscription, where they stood to the side to see it better.

'As I told you, this band contains the cream of Mulani wisdom, though much of it is borrowed from others. This last aphorism is one such borrowing. It's the one I live most by, thus its position atop the rest. You will be pleased to know it is human. Attributed to a Sir Francis Bacon, a British philosopher and statesman born in 1561. What it says is: *"Nature to be commanded, must first be obeyed."* Leastwise that's our version of it. Any comments?'

Puzzlement and annoyance competed for attention. Raif usually didn't waste much time on deep thinking, but recent events had forced such in-depth analysing upon him, which perhaps made it easier for him consider the question of why Unarad was so smitten by *that* particular saying?

As if reading his thoughts, Unarad added, 'Fully grasping the wisdom in Sir Francis' words will allow you to better appreciate our ship's name, and possibly, its greater purpose.'

'Bwal Narjim? It means nothing to me,' replied Raif with hints of annoyance. He was beginning to tire of Unarad's riddles.

Unfazed by his sour tone, the Mulani commander-in-chief explained, '*Bwal Narjim* means: *The Glorious Enlightenment!* ... an enlightenment that only comes from understanding and implementing Sir Francis's wisdom. But you grow tired, let us go inside. Follow me. Naturally, our path to safety lies just past "enlightenment"!'

Raif wasn't sure if Unarad was being condescending, or what? But he was past caring much either way. He *was* tired, more so mentally than physically, and so said nothing, merely trudged behind the Mulani, looking forward to doing a bit of nothing for a while.

By the time they had extricated themselves from their spacesuits and returned to Unarad's suite, it was midmorning. Unarad suggested they have a hot beverage and a snack before they went their separate ways. Raif would have preferred an earlier exit, but assented because Unarad gave the appearance of still having something important he wanted to say.

The coffee and the cake duly revived both his body and his spirit.

It was a pleasing development not lost on Unarad, comfortably sprawled upon his saddle/chair on the other side of the coffee table. A subdued flow of colours preceded his announcement: 'Ms Sorensen mentioned to me she had a senior position available that she was considering offering to you. It would involve overseeing modifications to her product lines and their marketing. She wanted my opinion of your *nature*. Specifically, whether it is compatible with hers, and the long-term goals of her organisation.'

'And?' was all Raif could offer up as a response.

'Before I answer, tell me what you know of the biological world, especially regarding the *roles* each organism performs. Earlier we mentioned two: predators and prey.'

High school science was a long time back and he'd concentrated more on English, History and Psychology, which had some connection to biological roles, in the sense that people play roles in society. Sadists and masochists could be seen as the equivalent of the animal world's predators and prey. He'd done psych in the hope of better understanding how to judge the trustworthiness of people, and whether they were the type to pull you down, not up. He'd never considered humans as being like any other animals, as occupiers of a biological niche that fulfilled a definable ecological purpose.

Unarad interrupted Raif's mental explorations.

'Let me give a clue. The Altlani are a relic phase of Mulani evolution; they are stuck in an evolutionary adolescence, hence are self-obsessed and happy to trample on the feelings of others for their own progress and advancement. They have plenty of energy and imagination and hence have conquered, used, and parasitised many. We Mulani ended up preferring ways that lead to peaceful co-existence. By doing so, we have increased our life-spans and reduced our birth rate. This has made us rare and hence vulnerable to sudden large losses. We understand our nature, and needs, and so try to persuade younger, energetic and more imaginative cultures to work with us, to our mutual benefit.'

Raif was surprised to hear himself arguing: 'One could say that the Mulani also live *off* subordinate races. That you enslave them for your benefit! Hmm?'

'Well said master Raif! You are partially correct. But consider your life with Lisle. Are you not benefiting from her? She provides companionship to ward off loneliness. The babies she will produce will carry your genes into the future. Likewise, you "use" others to grow your food, make your clothes, et cetera. Do these behaviours make you a predator, a parasite, or a symbiote – one who balances your needs with those of your associates and host society? The answers depend much on *how* you make a living, and *what* you live for.'

Unarad was making things awkwardly cloudy. Raif said nothing.

'The Mulani eventually chose to be symbiotes. It is a more comfortable life, and generates more beauty than the others. Ms Sorensen wishes to know what is *your* nature, and by how much do you command it. Or are you one who allows their unexamined nature to lead them down regrettable roads until unable to escape from them?'

Raif's uncertainty manifested itself in delayed breathing, which ended in a deep inhalation, and, 'I don't really know. I'd have to think about it. How long have I got?'

'I will be leaving Earth's orbit in three days. I suggest you forget about me and concentrate on speaking directly to Ms Sorensen and to Lisle, of course, since they are the two people whose opinions are vastly more important than mine. Farewell, Mr Hautman.'

§

Instead of returning directly to his cabin to help Leese get ready for their afternoon shuttle back to Earth – back to

Rockingham – Raif diverted to the observation deck.

At this in-between hour, post-morning tea and pre-lunch, it was relatively deserted. Most of the windows held the cold, empty black of space; only two were lit, one with the harsh white of the moon, the other with the living brilliance of planet Earth.

Australia lay directly below, an immense island grinding north into the tropics, its vast brown interior fringed by patches of green where life flourished, life that, to succeed, required basic requirements to be continually met. But what were they?

"The balance of nature", that long forgotten descriptive first encountered in high school science, came into Raif's mind, but now with new associations.

"Balance" was the key.

He had to balance what his body blindly and unthinkingly desired with what the living and inanimate worlds desired, a balance best reached via accumulating accurate knowledge.

The ancient Greeks had proclaimed to those seeking advice from the oracle at Delphi, "Know Thyself". Sir Francis Bacon had expressed it similarly a thousand years later.

The truth is the truth is the truth. It can't be escaped. It must be embraced.

Was this his moment of glorious enlightenment?

Time would tell!

Author's Note:

This story began ten or so years back, but refused to be born due to the author's lack of understanding of its theme: enlightenment. Hopefully, this rendition demonstrates that the author has made some progress towards that noble goal and state of being!

About the Author

D. Alan Petersen spent his formative years in New South Wales. In the late 1980s, he moved to Western Australia. There he found a wife and soulmate, and came to realise the veracity of Voltaire's assertion that: "Paradise is where I am."

His paradise is located at their home in Rockingham, Western Australia.

Previous titles by D. Alan Petersen are *Tarkine Mist*, a crime thriller set in Tasmania, and his philosophical memoir, *Why I Don't Like Sex, and Other Conundrums*.

He can be contacted by email at: petersenalan59@gmail.com